'Juana! Keep very still!' I called hoarsely.

My heart seemed to fall clean out of my body into the gorge below. There she was, defenceless, in deadly danger, and here I was, strung on two ropes over the gulf, with my gun strapped out of reach, useless on my back; however fast I moved, I would never be able to get back in time to save her if the bear flew at her.

The massive bear turned, at the sound of my voice, and eyed me intently. I joggled frantically on the rope, to hold its attention, and shouted, 'Ho! Ho! Hilloo! Yah! Bah!'

Juana remained still as a stone, but the wind was rising, and blew the folds of her blue hood about her face. The movement caught the bear's eye, and it turned again slowly in her direction.

'Bear! Bear!' I yelled. 'Look at me! Look at me on the bridge. Come and get me, bear! Here I am!'

JOAN AIKEN

THE TEETH OF THE GALE

THE FELIX TRILOGY: BOOK 3

RED FOX

THE TEETH OF THE GALE
A RED FOX BOOK 978 1 849 41829 4

First published in Great Britain in 1988 by Jonathan Cape Ltd,
an imprint of Random House Children's Publishers UK
A Random House Group Company

Red Fox edition published 1997
This edition published 2013

1 3 5 7 9 10 8 6 4 2

The Random House Group Limited supports the Forest Stewardship Council®
(FSC®), the leading international forest-certification organisation. Our books
carrying the FSC label are printed on FSC®-certified paper. FSC is the only forest-
certification scheme supported by the leading environmental organisations, including
Greenpeace. Our paper procurement policy can be found at
www.randomhouse.co.uk/environment.

Set in Sabon

Red Fox Books are published by Random House Children's Publishers UK,
61–63 Uxbridge Road, London W5 5SA

www.randomhousechildrens.co.uk
www.totallyrandombooks.co.uk
www.randomhouse.co.uk

Addresses for companies within The Random House Group Limited can be found
at: www.randomhouse.co.uk/offices.htm

THE RANDOM HOUSE GROUP Limited Reg. No. 954009

A CIP catalogue record for this book is available from the British Library.

Printed and bound in Great Britain by Clays Ltd, St Ives PLC

To Else-Marie Bonnet

Go saddle the sea, put a bridle on the wind,
before you choose your place

Proverb

1

In which I receive a message from home; travel with Pedro; am followed by Sancho the Spy; see a spoiled child and her fat father; give our pursuers the slip; and witness a fearsome landslide

It was on some saint's day – whose, I don't remember – that Pedro came knocking at the door of my lodging in Salamanca. The townspeople had been celebrating since dawn, with processions, fireworks, bullfights, and dancing in the streets; the students at the University had a holiday, and most of them had been out, waving banners and demanding more liberal laws. Many of them had by this time been arrested and were probably in bad trouble. By nightfall, most of the town's activities were concentrated in the Plaza Mayor, the main square, on to which my window faced. People who still had the energy – and there were plenty of them – were dancing; the older citizens sat at tables under trees in the middle of the plaza and drank wine and coffee and talked.

People talk more, in Salamanca, I have heard it said, than in any other town in the world. The sound of their conversation came up through my window – open, for it was a mild spring evening – in a solid clatter, like the tide breaking on a pebbled shore, just sometimes overborne by bursts of music on pipe, drum, and guitar.

For this reason it was some time before I noticed the tapping and scratching at my door, and heard Pedro's voice.

'Felix, Felix! Are you in there? *Ay, Dios*, what a struggle I've had, shoving my way here through the crowd—' as I opened the door and let him in. 'I reckon the whole town is packed into the square down below. Why aren't *you* out there, drinking and dancing with the girls? Or carrying placards with the students? Mind, I'm just as glad you are not; it would be like trying to find one leaf in a forest.'

'Pedro! What in the wide world are you doing here, in Salamanca?'

It was at least eighty leagues from home, two and a half days' riding at a horse's best pace. And Pedro, I knew, could not easily be spared these days; he had risen from stable-boy to a position in the estate office under Rodrigo, my grandfather's steward, and everybody was very pleased with his work. So what was he doing here, such a distance from Villaverde?

'*Quick* – tell me – there's nothing the matter with Grandfather?'

'No, no, set your mind at rest; Don Francisco is in good health; at least his *mind* is as active as ever, if his body isn't.' For many years my grandfather had been confined to a wheelchair because of rheumatism and wounds from old battles.

'Then why—?'

'He wants you home, and in double-quick time, too. We must leave tomorrow at dawn. It's a bit hard, I must say,' grumbled Pedro, 'year in, year out, I'm stuck up there on a windy hilltop in the middle of the sierra, not a girl to pass the time of day with, apart from country bumpkins smelling of goats' milk. And when I do get sent to what looks like a decent town, full of jolly senoritas, I'm obliged to turn straight round and gallop home, not even allowed time to buy a gift for Aunt Prudencia.'

'You can buy her something tomorrow while I see my tutor. *Why* does Grandfather want me home so urgently?'

'How should I know? A letter came—'

'From France?' My heart leapt – foolishly, I knew.

'No, from Bilbao.'

In deep anxiety I asked, 'Is it politics?'

Pedro shrugged. 'I don't know, I'm telling you! But, half an hour later, I was ordered off to fetch you back as fast as the Devil left St Dunstan's dinner table. The Conde didn't even take time to write you a note.'

'Well, he writes so slowly these days, with his stiff hands. But you'd think he could have got Don Jacinto to do it.'

'Didn't want Don Jacinto to know, maybe. And I've half killed three mounts on the way,' said Pedro, glancing round my room, 'and I'm half dead myself. Is there somewhere I can sleep? And I'd not say no to a glass of wine and a mouthful of ham—'

'Of course.' I fetched food from a closet and said, 'You can have my bed when you're finished. I'll sleep on the floor.'

He was scandalised.

'What? You, the Conde's grandson – and an English milord as well – Lord Saint Winnow,' he mouthed the English syllables distastefully, 'give up your bed to the *cook's nephew*?'

'Try not to be more of a numbskull than you are,' I said, pushing him on to the cot, which was narrow and hard enough, certainly, no ducal couch. 'Go to sleep, you're tired out. And I've bedded down in plenty of worse places.'

He argued no more, but kicked off his boots.

4

'Beggarly sort of lodgings for a Cabezada,' he grunted, looking disparagingly round my small untidy room.

'I like the view. And money's not so plentiful these days. *You* know that.'

'Ay, ay. Since our dear king was put back on the throne, with all those French and Russians to hold him there and see he doesn't get pushed off again—'

'*Hush*, you fool!'

'Who could hear, with all that blabber going on outside? And the taxes going up crippling high, and your granda's Mexican estates lost in the uprising there – times are bad—' Pedro gave a great yawn and closed his eyes. In two minutes he was asleep.

I pulled my clothes out of the chest, ready for packing, piled them into a heap on the floor, and flung myself down on top of it.

Hours had dawdled by, though, before I slept. It was not the roar of chat from the Plaza Mayor, nor the lumpy layers of shirts and breeches below me, but sheer worry that kept me awake.

Was Grandfather in trouble with the authorities? He made no secret of the fact that he despised King Ferdinand, now back on the Spanish throne, and all the men chosen for his ministers. Villaverde was a tiny, unimportant place, high on the sierra and far from Madrid; but that made no difference. All over Spain men lived in fear these days. My grandfather's crippled condition, his old age, his noble birth, and known patriotic fervour would be no protection. Empecinado, who had bravely led guerrilla troops against Napoleon, had been imprisoned at Roa for ten months, brought out on market days in an iron cage to be spat on by the peasants. A lady of aristocratic family had been put under arrest, simply because she had permitted patriotic songs to be sung in her house. Men had been sent to the galleys at Malaga, just for having Colonel Riego's picture on their walls.

And Riego had been my grandfather's close friend from boyhood.

If Grandfather was in danger of arrest, his future did not bear thinking about.

What could have been in that letter from Bilbao, that caused him to send for me at such racing speed?

Long before daylight, we were up. Seeing me put on my hat and jacket, Pedro said, 'I suppose you'll want to say goodbye to your sweetheart?'

I answered rather shortly. 'I have no sweetheart in Salamanca.'

'Oh, ay,' he muttered, 'there was that French girl. I forgot. Years ago, that was, though . . .'

To which I made no reply. Juana was not French, I

thought, she was Basque. Pedro, seeing my face, I suppose, smiled his wide apologetic grin – his teeth fanned out like a hand of cards, but the effect was not unpleasing – and said, 'I'm sorry, Senor Felix. You know me – I'm a clod. What I say is nothing but nonsense. Would there be any breakfast?'

'Buy yourself what you like.' I tossed him a couple of coins. 'I have to see my tutor and explain that I shan't be able to attend his classes for a while. I'll not be long – back in twenty minutes.'

Having descended the three flights of stairs I set off running along the Rua Mayor which led to the University.

I found my tutor, as I had expected, already in the classroom where, two hours later, we would assemble for his lecture on the Greek drama. His own lodgings were small and frightfully cold – the pay of a university lecturer was not high – so he often came into the school halls long before dawn.

'Glory be to God!' he exclaimed at the sight of me, hot and panting, 'here's one of my students shows real enthusiasm at last! And thankful I am to see you weren't one of those hotheads who are now cooling their heels in the jail.'

He was a small, round-faced, red-haired Irishman, with a soft voice and more learning in him than I would be able to pick up in several lifetimes. His name was Lucius Redmond.

He smiled at me very kindly as I began to gulp out my explanations.

'N-no, sir – I'm afraid it's not – though I *am* enthusiastic – and I would have been out with a placard but I promised my grandfather – the thing is, he has summoned me home, most urgently—'

'Is it the politics?' He gave a quick, wary glance round the ill-lit, empty classroom – at whose battered desks students had been sitting for more than 300 years. Craftsmen built good desks in the sixteenth century!

'I – I can't tell, sir.'

'Eh well – let's hope not.' He crossed himself. So did I. Politics had closed down the whole University at Salamanca for several years after King Ferdinand returned to Spain from exile, and, when it did reopen, a number of the teachers were missing, and never re-appeared. 'Give my very kind regards to the Conde,' said Dr Redmond, who had occasionally corresponded with my grandfather on learned subjects. 'And return to us as soon as ye can, Felix, dear boy, to take your degree. We'll miss ye, faith, in the classes. Like a sunbeam, ye've been.'

'And – and I'll miss the classes too, sir! But sir –

please tell me one thing—' I had been reading the plays of Sophocles that week, and for a moment thirst for information made me forget the urgency to be gone – 'why, *why* did all those troubles fall on poor Oedipus? None of it was his fault – he did not know that Laius was his father and Jocasta his mother—'

'Yerrah, dear boy, ye've read the classics with me now for three years and ye still expect justice in human affairs? Divil a bit will ye find in this world – justice is only guaranteed in the world to come! No, no,' Redmond went on, shepherding me out of the door, across the cloisters, and out into the street '– I'll walk with ye a step of the road and take my breakfast coffee in the Plaza Mayor; no, my child, the misfortunes that fell on poor King Oedipus were kin to those that have fallen on poor Spain. Whose fault? Nobody's, that we can see. Who could guess, when the English drove out Napoleon and kicked his brother Joseph off the Spanish throne, and brought back the rightful king Ferdinand, that the man would turn into such a bloody tyrant?'

'Oh, sir, mind what you are saying, for God's sake!'

'Ne'er fret your head, boy. 'Tis early for the Gardai to be about.'

Indeed the night was still black. The streets were empty. No Civil Guards were to be seen.

''Deed and I sometimes think,' went on Dr Redmond, 'that the ancient tales, such as that of Oedipus, were given us so that we may measure our own troubles against the ills of former times. That way, our own lot may not seem so bad.'

'What can help Spain now, sir?'

'Time alone is the cure,' he answered gravely. 'No use expecting a sudden rescue, for there won't be one. Maybe in a hundred years . . . Ye have English kin, have ye not?'

'Ay, sir, a grandfather living near Bath. But he is old, and out of his wits.'

'If it were not for the Conde,' he muttered, 'I'd say, take ship for England, and live there where folk of liberal views may speak as loud as they please. But ye'd not want to leave your granda.'

'*Indeed* I would not!'

'Well, God go with you, my child. *Vaya con Dios!*' he added, breaking into Spanish – hitherto we had spoken English, to lessen the risk of being overheard – 'ye have been one of my brightest students, don't forget what ye have learned.' He waved me a friendly goodbye as he turned into one of the cafes that lined the square, just beginning to open for business.

Back at my lodgings I found that Pedro had capably packed up my clothes and books, and had ready a pair of mules which stood waiting to take us on the first stage of our journey.

'Mules?' I said. 'Was that the best you could do?'

'Now who's being high and mighty? These are a good pair, from la Mancha, they can outpace any of your high-stepping Arabs; and will take longer to tire. Also—' he glanced about the street – 'mounted on a pair of mules, we won't attract such notice.'

'Well: there's something to that.'

I swung myself on to one of the long-eared beasts and Pedro, doing likewise, added with a grin, 'Anyway, I seem to remember that you weren't too proud to leave home on a mule, once before.'

Laughing, I kicked my mount into a swinging lope. It was true that, six years ago, at the age of twelve, I had run away from home, riding a canny, cross-grained mule from my grandfather's stable, who had been my faithful companion through various hair-raising adventures, and had saved my life at least twice.

'Everything you say is perfectly correct, Pedro. Did you manage to buy a keepsake for your aunt?'

'Got the old girl a bit of lace from a stall in the Calle de Zamora.' He patted his saddle-bag.

So we set out northwest, along the highway to Leon and Oviedo.

For a couple of hours we rode in silence. As Pedro

had foretold, the mules went well, covering the ground at a smooth, steady amble, five leagues to the hour. By the time full day had dawned we were well away from Salamanca, in open country. Then Pedro's tongue was loosened, and he chattered with his usual vivacity, telling me all the news of Villaverde, my grandfather's household, the great fortified house, and the tiny town that clung to one side of it and was encircled by the same massive wall, high on the Picos de Ancares. Who had been married to whom, who was sick, who was well, he related, which horses had foaled, how my grandfather did these days, and my five aged great-aunts; no, only four of them now, Great-aunt Feliciana had been carried off by the croup at the age of ninety-four last month, leaving Natividad, Adoracion, Josefina, and Visitacion. And Dona Mercedes, my grandmother, Pedro said, was now like a little child, had to have the simplest matters explained to her, and asked the same question five times in as many minutes.

'It's hard on your grandfather,' Pedro concluded. 'But everybody else in the household finds it a change for the better. Such a Tartar she used to be! Now she's peaceable as a duckling, smiles and pats your head if you so much as pick up her fan.'

Pity she wasn't like that fifteen years ago when I was a young child in her household, I thought;

many was the beating she ordered for me then.

'So how do you like college, Felix?' Pedro asked. 'Are you growing mighty learned? Are you going to be a great man of law? I reckon it's better than being rapped on the knuckles twenty times a day by old Father Tomas, eh?'

'Just about ten thousand times better. I like it very well. Though there's a deal to learn. The full course of study for a barrister takes thirteen years.'

'*Thirteen years?*' Pedro turned to me a face of horror. 'You're joking, Senor Felix!'

I shook my head. 'It's true. But you have to be aged twenty-five before you can apply . . . I'm just working for a bachelor's degree. I'd like to be a barrister, though. You have to swear to defend the poor for nothing—'

'You always were mad on finding out about things that are no use,' Pedro said rather disparagingly. 'Now I—' he thumped his chest – '*I* can only reckon if I can see the things right there in front of me. Or know they are in the barn: so many head of goats, so many tons of hay.'

Pedro, I remembered, was lightning-quick at figures; calculation always had a great appeal for him. So I told him that, back in the fifteenth century, Cristoforo Colombo had travelled to Salamanca to ask the astronomers and mathematicians there for help in planning his voyage in search of the New World.

'Is that true?' he said, only half believing, and when I said yes he burst into ribald song:

> Cristoforo Colombo
> Es verdadero
> Una grasa Senora
> Se senta en mi sombrero!

Then he asked, 'But you aren't studying *astronomy* are you, Felix? That would be *really* useless!'

'No, only law. And some other things which I hope will come in useful.' Like plays of Sophocles, I thought, and fell silent, recalling, as I had many times, the day when it had been decided that I should attend the University at Salamanca.

I had been out on the grasslands, beyond the town wall, exercising a half-schooled Andalusian colt, when Pepe, one of the stable-boys, came racing to tell me that Grandfather wanted me urgently. And indeed, as I cantered towards the arched gate in the wall, I saw the Conde come through it, pushed in his wheelchair by Manuel, his personal servant. There was a stretch of paved road outside the wall, and here they halted. My grandfather made urgent beckoning gestures, and motioned Manuel to go back inside, so I dismounted and tied my horse to a stanchion in the wall.

'What is it, Grandfather? Are you ill?'

Even from a distance I could see how white his face was. And, coming closer, that his mouth trembled and shook in a way that frightened me. For, as a rule, he was a man of iron self-control. He had a paper in his hands.

'No,' he said. 'I am not ill. But I have had terrible news.'

I waited in silent suspense while he made several efforts to speak. At last he brought it out.

'They have killed Rafael Riego. The best man in Spain. Killed him like a dog.'

'Oh, Grandfather—'

Riego was a Liberal leader, a man of great courage and nobility. In the wars against Napoleon he had served with gallantry, and had been taken prisoner. Back home, when peace returned, he was elected to the Cortes, the Spanish parliament, and, in 1820, appointed its president. That same year, he proclaimed the validity of the Spanish Liberal Constitution, which had been drawn up in 1812, while King Ferdinand was still a captive in the hands of the French.

But then, later in 1820, history repeated itself and French troops again invaded our country, for the other

European nations refused to acknowledge a democratically elected Spanish government. Colonel Riego led the fighting against the French, and was captured at Malaga. The restored King Ferdinand, who had at first pretended to accept the Liberal constitution, now completely turned against it, and sided with the French, who supported him in all his tyrannical acts.

'Not only have they killed Riego,' said my grandfather with white lips, 'but they did it in the most shameful, degrading way. He was dragged along the streets of Madrid in a basket, at the tail of an ass. Imagine it! The president of the parliament – the man who could have saved Spain! Then he was hanged, drawn, and quartered like a – like a cut-throat! This country, I truly believe, is turning into a hell on earth.'

There was no possible way to comfort my grandfather.

Riego, a neighbour, a man of Asturias, had been a close family friend. I know Grandfather felt his horrible end all the more keenly because, if he had not been prevented by his crippled state, he would have been Riego's active ally.

'What can we *do*?' I said. I was wild to make some demonstration – put up a placard – write a letter to the king – hit somebody.

I was only fourteen at that time.

But my grandfather said, 'Nothing. There is nothing we can do. King Ferdinand is backed by the French – the "hundred thousand sons of St Louis". If the Spanish people did rebel, I have no doubt that the Tsar of Russia would send Cossacks into our country. We should be beaten into submission. The other kingdoms of Europe do not *want* Spain to become a free and liberal state.

'But, Felix, it is for you that I fear. My political views are known. If I were to be carried off to prison, they would take you too. Then who would care for your grandmother and your great-aunts? It is best that you leave Villaverde, my boy, and go away, at once, to college in England.'

This, however, I flatly refused to do. My grandfather argued in vain.

'You have relations there—' This was true, for though my mother had been Spanish, my father was an English officer, killed in the French wars, and I had travelled to England to visit his family home. 'You could go to Oxford or Cambridge University,' my grandfather said.

'Those places are too far from Villaverde. Besides, I don't like England.'

In the end, after much argument, I agreed to go to Salamanca. For I did, in truth, wish to learn. And my grandfather felt that, if I were at least that far away from Villaverde, it could not be argued that I was under his influence. He begged me not to involve myself in politics while I was studying; and, as I loved him, I gave my promise, and kept it, though it went against the grain. Which was why Pedro had found me at home and studying, instead of out rioting with my comrades.

As it turned out, the authorities had *not* imprisoned Grandfather – perhaps because it was so plain that, in his severely crippled state, he could play no part in any uprising. But for several years he was under house arrest, forbidden even to go out of doors, That was in 1823. And I went off to Salamanca early next year and had remained there for the following three years, often homesick and heartsick enough, but glad of the chance to acquire knowledge, for which I had a deep hunger.

If you can only discover the causes of things, I often thought, surely you can also discover their cure?

Now, despite my worry over Grandfather, I was deeply happy to be riding north again, back to Galicia. Among other reasons, because Galicia was a little nearer to France.

Five years had passed by since I had met 'that French girl' referred to by Pedro. I had no reason to hope that I would ever see her again; yet still, how fervently I did hope! She and I had shared a strange adventure; we had each saved the other's life, several times over. And, as surely as spring follows winter, I felt certain that our fortunes were, in some way, knit together and that we must, some day, meet again. I felt about no other person in the whole world as I did about Juana – we had grown to know one another so well, had become in the end – though not at first – such good friends.

Sometimes – in periods of doubt or despondency – it did occur to me that by now, after five years, she would be greatly changed. As, I suppose, I was myself. She would be grown up, she would have become a young lady. But still, but still, how I longed to see her!

Twice, during the five-year period, I had written to her, the first time in care of a firm of lawyers, Auteuil Freres, at Bayonne, who had been in charge of the affairs of her uncle, Senor d'Echepara.

After long delay I had a reply from the lawyers.

Following the recent death of our esteemed client, Senor León d'Echepara, his niece and heiress Mademoiselle Jeanne Esparza has announced her intention of entering the Convent of Notre Dame de Douleur in Bayonne as a postulant, and instructed us to dispose of all her uncle's property.

This was done and the resulting funds of 30,000 *reales* assigned, at her request, to the convent as her dower. Any communication to Mademoiselle Esparza (now Soeur Felicitee) should now be addressed in care of Mere Madeleine, the Mother Superior of the Convent.

That, for a year and a half, had put a stop to my efforts to communicate with Juana. A novice! In a French convent! Now indeed she was really cut off from me.

But, at the end of that time, as my yearning to talk to her did not abate, I wrote another letter, addressed to the convent. Nothing of importance: asking how she did, describing the course of my own studies, recalling some of the events of our wild journey over the Pyrenees from France into Spain.

And then waited months, hoping, longing for an answer.

None came; only, at long last, a curt note, unsigned but indited in exquisite copperplate script, instructing me that 'novices under the discipline of the Convent de Notre Dame de Douleur were not permitted to enter into correspondence with outsiders except on urgent family affairs'.

Feeling snubbed, rebuffed, and wholly cast down, I

yet took a grain of comfort in that word 'novices'. At least, then, Juana had not yet taken her final vows.

But two years had passed since that time; there was a strong probability that by now she had done so.

'Senor Felix,' said Pedro, interrupting my glum train of thought as we plodded through a small town called Corales, 'my stomach rumbles like Mount Vesuvius. How about a bite to eat?'

'With all my heart. And it is time we gave the mules a rest.'

It was a poverty-stricken little place, containing, perhaps, fifty families dwelling in mud huts and set in the midst of dry, dusty flatlands where young corn was beginning to sprout. We asked which was the *posada*, for there was nothing to distinguish it from any other house, and were directed to one in the middle of the village. Here we dismounted and entered, calling for food. A sullen-looking man said there was nothing to be had.

'What?' said Pedro, pointing to some dried bacon flitches hanging from the rafters. 'What about those? And have you no eggs? Bacon and eggs would suit us very well.'

Muttering and grumbling with the most cantankerous ill-will, the man at length hoisted down a side of bacon and cut a few slices from it. These he set sizzling in a pan while he growled his way out to a weedy yard at the rear, from which he presently returned bearing a basket of muddy, dusty eggs. These he fried in a great pan of oil so rancid that the smell was horrible.

'I am sorry now that I asked you to stop here,' muttered Pedro. 'We should have gone on to Zamora.'

While the eggs were cooking I strolled to the doorway, to get away from the smoke and stink, and stood gazing along the dusty, empty main street of this gloomy little hamlet.

By and by, in the distance, coming from the same direction as we had done, I discerned another traveller. He was mounted on a big, bony stallion, and, though his pace was slow enough now, he had evidently been travelling at a much faster rate, for his horse's shaggy grey coat was soaked and streaked with sweat. The man did not pause in Corales, though he eyed our two tethered mules with attention, I thought, as he rode past.

'What a weedy little fellow!' said Pedro, joining me in the doorway, attracted by the sound of hoofs. 'He does not look as if he'd have the strength to master that big brute. Why do you stare after him so?'

'I felt I knew his face. It seemed in some way familiar.'

At that moment the innkeeper called out in a surly tone that our food was ready, so we returned to eat the unappetising meal. The bacon was burned, and the eggs drowned in evil-smelling oil. All the while we ate, the man stood eyeing us and grumbling. as if we had done him an ill turn by stopping to eat at his posada; it was plain that, as a rule, he reckoned to serve only liquid refreshment, and that only in the evening. Pedro responded to this usage by a smile of beaming good-will. He commented loudly and flatteringly on the delicious flavour of the food as he munched each disgusting mouthful, and, when we left, cordially shook the owner's hand, assuring him that it was the best meal he had ever eaten, and that he would be sure to recommend the place to all his friends, of whom he had a great many, he assured the man, all over Spain.

'So you will soon have hundreds of customers for your superb bacon and your incomparable eggs.'

The ruffian gaped at him, incapable of thinking up a suitable reply, since, though Pedro's words were patently untrue, they were delivered with such smiling affability.

When I asked for the *cuenta*, it was at least double what it should have been, but, rather than fall into an argument with this disagreeable fellow, I paid it without haggling. I was still puzzling my wits, as I had done throughout the meal, as to where I could previously have seen the small man on the big grey stallion. He was a weaselly-looking character, who might have been an apothecary, or a lawyer's clerk . . .

An hour later, as we travelled on towards Zamora, descending, now, into the valley of the River Duero, I exclaimed, 'I have it! Of course, he is Sancho the Spy!'

'Sancho the Spy?' said Pedro, very startled. 'Who is Sancho the Spy?'

'That little fellow who rode by on the grey horse. We used to see him in Salamanca; very often, if a group of students were talking in the street, he would sidle past with his ears cocked like a terrier, and some of my mates believed that he was a police informer; if people were arrested it was thought that he had a hand in it; though nothing certain was ever proved. But they gave him the name of Sancho the Spy.'

Pedro frowned.

'Are you sure it was the same fellow?'

'I'd place a wager that it was. I wonder what in the world he was doing, so far from Salamanca?'

'Why wonder? For sure, he was following us.'

'But he has gone on ahead.'

'And he will certainly be waiting at some point farther on to pick up our trail again. It is a pity we must go to Zamora to cross the river. But perhaps after that we can give him the slip.'

'If he is really following us, I would rather knock his head off.'

'No, Senor Felix, that is not sensible,' said Pedro, shaking his own head. 'To kill a spy is like killing a spider. It brings bad luck.' Where he had his odd superstition from, I do not know. I never heard it before. 'No – what we must do,' he went on, 'is to try and lose him after Zamora. We can leave the main highway, strike westwards to Pueblo de Sanabria, and cross the mountains, the Sierra Cabrera; he'd be clever if he could follow us there.'

'Whatever you say, Pedro. How do you come to know the roads so well?'

'Oh, I've ridden errands for your granda in these parts; buying wine and selling wool. It's a fine wine country.'

Indeed the region around Zamora, very different from the desert plains north of Salamanca, is known as the Tierra del Vino and famous for its fertility, its vines and orchards. By and by we came within sight of the Duero, a wide swift blue river, here brawling over stones, there winding among white sand-banks. It was deep from melting winter snow, and its banks were well grown with trees, all in new spring leaf; among them, dozens of nightingales were singing at the tops of their voices.

'What a row!' said Pedro, blocking his ears.

'But their song is beautiful, Pedro!'

'*Beautiful?* All that chuck-chuck, tizz-wizz-wizz? Give me the old parrot any day! She, at least, talks good Spanish.'

When I ran away from home at the age of twelve, I had spent a night in the jail at Oviedo; there an old man, who helped me to escape, gave me his parrot, Assistenta. As I was at that time on my way to England, I had left Assistenta with some kind nuns in a convent at Santander, but later went back to reclaim her. She became my grandfather's favourite companion; he was tickled by the Latin words I had taught her, and taught her a great many more himself. When I went to college I had been glad to think they would keep each other company; she spent all her days clambering about his bookshelves.

We crossed the Duero by the great stone bridge (the only one for miles) and so up into the fortified town of Zamora, tightly crammed inside its high walls. Despite which walls, the French had captured it in Napoleon's wars, and remained there until fourteen years previously.

By now it was not far from dusk. Pedro said in a troubled tone, 'Our wisest course would be to ride straight through the town and continue on our way. But I am not certain that I could pick out the road to Pueblo de Sanabria in the dark.'

'No, it had better not be thought of. We'd get lost and waste time. Besides, the beasts need rest and fodder. What we should do is find some small *venta* near the northern edge of the town where we may pass the night inconspicuously and be off by dawn.'

Pedro agreed, so we rode on, along streets which, at this time of the evening, were crowded with towns-people taking their *paseo*, or twilight promenade. I looked carefully about me for the weaselly man on his grey horse, but saw them not. Near the north wall we found a small, humble inn, with a tumbledown stable where we left our animals. Now our plans received a check, for when we unsaddled we found that the belly-band of Pedro's mule was nearly worn through; another hour's riding would have broken it.

He exclaimed with annoyance.

'How could I have been such a dolt as not to notice that when I bought the beast? It was that cunning Granada gypsy who distracted me, when I began to inspect the harness, with a long tale about the beast's pedigree—'

'Never mind,' I said. 'The belly-band can be replaced. All we need is a saddler.'

'And where are we likely to find one open at this hour?'

However – having ordered a meal – we walked towards the market square, which lies to the east of the town, and were lucky enough to come upon a harness-maker's shop still open for business. The master of the establishment was attending to another late customer, but his boy came to serve us; Pedro, who had brought along his saddle, showed the rotted girth-strap and the boy went off to find a replacement. Meanwhile I amused myself by watching the other customer's child, a petulant looking little girl of perhaps four or five, with black hair plaited up on top of her head, fastened with red ribbons. She had a pert, pale, self-willed little face, its elfin prettiness quite spoiled by her expression. When, after listening with a sharp intelligence quite in advance of her age, she suddenly realised that the fat customer was purchasing a saddle with a *pillion*, she at once burst into ear-splitting shrieks of disgust and fury.

'No – and no – and *no*!' she yelled. 'I will not! I will *not*! I will *not* ride behind you like a beggar's child! I wish to ride in a carriage. I want it very much. *Very much!*'

The fat customer appeared almost out of his wits at having to deal with her temper and her tantrum.

'But, *hija*, you cannot! *Querida*, I fear it is impossible. Do not scold poor Papa!'

'You are not my papa! I want my proper papa.'

'Indeed, *hija*, I am your proper papa. You know how much I love you.'

'I want him. I want him very much!' she cried, ignoring the fat man's remonstrances.

'But that man is not your real papa—'

'I want him!'

'Well – we'll see – if you are a good girl,' he told her rather hopelessly. 'You shall have all the treats you want at the end of the journey, I promise! Sugar plums! And a new dress to wear—'

'And a fan as big as Mama's?'

'A fan – if you wish – and shoes of the best red leather—'

'But I wish to ride in a carriage!' she stormed. 'Not on a nasty hard pillion!'

'But *chica*, we cannot!'

'Why not? We rode here in a carriage.'

'But that was along an easy road from Salamanca. Now we must cross mountains – where there may be no carriage road.'

Idly watching this scene, I had been plaiting together some scraps of broken leather thong that lay scattered over the floor – a skill picked up from sailors on the tiny Biscay hooker which had brought me from England to Spain five years ago. Now, threading over

29

these a large blue bead, fallen from my mule's brow-band, which came from my pocket, I tied the thong-ends together and dropped the whole circlet over the child's head. She whirled round to stare at me, wide-eyed, clutching the leather necklace in astonishment – in her absorption over the affair of the pillion, she had not noticed me before.

'Why did you do that?' she hissed, scowling up at me.

'To put a spell on you,' I suggested.

'What do you mean?' She stuck out her lower lip, frowning down at the plaited necklace, pulling it up so as to study the blue bead. 'What is this? It is like the beads that oxen wear – to protect them from the Evil Eye.'

'Well,' I said, 'perhaps it will protect you likewise. Or perhaps it will help you to enjoy riding on that pillion!'

Then, seeing that Pedro had completed his purchase, I joined him among the dangling saddles at the shop entrance as the child still stared after me – meanwhile, I noticed her father hastily handing over silver coins for his pillion saddle. Flustered, sweating, and anxious, he had never even noticed my conver-sation with his child. Glancing back, I saw her quickly push the blue bead out of sight, under her tucker.

'Good, that was a piece of luck,' said Pedro with satisfaction. 'Heaven only knows what we would have done if that girth had broken somewhere on the mountains between Pedralba and Ponferrada.'

At our little inn they had a great dish of stewed hare waiting for us – a far better meal than our midday bacon and eggs.

While we were eating in the dim-lit downstairs room, the only one the place boasted, I overheard some inquiry taking place at the front door, and, craning so as to see past the back of the fat innkeeper who stood there, I caught sight of my small man from Salamanca, apparently putting questions to the posadero.

This seemed a perfect moment to take the bull by the horns – if bull there were – so, rising from the table, I walked to the entrance as if wishful to take a breath of air. Then, appearing to observe the small man for the first time, I gave a great start of assumed wonder, and cried out, 'Why, senor; what a pleasant surprise! How good to encounter a familiar face in a strange town! My dear friend, I have seen you so *often*, week after week, month after month, in the streets near the University in Salamanca that I feel you are, indeed, quite a friend! Will you not come in and take a glass of wine with me? It is such a joy to meet an acquaintance when far from home!'

The small man seemed startled out of his wits, and gaped at me, not in the least gratified at my recognition of him.

'Er – ha – hum – I fear I don't understand you, my young senor. Know you? I've never laid eyes on you in my entire life!'

'Oh, senor, how can you say such a thing? When I have so often seen you looking at me! Do you not come from Salamanca?'

'Why – yes – but—'

'Then what can you be doing in Zamora?'

At this he looked very put about. 'May the foul fiend fly away with you!' he burst out crossly. 'What affair is that of yours? I have a right to be in Zamora if I please! My – er – my sister lives here!'

'But you were asking, senor,' said the innkeeper patiently, 'you were inquiring if a certain young gentleman were staying here – was this the young gentleman you had in mind? You were telling me that he—'

'No, no, no, Devil take you, and him, this isn't the one. This isn't he at all. A – a tall big-built black-haired man – I was about to say – with a scar on his cheek—'

Outside the inn doorway there was a lantern suspended, and, now that my eyes had grown used to its dim glow, I could see that the Salamanca man had two companions, who loitered in the shadow just beyond the first circle of light. The smaller one I recognised at once by her movements – it was the child from the saddler's shop, dancing up and down, dragging and twisting her companion's arm. And he, from his bulk, must be her fat father.

The child knew me directly. I saw her intent little face look up, her eyes flicker, her hand move to the neck of her dress, as if she expected me to ask for the leather circlet back.

'Would you wish to come in and wait, in case the senor you are looking for comes later?' suggested the landlord.

'No, no, no!' cried the other man again. 'How do I know that he is not at some other posada – I must be on my way without delay—'

'Can I have his name – or yours – so that a message may be left?'

But, whisking his companions away from the circle of lamp light, the small man departed at speed. I returned more slowly to the table and my unfinished plate of hare stew.

Pedro made no comment at the time, nor did I. But, later, when we were abed – the small bare bedchamber had but one couch in it, a big sagging one with a tester and a flock mattress which we had to

share (it was damp and soggy as a tidal marsh) –
'Well,' whispered Pedro, 'I always say that it is an
advantage to know your enemy.'

'Ay – and for *him* to know *us*.'

'We had better set off before dawn.'

'I am of your opinion.'

Accordingly we were up and stirring, as on the
previous day, long before daylight, had drunk a cup of
greasy chocolate, paid our reckoning, and saddled our
beasts before anybody else was abroad in the streets.
Or, at least, anyone that we could see.

Guided by the dawn star, on our right, we set off
northwards.

'The turning for Pedro de Sanabria should be about
seven leagues farther on,' Pedro said. So we rode at a
good pace, in silence, for about an hour and a half,
listening hard for any sound of pursuing hoofbeats.

By that time, a grey and misty day had dawned.
Ahead of us now, to the north-west, we should have
been able to see high peaks, the Cabrera, and perhaps
the Montanas de Leon; but all was veiled in
cloud.

'This weather favours a notion I have,' said Pedro.

'Which is—?'

'We made very poor time yesterday. At this rate, it
will be four days before we reach home. Your grand-

father will be growing anxious. And if we take the mountain road, that is bound to slow us down—'

'What do you suggest?'

'We play the hare's game, and double back.'

Luck favoured us. Just before the left turn that would take us to Pueblo de Sanabria – which is in open country – we encountered a shepherd driving a great flock of sheep southward towards Zamora.

'Can you tell us, friend, which is the road for the Valle de Sanabria?' Pedro called above the bleating of his flock. In reply the shepherd gestured with his crook.

'Four bowshots ahead, to your left, senores,' he called back.

We were still in the green valley of the River Esta; there were orchards and vineyards all around. When we had reached the turn indicated by the shepherd, taken it, and ridden a hundred yards or so, Pedro said, 'Quick, now, while nobody is in sight. Off the road, and let us tie up the beasts at a good distance, out of sight and earshot.'

We led them among the trees, hobbled them, and left them grazing in the midst of an immense orchard of flowering plum trees; then returned to a point from which, hidden among the trees ourselves, we could watch the road. There we waited patiently.

Our patience was rewarded. Not half an hour after we started our vigil, who should come along but the small man on the big grey stallion. Without hesitation he took the left-hand fork, north-westwards for Pueblo de Sanabria.

'Good,' said Pedro. 'He has interrogated the shepherd, and the shepherd told him what he told us. Now, let us make haste the other way.'

So we retrieved our beasts and set off at full speed on the carriage road northwards towards Leon. 'And at Beneventa,' said Pedro with satisfaction, 'we join the great highway from Madrid to La Coruna. So our road becomes easier still. While Sancho the Spy has ahead of him a weary clamber over mountains.'

'You think he knows our destination?'

'Who can tell?'

'Why does he follow us?'

'How should I know?' said Pedro. 'That's not my affair.'

And he fell to singing, horribly out of tune, the verse:

> Santo Cristo de Lezo
> Tres cosas piso
> Salvacias y dinero
> Y una buena marida.

Pedro was good-natured, easy-going, cheerful, and shrewd as need be over all practical affairs; in many ways the best possible companion for a journey; yet there were boundaries to his nature, and beyond these he never made any attempt to venture. If the explanation of some matter was unknown to him, he would never try to seek it or guess at it. Things that he could not see were of no interest to him. And even things that he *could* see were valued strictly for their utility; you would never catch him admiring a sunset or a blossom-covered tree. I, as we rode in the mist among pink and-white starry plum trees, would have liked to exclaim over and over at their mysterious beauty; but I knew that Pedro would be both embarrassed and perplexed if I did so, or turn it off with a laugh; so I remained silent. Yet he was very fond of me, I knew, and so was I of him; he was the older by two years, and we had played and tumbled about together, and fought, sometimes, ever since I was born. And he was devotedly attached to my grandfather.

I thought of Juana. If she had seen this vast plain, covered with fruit-blossom, she would have wished to write one of her poems about it. In many ways her nature was as far removed from mine as mine was from Pedro's. Did *she* find *me* as limited as I found Pedro? That was a chill, uncomfortable notion. I feared it must be so. Perhaps she had done rightly in deciding to shut herself up alone with God? Perhaps God was the only person who could truly appreciate her?

Then I grinned, remembering some of her other qualities: she could lie like a tooth-puller if there was need (even, sometimes, without the necessity); she could be very bad-tempered and moody; she had a fierce pride, and was often impatient with those of less wit than herself. Indeed, I felt not a little sorry for God, in His dealings with Juana, shut up alone with her . . .

We made excellent speed that morning. After five hours' hard riding we came to Astorga, where we sold our mules, since they, poor things, were spent for the time, and would need several days' rest before they were fit for more work. However, since, they were fine animals, Pedro, who took care of the sale, obtained a decent price for them, and we managed to procure another pair, almost as good, big and strong, the larger one standing nearly sixteen hands.

Astorga, a small walled city with an arcaded plaza, is set on moorland with great mountains not far away. The cathedral is in ruins, and the people are grim and unfriendly. Hereabouts live the tribe of Maragatos, descended – so I have heard – from the Moors and ancient Goths. They carry the mails all over Spain, and are very faithful to their task, but otherwise surly and brutish.

We did not linger in Astorga, for there we had the great good fortune to fall in with the grand post from Madrid to La Coruna. We had been told that the road ahead was infested with robbers, so the chance to travel with some fifty companions, under armed escort, was not to be lost. A troop of soldiers accompanied the government courier, who carried, on his sturdy pony, two great leather sacks of official papers. We asked permission of the sergeant in charge to ride with the party, leave was given, and we all set forward together, Pedro and I congratulating ourselves, for, with luck, our presence in such a cavalcade would pass unnoticed, should anybody inquire about us after we had gone.

I had been wondering why the fat man with the little girl was not with Sancho the Spy that morning? Were they to follow him later? Or were they, after all, nothing to do with his interest in us, merely chance companions? Could Sancho have spoken the truth about his sister in Zamora? But then, why was the fat man planning a journey over the mountains? Or was that just coincidence? From time to time I put some of the questions and communings to Pedro but he, as I had known he would, merely shrugged, threw up his eyes, and answered, 'How can I tell?'

Meanwhile we continued at a rattling pace, the soldiers who accompanied us singing a great many songs, mostly bawdy ones. Once, for a moment, one of the men struck up the Revolutionary Hymn of Colonel Riego:

Tragala, tragala, tragala
Cara de morron—

but the sergeant immediately silenced him with a terrible look, and a great blow on the shoulder, struck with the flat of his sword.

Now the road began to seesaw, climbing sometimes over mighty and formidable mountains, dropping again among wide valleys where walnut and chestnut groves flourished, where nightingales sang and cuckoos called. At the village of Bembibre, a beautiful spot set among groves of oak and willow, we exchanged our martial escort for another, but there was no time to halt, the whole manoeuvre was performed at speed and we had no chance to buy food or bait our mounts. The same thing happened at Ponferrada, a mining town with a great castle high above it. Here, some members of the party fell out, as their steeds were exhausted, but we decided to press on, as far as our good beasts would take us.

Now we were ascending one of the loneliest roads that may be found anywhere in Spain, and skirting the shanks of some of the highest mountains. Great gorges and precipices lay all about us, and we had to tilt our heads far back to look up at the high snowy peaks. The villages, scanty and far apart, were small and grim, built of slate, with great stones on the roofs to keep them from blowing off in mountain storms. Down from the crags tumbled white waterfalls, often dropping a hundred feet to the beds they had carved out for themselves far below. We were warned by our escorts to be on the watch for wolf or wild boar, as the mountain-sides were often covered from peak to foot with dense forest. A few tiny fields, scattered here and there, hung almost vertical; on such steep slopes the crops must be dug and reaped by hand.

Joy filled my heart, for I knew we must be near the border of Galicia; the language of the folk we met along the way (few enough) now had the rough Gallegan accent, rather than the smooth Castilian they speak farther south.

Then a thought struck me: this road we travelled was the hard and terrible way taken by General Moore's armies when, eighteen years ago (just before

41

my birth), the English troops were forced to retreat, through bitter winter weather, with Napoleon's cavalry hard on their heels, sabring and shooting down any stragglers. All the way to La Coruna, more than 150 miles, the English retreated with General Soult close behind them; the Spanish baggage-drivers forsook their mule-carts, and the provisions had to be abandoned, since the draught animals did not understand English words of command. Bodies of dead men, mules, oxen, were scattered all along the way. And at one point, farther along that grisly road, among the highest peaks, a great treasure in gold and silver dollars, worth 25,000 English pounds, had to be jettisoned, rolled down the mountain-side in barrels, so that the pursuing French should not seize it.

That treasure had never been recovered.

This story I had heard many times, from country people on my grandfather's estate, and also from a renegade English soldier named Smith, whom I had met five years ago in strange circumstances on the mountains near Oviedo. Smith and some comrades of his had actually known where the treasure was to be found – or so he told me – and they had fought one another for the prize, two by two, until at last only the man Smith was left. I had been the accidental witness to the last of these duels. Smith, after killing his opponent, had planned to go and take the treasure for himself; but he died of the lung-rot before he could so do.

Who had it now, I wondered? Perhaps it had been discovered long ago; but whoever came across it must have kept the news to himself. If you found 25,000 pounds' worth of gold coins in a mountain gorge on the border between Galicia and Asturias, would you not keep a still tongue about it, lest the authorities descend like mountain ravens, and rob you of your prize?

Everything in this region was wild, strange, terrifying, and beautiful; the track grew narrower and narrower as we climbed (going more slowly now) up and up to the very top of the highest pass. A thick mist, up there, enwrapped us – what in Galicia is known as a *bretima*. Luckily the ground at the top of the pass was level, a flat plain studded with thorn-thickets, for now night fell, and we were obliged to make our way through a profound darkness, without moon or star. If Pedro and I had been on our own, crossing one of the loftiest peaks in Spain, carved by ravine and precipices, we must have sat down and waited for daylight; but the armed guard, well used to this road, merely lit flambeaux and continued, a little more warily, yet still making good speed.

43

After more hours of travel, descending the northern slopes of the mountains, we came to the village of Los Nogales, where the escort was again exchanged for another set of soldiers. Nogales was a pleasant little place, half buried in chestnut woods, with a brawling river – but little of it could be seen, for the hour was now very late, and all the houses were dark, excepting the posada, where the new guard awaited us. Pedro was for spending the rest of the night here, but I said, 'Come! Surely we can make shift to keep awake until daybreak. By now we must be little more than seven leagues from Villaverde; let us press on.'

'Ay,' said Pedro doubtfully, 'but the road from Becerrea is little more than a track—'

'Well, let us make a try, at all events.' Now that we were so close to home, I was wild with impatience to finish the journey.

So at Becerrea we left our companions, who all shouted a friendly farewell, and turned north-east off the main *carretera*.

Happily for us, the mist had thinned as we descended the mountain, and there was moonlight to guide us on our way down a narrow valley beside yet another foaming torrent. We must follow this valley to where it was joined by a second, then turn south-east up that one; the cart tracks in this region follow the valleys; only sheep tracks cross the mountain ridges.

At a little village called Navia we had to make the turn, but here Pedro said apologetically, 'I must rest a while, Senor Felix. My eyes keep closing. And my poor beast keeps stumbling. An hour's sleep will see me fit to finish the journey.'

'*Vaya*. Sleep then. My mule can do with a rest too. I'll keep watch – I'm too restless for sleep.'

Navia was too small to boast even the meanest *albergue*. But there was a farmyard with an open shed where, amid a thin litter of last year's hay, two scrawny cows were stabled. In half a minute Pedro had fed some of the hay to the mules and scraped himself a pile of it on which to cast himself down.

Far from sleep myself, I sat down upon another truss, elbows on knees, and listened to the peaceful sound of our tethered mules munching the stale fodder. Poor things, they had travelled more than twenty leagues at a spanking pace; they deserved a better meal. If the farmer showed himself early enough, we could ask if he had barley or oats.

The great stars paled and sparkled overhead, the mountain ridges on either side of the valley showed blacker as the eastern sky began to lighten. But down here, in the valley bottom, it was still pitch dark when I began to hear the shod hoofs of two horses come rapping along the road from Becerrea.

My mind had been rambling vaguely over many subjects – Juana, shut away in her French convent; my grandfather and his friendship with Rafael Riego, the Liberal leader; the story of King Oedipus that I had been reading; the gold treasure lost during General Moore's retreat; the brigands who infest these mountains, and indeed all of Spain; my tutor saying in a resigned tone, when I asked him what could help Spain, 'Time alone is the cure. Maybe in a hundred years . . .' A hundred years is a long time, a very long time . . . I thought, beginning to nod off, but the sound of the hoofs brought me full awake, all in a minute.

I could just see the two mounts, with their riders, pass the entrance to our yard; they were little more than shadows, but I caught the gleam of a stirrup and heard the clink of a bit. They did not pause, but rode quietly on their way.

I touched Pedro's arm, and he was awake in a moment.

'Psst! Two riders have just gone past!'

'*Maladetta!* Did you see their faces?'

'No, it was too dark. But, more important, they did not see us.'

'Are you sure?'

'Yes.'

'How can we make use of that?' Pedro fell silent, gnawing his lip in thought.

The farmer's pair of heifers had been lowing for some time, clamouring to be milked, and the man himself now made his appearance, yawning and surly – but was appeased when we gave him a *cuarto* for the use of his fodder, and told him that we were on our way to Villaverde. Everybody for miles around knew my grandfather and respected his name. Pedro asked the man if he had any idea who the two travellers could be that had passed so secretly in the dead of night. Did people often pass through Navia at such an hour?

'No: it was probably friars,' he said, scowling. 'Friars are the cause of all the miseries in this wretched land. Until a few years back they had a monastery, up there on the mountain. It is empty now, but they still come round to claim rents and rob us poor farmers of half our income. They travel at all hours and mind everyone's business but their own.' He would have gone on much longer, grumbling about the friars, but we cut him short by asking if there was another way that would take us to Villaverde, besides the road along which the horsemen had gone.

There did exist a track, he told us, up over the shoulder of the mountain; but we would have to walk the first part of the way, leading our mules. 'It is far too dangerous to be ridden, you or your beasts would be certain to fall down the mountain.'

After reflecting a moment, he added, 'For another cuarto I will put you on your path, if you don't mind waiting till I have milked my cattle. I wouldn't mind a chance to see those night travellers for myself. The track is a short-cut although so steep, and will take us over a height from which we can look down and see them winding their way along the valley road.'

This offer was agreeable to us, so we waited, and he gave us a drink of warm milk. Then, the milking finished, he led us along a steep zigzag path which climbed straight up from the valley and over a wooded shoulder of the mountain. We would never have been able to find it for ourselves, even in the dawn light which was now creeping over the hilltop, for it was hardly more than a rabbit-track, scarcely visible, save to one who knew it well.

By and by we were out in the open, on bald scrubby hillside, and paused a moment to get our breath. The farmer would not permit us to wait longer. 'We must make haste,' said he, 'or those fellows will have turned the comer of the road and we shan't be able to see them,' leading us onward along the threadlike track at such a pace that both we and the mules were hard put to it to keep up with him. The path, as he had warned, was horribly unsafe, since it crossed a bare steep shoulder of mountain which was formed of loose shale that crumbled and slid away under our feet and our mules' hoofs. We had to move with infinite care, studying every foothold. After some half-hour of this perilous and unpleasant progress, the farmer let out a triumphant cry.

'There are the pigs, down below. I see them! Ay, they are most certainly friars – just look at their black cloaks.'

With extreme caution, I lifted my eyes from the pathway and looked down the hillside where he pointed. As he had promised, up here we commanded a view of the cart-road, which, a hundred feet below, wound its way along beside the river in the bottom of the valley. And there, sure enough, were two riders who looked, from so far above, like mere beetles creeping along the road.

'*Bueno!*' said the farmer. 'God certainly sent you two gentlemen to tell me about those wretches. They shall do no more harm in this world.' And, with careful deliberation, he pulled a largish rock, about the size of a melon, from a spot below the path and, before we realised what he intended, tossed it downwards on to the hillside above the two unwitting travellers.

What followed was terrifying, almost unbelievable

to behold. The rock, thrown down on to that slope of unstable scree, started a spurt of small stones cascading down which, in a matter of seconds, increased to a huge pouring cataract of rubble, deadly and unstoppable. Alerted by its roaring sound, the two travellers looked up, and, terrified, spurred their horses – but they were far too late. There was no escape for them. In moments both they and their beasts were completely engulfed in a smoking torrent of earth and rock which covered the road entirely and poured on into the river below.

'Merciful God, man – what have you done?' I cried. 'You have murdered those two men – who, for all we know to the contrary, may have been two perfectly harmless, innocent wayfarers!'

'Not they!' he said with satisfaction. 'Did you not see their black cloaks? They were friars for sure.'

'But others besides friars wear black cloaks!'

'If they were *not* friars, what were they doing, sneaking about in the middle of the night like brigands?'

'Well, but *we* were travelling at night, and we are not brigands.'

'I know you are honest folk,' he said, 'for you are going to the house of the Conde de Cabezada at Villaverde; everybody knows that the Conde is a good and just administrator. My niece works in his dairy and says the old ladies are holy angels. Here I will bid you goodbye, senores; you cannot go wrong now the sun has risen. Keep south-east, with the sun on your left, cross two ridges, and you will see Villaverde straight ahead.'

So, picking his way carefully past us, he took himself off homewards.

We too continued, tiptoeing along the track as if we were walking on razor-blades. Our beasts snorted and shivered, no happier than ourselves. However, another half-hour's inching, cautious advance brought us to the end of this frightfully dangerous portion of the path, and we were able to stop, wipe our sweat-soaked brows, and fondle our mules, likewise sweat-soaked and trembling.

'Well,' said Pedro in a devil-may-care voice – though I could see from his pallor that he was as shaken as myself – 'I daresay we shall never know who those two men were. But – as the farmer said – they were probably up to no good. And they may very well have been on our trail. If they had found out that we travelled with the grand post, they must have guessed that we'd take the road from Becerrea.'

'I suppose so.'

I could say no more. Already, in my short life, I had

witnessed a number of deaths – these were wild and heartless times – but the calm, callous way in which the farmer had tossed that rock and despatched those two into the next world, neither knowing nor caring if they deserved such an end, had left me shaken to the marrow.

For a long way we rode in silence. Now the risen sun warmed us and dried the shaggy coats of our beasts; birds began to sing, mountain larks, and I smelt a hint of smoke from a steading in the valley below. A great eagle floated past us, on nine-foot wings.

Another two ridges crossed and, as the man had promised, we could see, ahead on the farthest height, the town wall of Villaverde, like a scroll of rock, gilded with morning light, encircling the houses within.

Pedro gave a great yawn.

'Your grandpa will have been up for hours,' said he. 'Looking for us all over the landscape with his spy-glass. And I can eat every crumb of the breakfast my aunt Prudencia will have prepared.'

2

*I return home and hear heart-warming
news from a convent in Bilbao; Pedro
and I prepare for another journey;
strange tidings of Sancho the Spy*

It was a great joy to be with my grandfather again.
Every time I left him, I had a secret dread that it
might be for the last time, that I might never see him
again, for he was very frail these days, thin, wrinkled
and veined as a withered leaf, and his hair, which
during my childhood had been iron grey, thick and
burnished, had since turned to frosty white and was
growing very scanty. At each of our partings I put up a
silent prayer to God that we would be permitted to
meet again; and so far God had been indulgent to me.
But, this morning, I noticed with grief the thinness and
pallor of the Conde's face, seamed now with many new

wrinkles, and the tremor in his hands as he held them up to embrace me.

His dark eyes were fiery as ever, though, and his voice had its accustomed dryness.

'Good heavens, my dear grandson! Here have I been praying for the last three years that you might be returned to me safe, and the Almighty has listened so favourably to my petitions that He has granted them twice over. You have doubled in size!'

'Why, yes, Grandfather – I – I suppose I *have* grown. I never gave it any thought.'

'The air of Salamanca must be healthy,' he said as I stooped to kiss his brow.

'And I am glad to see *you* looking well, dear Grandfather.'

This was not really true, but he sniffed, waved a dismissive hand, and let it pass.

'How extremely fortunate,' he said, 'that your grandmother and great-aunts are still asleep in their beds. They lie long, these days, the old senoras. We can discuss our affairs before they all come cawing and pecking about you.'

'I shall be glad to do so, sir.'

'You were a good boy to make such admirable speed. And so was Pedro. Both good boys—'

At this moment Gaspar, the major-domo, brought in

a great breakfast for me – we were in my grandfather's library, with the parrot, Assistenta, clambering about the bookshelves as was her habit – so the Conde waited until he had withdrawn.

'Eat, my boy – help yourself to chocolate and *churros* – you must be half starved if you have been riding all night.'

'How about you, sir?'

'Half a cup of chocolate – no more. I eat sparingly these days.'

'Now, sir,' I said, when he was served. 'Do, please, tell me what the matter is, for I am dying of suspense. Is it some trouble? Government business? Does it relate to the Liberal party? To politics?'

The Conde shook his head.

'Not exactly. Yes and no. *Trouble* there is, yes, but it relates to your friends rather than to mine.'

'My friends?'

'Your help has been requested.'

I was running my mind through the small tale of my friends, trying to think who could have asked for my help – the miller's family in San Antonio, the English sailor, Sam, married to the blacksmith's daughter at Llanes, the priest in Santillana?

Suddenly a notion, burning and improbable, flashed like a comet across my mind.

'*Who* has asked for my help, sir?'

My grandfather had the most elaborate wheelchair, constructed out of oak, steel, and damask. It was equipped with a hinged writing desk, a side-table, a lamp, and a mirror. He now pulled forward the writing desk and searched methodically among the neatly piled papers, each pile tied with a differently coloured thread of silk.

'I have had a letter,' he said, finding a packet tied with a blue thread and selecting a paper from its contents. He put on a pair of silver-rimmed spectacles and peered through them. 'A letter from a convent—'

'A *convent*? In Bayonne?' My heart shot up and lodged in my windpipe.

My grandfather squinted at me over the top of his spectacles.

'Bayonne? No, in Bilbao.'

My heart sank down again.

'Bilbao? I – I believe that I know nobody in Bilbao.'

'I had better read you the letter,' said my grandfather. 'It is from the Reverend Mother at El Convento de la Encarnacion, Bilbao.' He cleared his throat. 'Ahem! "Esteemed Senor: It is with the most humble apologies and the deepest diffidence that I take the liberty of approaching your gracious self, and I would hardly venture to do so if the matter were not one of life and death."'

'Life and death!' I gasped.

'Humph.' My grandfather again looked at me over his glasses, then resumed reading. '"One of the novices in our sister convent of Notre Dame de Douleur, in Bayonne—"'

'Ah!'

'"— in Bayonne, Sister Felicita, has been appealed to by a female relative of hers who is in extreme distress. The name of this female relative is Dona Conchita de la Trava y Escaroz. You may recall the name of her husband, Don Manuel de Morales de la Trava, who was consigned to prison in Barcelona last year for expressing revolutionary and anti-royalist opinions of the most disgraceful nature."'

'*Did* he do so, Grandfather?' I asked, partly to quell the frantic beating of my heart.

'It depends upon your own views as to whether you consider his disgraceful,' replied the Conde, pursing his upper lip. 'I certainly knew of Manuel de la Trava, and that he had been imprisoned.' He continued reading. '"Upon the imprisonment of her husband, Dona Conchita, whose political opinions are of the most exemplary nature, was obliged to sever all connection with her husband. She retired to live with relatives here in Bilbao, accompanied by her three children, who are all under the age of nine. But, last month, her renegade and ruffianly husband succeeded in escaping from Montjuich prison in Barcelona, where he had been incarcerated, and then managed to abduct the three little ones from their mother's care. He has absconded with them to some cave or ruin in the vicinity of Jaca, where his family formerly owned property. He has written a letter to his poor wife declaring that he will never give up the children, but will sooner put an end to his existence, and theirs too."'

'Good heavens!'

'"Dona de la Trava, who has the deepest and most devoted attachment to her children, is, consequently, in terrible distress. She wrote appealing for help to her cousin, Sister Felicita (in the world formerly known as Senorita Juana Esparza)."'

'I wonder why she did that?' I said thoughtfully.

It was true that Juana had been a most resourceful and redoubtable girl – none knew that better than I – but how, from her convent, could she possibly assist in the rescue of those unlucky children from some cave in Aragon?

Grandfather continued reading: '"It appears that, for a portion of her life, Sister Felicita had the care of these young ones, knew them well, and was sincerely attached to them. Mere Madeleine, the Superior of the Convent in Bayonne, therefore gave her permission for

Sister Felicita to travel from Bayonne to our House in Bilbao, where she is at present, in order that she might discuss the situation with her cousin, Dona de la Trava, and give advice."

'Conchita de la Trava,' remarked my grandfather, pausing at this point and again looking at me over his glasses, 'before her marriage was Conchita Escaroz, daughter of one of the richest mine owners in Bilbao.'

Grandfather always knew about families, who had married whom.

'Oh, I see. *That* is why the Reverend Mother is being so obliging.'

'One of the reasons, perhaps. "Sister Felicita, horrified, as we all are, at the plight of these poor innocent little ones, snatched off into the wilderness by a madman, has offered all the help in her power, and has been granted permission to travel to Jaca with her cousin, in case her intercession may be of use. Another nun, Sister Belen, will accompany her, but a male escort will also be necessary. Dona de la Trava's father is too old and unwell for such a mission; Sister Felicita therefore suggested that we appeal to you for the good offices of your grandson, Senor Felix de Cabezada y Brooke, who, I am informed, displayed the greatest possible enterprise, courage, chivalry, and resource upon a former occasion when he escorted Senorita

Esparza (as she then was) across the Pyrenees and into the safe-keeping of her uncle Senor León d'Echepara."

'Ay, ay,' commented my grandfather, breaking off to wipe his glasses and take a sip of chocolate, 'they can pile on the compliments fast enough when they want to wheedle a favour out of you. While, at other times, they take the greatest delight in slamming a hammer down on your fingers.'

I reflected that, in his views on the clergy, Grandfather was not so far distant from the farmer this morning, coolly unleashing an avalanche upon the two travellers who might or might not be friars.

'Do you think that I ought to go, Grandfather?'

But of course, of course I would! My heart was bursting with joy and excitement. *I shall see her. I shall see her again!* sang its senseless refrain inside my head.

'How could you possibly resist such an appeal?' said the Conde, raising his brows. He removed his spectacles, eyed me sharply, and inquired, 'Why did the young lady become a nun in the first place? Was she so very religious?'

'No . . . I do not think it was that. But she had had all those terrible experiences – abducted by the Mala Gente – nearly hanged – her own brother hiring assassins to kill her and being murdered himself; and there had been a cousin of hers, Laura, who had also died violently. I think Juana felt that her taking the veil might in some way atone for all these crimes . . .'

'I see.' He resumed his glasses and glanced at the finish of the letter. 'There is little more – except a great many professions of gratitude and so forth, which we may take for granted.'

He handed me the paper, which was headed by a great conventual seal, and I read the lines again for myself.

Then I said, 'Would you wish me to go upon this errand, Grandfather?'

'My boy, I leave that decision entirely to you.'

Yet he had brought me home at racing speed.

I asked, 'Do you know anything about these people, sir? Manuel de la Trava, and his wife?'

The Conde pursed his lip again.

'He is of good family – noble blood of Aragon. He wrote some intelligent pamphlets on the backwardness of our educational and medical services. I daresay those were enough to get him jailed. He is, I believe, a friend of that Jose de Larra who writes in Madrid under the name of Figaro.'

'Of course I have heard of *him*.'

'Somebody told me that Manuel de la Trava had gone mad in prison. A not infrequent occurrence at Montjuich,' added my grandfather gloomily. 'They say it is a hell on earth. As to his wife, I know nothing, except that she was very rich and reputed to be a great beauty. Her family were not so well born as her husband's. *New* money, from coal mines.'

I smiled a little, inside myself. Grandfather, despite his views on progress and reform, would always look more kindly on somebody who came from an ancient line. His attitude towards me had changed decidedly for the better when he found that I was not born out of wedlock, son of a penniless English army captain, but was, on the contrary, the legitimate grandson of an English duke. I could not hold this against him. For one thing, he loved and respected the peasants just as much as he did people of aristocratic descent.

'The peasants, you see, are well-descended too,' he had told me seriously. 'Their forefathers have always been here, in Villaverde, since long before the Romans. Since Adam. They and I understand one another very well. It is only those jumped-up nobodies in the middle – people whose ancestors come from God knows where, foundry owners and shopkeepers, people who don't know their place – that I cannot abide.'

All these things were passing through my head as I said, 'Well – I should like to go on this errand, if you approve, Grandfather. I do not at all see how I can be helpful in getting these poor children away from their crazy father, but there is no sense in trying to make plans until I have seen what the circumstances are. And I must confess I shall be glad – very glad – of the chance to see Senorita Esparza once more.'

'You must be prepared, don't forget, to find great changes in her. Young ladies at that time of life grow up much faster than their male counterparts.' His wise, ironic eye dwelt on me, I thought, with sympathy.

'Yes, I suppose so . . . And she is a nun, after all.'

My heart sank again at the thought. To distract myself, I asked, 'When did you receive this letter, Grandfather?'

He counted on his fingers. 'Seven days ago now; I delayed answering until I had discovered your feelings on the matter. Now, since you wish to go, I will dictate a letter which you may write for me if you will – my fingers are so wretchedly stiff these days that they can hardly grasp a quill; then you may carry it with you to Bilbao, to this Reverend Mother at the Convento de la Encarnacion.'

'How long will it take us to get to Bilbao?'

I had never been to Bilbao, which is a seaport on the Biscay coast, not far from the border of Spain and France.

'It is farther than Salamanca – I suppose five or six

days' travelling. You could go part of the way by sea – take ship from Aviles or Gijon.'

A week from now, I was thinking, perhaps a week from this very day I may see her.

I still kept a remembrance she had left with me: a little snuffbox containing four tiny stones, ruby, ivory, agate, topaz, and a dried ilex leaf. I carried it with me always.

My grandfather gave me another long, considering look, and said, 'I should like you to take Pedro with you.'

'*Pedro? Why?*'

I was not pleased. True, Pedro was a good fellow, we got on well, and I was fond of him; but for an errand of this sort, where great delicacy might be called for, and who knew what kind of complications might arise, I did not see the necessity for his company. Juana and I had been alone together on our previous adventure, and we had come through it very success-fully. Pedro's presence had been all very well on the journey from Salamanca, but I could not help feeling that, on this new mission, he might be most wretchedly in the way.

But my grandfather said placidly, 'Pedro has grown into a very dependable, sensible fellow.'

'Yes; that is true. He showed plenty of sense, coming from Salamanca.'

'And you are going to have a pair of religious sisters on your hands; besides, I presume, Senora de la Trava.'

'True,' I said gloomily. I supposed the children's mother might wish to come along and have some say in our rescue plans.

'I shall feel easier in my mind if you have Pedro with you,' my grandfather concluded in a firm tone.

I suppose I must still have looked as if I disagreed. My longing to conduct this adventure on my own was so very strong. A glow of pride warmed me through and through at the notion that Juana, even though she might now be a nun, had thought of me, had needed my help, had singled me out and taken such pains to have me sent for.

'But, after all, it is only to entice some children away from a madman? There can be no great danger or difficulty about such a task?'

'How can we possibly tell?' said my grandfather. 'I recall meeting Manuel de la Trava fifteen years ago at Santiago de Compostela—'

'I can remember that journey,' I began impulsively, and then stopped. I had been nearly four at the time. The pilgrimage had been undertaken so that my grandparents might pray for the safety of my uncles Juan and Esteban, colonels in the Spanish army fighting in the War of Independence. But those prayers had gone unanswered; both of my two uncles, like their brothers Miguel and Jose before them, had been killed in battle. I was now my grandfather's sole descendant, for my cousin Manuel Isidro had died of the smallpox in Madrid last summer.

'De la Trava was a fine, handsome fellow, intelligent, honest, and brave,' my grandfather said slowly.

'But he may be quite changed now if he has gone mad.'

'His strength and courage may be unimpaired. You may find your task a difficult one. In all kinds of ways.'

I sighed, feeling certain that I would be able to manage it somehow, if only I were left to arrange matters to my own liking.

Grandfather smiled then, the rare smile that lit his face like the gleam of the dying sun.

'Bear with me, Felix! I am an old man and must be humoured. The years have been long while you were away at Salamanca. But at least, while you were there, I could feel that you were in no danger and were profiting from excellent teachers – I trust that was so?' he added, shooting a diamond-bright glance from under his bushy brows, which, unlike the rest of his hair, had remained jet-black.

'Certainly it was,' I replied stoutly. 'I have been working hard, Grandfather. I have learned a great deal.'

'But now you are my sole heir – I have lost so much – so much,' he muttered.

'I know, sir. And I am very sorry. I won't thwart you.'

Yet still, though ashamed of my childishness, I felt impatient at this weight of moral obligation which seemed to hang on me like a heavy collar; I had not asked to be his heir, after all!

'You will have to look after your great-aunts when I am gone. And your grandmother too, very possibly. And there is much less money than there was.'

Indeed I had noticed that many of the treasured objects of silver, china, and porcelain were gone from the places they had once occupied in the big, glass-fronted walnut cabinets. So had the ornaments of Toledo steel, and some of the big glossy paintings of fruit and fishes and dead hares that used to hang on the walls. Pedro had told me that many things had been sold. Now for the first time I realised that these had probably paid for my education at Salamanca. Well: those pictures of dead hares were no great loss, I told myself doggedly.

But perhaps Grandfather had hated parting with them.

I was glad that I really had worked hard.

'Are you sure, Grandfather, that you can manage without Pedro? After all, we do not know how long this business may take.'

'Yes, yes, this is an easy time, before the harvest. And, between you, I daresay, you will find some way of bringing the affair to a speedy conclusion. Though it's an unhappy matter.' The Conde sighed. 'But now, run along with you, my dearest boy, you look tired to death. You had best get some sleep before all the old ladies come swarming out, and before you need to start planning your new departure.'

'May I take this letter, Grandfather?'

'Certainly, certainly. Sleep well now—' He made the sign of the cross as I bowed and left him.

The paper, with its heavy seal, felt warm in my fingers. 'Sister Felicita therefore suggested that we appeal to you for the good offices of your grandson . . .' How those words danced in my heart!

Tucking the letter into my jacket pocket I went to the kitchen, where Pedro was being fed a huge breakfast by his aunt Prudencia, the cook. She at once rose and gave me a great embrace.

'Glorious Virgin! How the boy has grown! I never thought you'd fill out and shoot up so! But your hair is still as yellow as a gold *duro* and your eyes blue as flax.'

Annoyed with myself, I blushed. When I was younger I had hated my yellow hair, so different from that of everybody else; and I still thought that it made me seem younger than my age.

'How is everybody?' I asked quickly. 'Rodrigo – Gaston – Sancho – Manuela – Maria?'

'All well, all well – all agog to see you too, only the Conde said you'd go straight off to your bed after you had eaten.'

'And so I shall, only first I must go and see if old Gato is somewhere about. He is – he *is* still alive?' I asked Pedro.

'Who? Oh, the old cat, yes, he'll be somewhere out there in the stable-yard, so far as I know, he was here when I left to fetch you. But very old now – so stiff he can't jump on to the mounting-block any longer.'

I went into the stable-yard calling, 'Gato! Gato!' And saw him, sitting in a patch of sun and straw, my old yellow cat. He must be an immense age for a cat now, even in human years older than I. He was one of the first things I could remember.

He stood up, stiffly, and started towards me. I saw with grief that he was lacking an eye, and that one of his ears was in tatters. He had always been a great battler, Gato. He walked very slowly indeed, stiff and skeleton-thin, with his tail straight upright, like a sword. I could see the shadows of all his bones, along his tawny side. And when he was within a yard of me, he suddenly lay down, on his side, on the dusty cobbles.

As I stooped to stroke him, I saw that he was dead. The one good eye, still yellow as amber, stared at nothing. He had waited for me as long as he possibly could.

I carried him to a far-distant corner of my grand-mother's garden, took a spade from a shed, and buried him under a neglected grape-arbour, wrapped up in one of my old cambric shirts. Sleep well, old fellow, I told him. Dream of mice. Rest there, in the shade. I won't forget you. Never, *never*. Once, you were my only comfort.

Suddenly my three years at Salamanca – learning, reading, talking, arguing, discussing – fell away and seemed as if they had been no more than three minutes. I was the Felix of an earlier time once more. The substance of home lapped me round. I belonged here, at Villaverde – like it or not.

Slowly, feeling all of my exhaustion now, I made my way to my room. Thoughts drifted past – Grandfather – Juana – my tired old Gato – and then, just before I slept, the memory of those two men, smothered to death under the avalanche, came into my mind. Poor devils – poor devils – had anybody dug them out yet? Very probably they might lie there for days, on such a rarely used road . . .

When I woke, the room was filled with reflected sunset glow. My windows looked south – in fact they pierced clean through the town wall – towards the great snow-covered mountain range round which Pedro and I had just skirted, the Picos de Ancares. I had always loved this room, even in my loneliest, most miserable days, for its silence and security and seclusion – few members of the household ever troubled to climb up here and seek me out.

But now I was aware of a small, scrabbling sound, before I opened my eyes, as if squirrels or mice had got into the place and were searching for eatables. I rolled over and sat up, startling my great-aunts Josefina and Visitacion almost to death. (Fortunately I had flung myself down with all my clothes on.)

The two old ladies huddled together, staring at me with bright beady eyes. They were like two dried-up old insects, wrapped in layers of silk, wool, and bombazine, with Manila shawls over all, enveloped in a cloud of lavender water that made me cough, hung

71

about with little pockets and laces, with clinking sets of keys, with fans and handkerchiefs and crucifixes and beads and needle-cases.

'Ah, *there* you are, Felix!' murmured Josefina.

Visitacion just stared. She, apparently, during my three years' absence, had suffered a slight stroke, for her face was a little lop-sided.

I said politely, 'Thank you kindly for coming to wake me, Aunt Josefina, Aunt Visitacion. I am glad to see you well. Can I – can I help you in any way?'

They looked at one another, then at me again. Then they both twittered together, in their high, husky voices.

'We wished to ask you – that is, we were anxious to know—'

'What did you wish to ask me, senoras?' I inquired, for they seemed to have come to a halt, and I wanted my room to myself.

'Is it *true* that you are going on this errand? Are you really going to search for that terrible man who has made away with his own children?' they said together.

And how the Devil did you learn that? I wondered. For sure, my grandfather never told you.

But I remembered that keeping any secret in this household was out of the question. The contents of a letter would be whispered around the house, almost before its owner had done reading it.

'Is your grandfather *really* in favour of such a mad, dangerous scheme? Francisco is so simple and gullible! The whole thing is a plot – a perilous, terrifying plot!'

'A plot, senoras? How can it be that?'

'Child, child, don't you see, it is a plot to involve you, and so also the Conde, in dangerous, democratic affairs. The Society of the Exterminating Angel will be after him directly, and the Military Commission. He will be a doomed man!'

'But why – I don't see—'

I knew, of course, about the Society of the Exterminating Angel. It had been founded by the Bishop of Osma and was secretly organised and most powerful. It was said that Don Carlos, the king's brother, and his wife belonged to it; that the meetings were held in the palace at Madrid, and its mission was to organise vengeance upon all the Liberals who had supported the democratic constitution.

'And *then* what will become of us?' lamented Josefina. 'If your grandfather is thrown into prison – and his estates confiscated – we and your grandmother will be forced to beg in the streets! We shall starve in degradation—'

I could hardly help laughing, their fears seemed so

selfish and irrational. But they were both as white as pastry and gazed at me with huge, haunted eyes. I did my best to reassure them, promised them that if I detected any evidence of such a plot as they envisaged, I would withdraw from the business; finally I succeeded in shepherding them out of my chamber.

Hen-witted old creatures, I thought, as they twittered and clattered their way down the flight of stone stairs outside my door, silly, self-absorbed old fools. All they worry about is where their next meal is coming from. As if I would let their remonstrances affect me in any way – specially in a matter such as this!

My grandfather had interviewed Pedro while I slept, and arrangements were already in preparation for our new journey. Pedro was so unaffectedly delighted at hearing he was to accompany me again that I had not the heart to let him know how contrary to my wish this had been.

'Look!' he said with pride. 'The Conde has lent me this pair of pistols which belonged to your uncle Esteban! What an honour! Are they not handsome? How far is it to Bilbao? I believe the people all speak Basque in that place. How in the world will we make ourselves understood?'

I remembered how Juana had attempted in vain to teach me Basque, or, as it should properly be called, Euskara. It is undoubtedly a language of the Devil. In all the weeks we were together I learned only about half a dozen words: *gab-boon*, *egg-en-noon*, for good night, good morning, *gizon*, a man, *khatten*, to eat, *erratten*, to drink. But, they say, Euskara is the language that our father Adam spoke in Eden.

'Don't worry your head,' I told Pedro. 'Nearly all the Basques speak some Spanish and some French.' My grandfather sent for me after dinner and presented me with a corresponding pair of pistols which had belonged to my uncle Juan.

'I hope you will not need to use them,' said he. 'But it is well to be provided against danger. And they are good weapons. Besides, if de la Trava has really taken refuge in the High Pyrenees, you may need to protect yourselves against wolves or wild boar. Ha! Now your eyes begin to sparkle. Well, I hope such beasts may prove the worst perils that you have to encounter. Wolves can be easier to tackle than wicked men.'

'Grandfather . . . my great-aunts, Josefina and Visitacion, seem to believe there is a plot.'

'I know,' he said seriously. 'Poor old ladies – they see plots in everything. Just the same, they need not be wrong. I have today heard a strange and troubling tale —' glancing at a sombrero hat which, for the first time, I noticed lying on the large table where he kept estate maps. The sight of it surprised me, firstly, because my grandfather had almost given up going out of doors since his house arrest, even though that had now been revoked; secondly, because if he did venture out, he wore an old-fashioned tricorne, never a sombrero. 'The villagers of Navia came to me, while you slept, to inform me that there had been a landslide on the road from Becerrea and that two travellers had been killed by it. The slide must have taken place after you and Pedro passed that way; I thank God that *your* lives were spared. The matter was reported to me as *Corregidor* of the district.'

Now I found myself in a severe dilemma; I had not told my grandfather about the action taken by the farmer of Navia. Ought I to do so? The man would have to be tried for manslaughter – or murder – would probably be executed—

While these thoughts ran through my head, the Conde continued.

'Men from Navia dug the road clear, thus discovering the two bodies. One of them, it seems, was El Caramanchel, a notorious brigand, and one of the greatest rascals in all Spain.'

I nodded. I had heard often enough, at Salamanca,

of El Caramanchel and his outrageous crimes.

'There was a price upon his head, which the people of Navia intend to claim, so his end will afflict nobody and will benefit many. But the other man, who was with him, did not appear to be a robber; he had papers on him showing him to be a government clerk from Salamanca.'

I glanced again towards the hat on the table. Now I knew why it was so familiar. It was the hat of Sancho the Spy!

'But what in the world,' said my grandfather, 'was a civil servant from Salamanca doing so far from home, in company with a notorious criminal? I do not like this, Felix. I do not like it at all. Can they have been following you?'

They can indeed, thought I, but decided not to trouble my grandfather with any further details of the matter, for it might change his views about my errand to Bilbao. And that I certainly did not wish!

'Well,' said I cheerfully, 'if they were following us, they will do so no longer. So we need not trouble ourselves about them.'

3

Arrival at the Convent – was it Juana? I take a dislike to the Reverend Mother; am received by Dona Conchita's parents; we receive permission to set out – and do so with too much luggage

A week later I was standing, sick and frozen with trepidation, at the top of a steep hill in Bilbao, in the pouring rain, pulling at the cord of a great brass bell that hung outside the visitors' gate of El Convento de la Encarnacion.

Nothing suspicious, or worthy of note, had occurred during our journey to Bilbao, which we had decided to make by land (since so many things may hold up a sea voyage – gales, fog, adverse tides, contrary winds). No harm befell us, we reached Bilbao on the sixth day, I delivered Grandfather's letter at the convent lodge, and received a message to return the following afternoon. So, for another night,

I had to contain my impatience.

For our lodging we had chosen ourselves a small, unpretentious *fonda*, down by the waterside. Bilbao is a bustling estuary town lying along the banks of the River Nervion; great ships ply in and out laden with coal and iron ore; it is a rich, black, dirty, noisy place, crammed into a deep narrow valley. The streets are thronged with cattle, horses, and people, and excessively muddy because of the damp climate. No carts or carriages are permitted in the centre of the town, because the streets are so narrow, and all goods must be carried on horse or mule-back, which adds to the congestion and foulness of the ways. The people are small, dark, busy, and surly.

On the following afternoon I left Pedro hopefully planning to try his chances with the senoritas of the city during the evening paseo. Wishing him luck (though I had a suspicion the Basque girls would not take kindly to strangers) I betook myself back up the slippery hill to the convent, which was right on the summit, and encircled by a high black wall.

At last, after I had rung and stood waiting in the rain for some time, a portress opened the massive door and beckoned me in. Ignoring a couple of beggars pleading for alms, she led the way across a courtyard. My throat tasted dry and bitter; a deep tremble ran all through my bones, from neck to ankle. Hoping that this state of terror did not show too plainly, I followed my guide along a passage into a small parlour where, it seemed, visitors were received.

There were pictures on the whitewashed walls – the martyrdom of St Sebastian, and St Martin dividing his cloak with a beggar. Why, if he was a saint, I wondered, did he not give the beggar the whole cloak? The floor was paved with stone flags, sweating in the damp atmosphere; on them lay two shabby rush mats. Two plain benches, two plain chairs, and a worn settee with curved legs were the only furnishings. They looked as if they had been picked up cheap at street markets.

Opposite the entrance door was another, white-painted, and beside it a window barred by a grille covering a closed shutter.

'Wait here; be seated,' said my guide. 'The Reverend Mother will speak to you shortly,' and she left me.

I was unable to sit down. I paced about on the slippery stone floor, trying not to trip on the rush mats. I felt sick with suspense.

About half an hour passed. Down below in the town I could hear church bells ringing for evening Mass; also factory whistles and the clang of iron-foundries.

By and by the portress reappeared, escorting a lady,

handsomely dressed, heavily veiled, who sat herself down on the settee, bowed her head, and began telling the beads of a superb gold-and-ebony rosary. She took no notice of me, so I thought it polite to avert my eyes from her. I could hear the regular click of her beads though, and a rustle of rich silk when she moved. In a brief scrutiny as she entered I had noticed how fine and stylish she was, in her velvets and laces; she made me feel shabby, though I had dressed myself as neatly as I knew how.

Every time the lady moved, a faint musky perfume drifted my way – very different from my great-aunt Josefina's lavender water!

After another interminable period of waiting, during which the lady devoutly told her beads and I perched myself uncomfortably on a bench, gazing at San Martin, a small bell rang once, sharply, and, with a loud clack, the shutters were folded back behind the iron grille. On the far side appeared the figure of a nun, in a black habit with a white headcloth. Her face was elderly, sharp-eyed, much wrinkled, and reminded me not a little of my great-aunt Isadora; I supposed that she was the Mother Superior.

I rose silently, and bowed.

In a dry, severe voice, she demanded, 'Are you Felix de Cabezada y Brooke?'

'Yes, Reverend Mother.'

'You are taller than I had been led to believe,' she said in a tone of suspicion.

Was I expected to apologise for my added inches? I did not know how to reply, therefore remained silent.

I had moved towards the grille when the shutters opened, and now could not see the woman with the rosary, who was behind me; I did not know what notice, if any, she was taking of this exchange.

The nun reflected. Next she seemed to beckon. Another white-robed form came into view, then quickly moved back out of sight.

The elderly nun said, not to me, 'Is that person Felix Brooke?'

After an infinitesimal pause a quiet voice answered, 'Yes, Reverend Mother.'

Had that been the voice of Juana? It was so soft, barely above a whisper, that I could not be certain. Nobody else in this place had known me before, though. It *must* be Juana.

I clenched my hands together.

The nun went on interrogating me.

'You have been informed of the purpose for which you were summoned?'

She addresses me as if I were a servant, I thought, with some resentment. Come here; go there; do this; do that. I was not summoned, I was invited. And no word of thanks for my speedy response . . .

'Yes, Reverend Mother.'

'You have seen the letter that was sent to the Conde de Cabezada and are acquainted with its contents? And his reply?'

'Yes, Reverend Mother.'

'You are prepared to undertake the rescue of the three unfortunate children of Manuel de la Trava, and remove them from the custody of their evil and demented father?'

I felt like saying, 'Senora, for the chance to get another sight of Juana, I would be prepared to liberate Don Juan himself from the clutches of Mephistopheles,' but contented myself with replying, for a third time, 'Yes, Reverend Mother.'

'It is well. By God's grace this mission will be achieved. Have you any scheme in mind for how it is to be undertaken?'

Rather taken aback, I answered, 'No, senora. It would be idle to make any plans until I am furnished with information about where the man has taken refuge and how he is armed. And what state of mind he is in.'

She nodded, slowly, twice, as if moderately satisfied with this reply.

'Have you a companion with you? Where are you staying?'

I told her that I had brought Pedro Gonsalez, assistant to my grandfather's steward, and named our posada.

'Humph . . . You don't have expensive tastes, I see. Just as well. And what have you been doing with yourself, during the years since you were able to be of assistance to Senorita Esparza?'

A little surprised, I answered staidly that I had been studying law, history, and literature at the University of Salamanca.

'At Salamanca?' she said as if this were news to her. 'Who were your tutors there?'

This is uncommonly like the Inquisition, I thought; and decided that if women were permitted to hold positions in the Holy Office, Mother Agnese would make an excellent member of its tribunal.

'Professor Lopez de Haro – Professor Enrique Mores – Professor Redmond.'

She pressed her lips together and frowned as if she could not recall any positively harmful information about these men, and rather regretted that this was so.

'I see . . . And what will you be doing with your self when your studies are completed?'

'What is that to your purpose, you old hag?' I felt

like asking. 'What has all this to do with the rescue of the de la Trava children?' But, trained by years of politeness to my great-aunts, I answered, 'I may very likely travel to England, senora. To visit once more the estates of my English grandfather, the Duke of Wells.' And what possessed me to reply thus, I cannot imagine, for I had no such intention, not the least in the world. Perhaps I said it *because* it was the very last thing I planned to do – since I had taken a strong dislike to the Reverend Mother and felt, instinctively, that she was a meddler, an organiser, one from whom plans had best be kept hidden lest she remake them to suit her own ends.

At all events, the introduction of my English ducal grandfather into our conversation certainly gave her a surprise; I saw her eyes open wide, under the snowy headband.

'Indeed?' she said slowly. 'That I did not know . . .' with a degree of displeasure, as if persons employed to furnish her with information about me had signally failed in their duty. Maintaining a very solemn and serious demeanour I gazed back at her while she sharply scrutinised me.

'You have an English title?'

'Yes, senora – in that land I am the Marquess of St Winnow.'

She tapped thoughtfully with her nail on the white-painted sill of the window. Then, apparently making up her mind, said, 'Go away now, Senor Brooke, and return at this time tomorrow. I shall need to take advice.'

Wonderful! I thought. Is there someone to whom even this dry old vulture turns for counsel?

Perhaps it might be God, of course.

Feeling horribly disappointed and thwarted, I would have liked to ask, 'Senora, may I not have a glimpse of Sister Felicita?'

But instinct again warned me that would be a very, very unwise thing to do. So I merely bowed, and was retreating to the door, when the Reverend Mother added, 'You may escort Senora de la Trava back to her residence.'

These words nearly startled me out of my skin. I had assumed that the well-dressed lady telling her beads on the settee was some unrelated visitor on some other errand.

The Reverend Mother's letter had said that Dona de la Trava was the cousin of Juana, which led me to think that they must be about the same age; Juana would now be about eighteen, I remembered. But this veiled lady was surely at least ten years older?

She had risen also, and said to me softly, 'If you

would be so good as to wait for me a short moment outside—' then turned for some low-voiced consultation with the nun. I walked into the passage wondering what I was supposed to do.

'Escort Senora de la Trava back to her residence,' the Reverend Mother had said.

Looking out across the courtyard I could see the rain still pelting down. Was I expected to walk with the lady through the deluge, or must I run down into the town and somewhere find her a sedan chair? My education at the University of Salamanca had not taught me how to deal with problems of this kind.

In fact the solution proved simple. When the lady joined me, it turned out that she had left a wet umbrella in the corridor. With this I was permitted to shelter her across the courtyard; and outside the gate a handsome carriage was waiting for her.

'I should be very glad, Senor Brooke, if you would give me the pleasure of your company to my parents' home,' she said. 'They wish so much to meet you. We have all heard about the gallant cavalier who rescued my cousin Juana.'

A fat coachman had jumped off the box and opened the door. He took the umbrella from me and guided the lady across the cobbles as if she had been made of sugar-icing. Then, when she was seated inside, he held the door for me.

Very reluctantly I climbed into the carriage, unable to think of any polite excuse for refusing. But I was hot with embarrassment. At eighteen one is not pleased to be complimented on actions undertaken when one was thirteen. And that journey had been a private transaction between myself and Juana; I did not like to think that it had been talked about by others. Of course I had told Grandfather about it, but that was different; he had received a letter of thanks from Juana's uncle, so all I did was confirm the letter.

'When did you last see your cousin, Dona de la Trava?' I inquired, in order to say something, as the horses moved forward.

'Oh, it was at least three years ago. When she was staying at her house in France, settling the affairs of her brother who died. Poor little Juana! She was so young to inherit all those cares.'

She would have had even more cares if her brother had not died, I thought; since he had paid some brigands to abduct and murder her. Apparently Dona Conchita did not know that.

'I went to stay with Juana in France when my children Nico and Luisa were six and five. Ah, they loved her so dearly! The youngest was not yet born.'

'Tell me about your children, senora,' I said. 'Why has their father abducted them?'

'The wretch! It is because he pretends to love them.'

'Does he not do so really?'

'How can he? He is mad! A madman! He has threatened to do terrible things – he said he would kill us with an axe! I am so afraid of what he will do to my poor babies—'

I asked how long Don Manuel had been like this, but she became vague. For a number of years, I gathered, he had steadily been growing more difficult, passionate, and ungovernable.

'And his opinions! So wild! And his behaviour harsh to me – uncivil – savage to my friends!'

'Where were you living at this time?'

'In Madrid.'

I asked if her husband had a profession and she replied rather coldly that he had no need to work for his living, being a nobleman, Grandes de Espana.

'And then,' she said, 'after – after he had become too wild and unreliable to be endured any longer; he – he was arrested and flung into jail for his seditious political opinions. So I returned here, with the children, to my parents' house. But Manuel – but he managed somehow to escape from the prison; and he followed us secretly – and one day, when I was out and my parents were not at home – he – he took them—' Her voice trembled, and she touched a handkerchief to her eyes, under the veil.

'How long ago was this, senora?' I asked quietly, when I judged she had had time to recover herself.

'Two months ago.'

'Two months – ay, *Dios!*' It had taken about four weeks, I supposed, for Juana to be transferred from Bayonne to Bilbao, and for me to be summoned from Salamanca. What had happened during the first month?

'Have you any idea where he has taken the children?'

'Somewhere in Aragon, I am sure. He went first to Berdun, where his brother lives, Don Ignacio de la Trava. But his brother would not permit him to stay in his house, and he wrote to me, telling that Manuel had been there. And then – then I had a letter from – from one of my children—'

The little sob she gave was very pitiful.

'Manuel kept them locked up. Would you believe it? But a servant girl at an inn was sorry for them and permitted Luisa to write a note, and arranged for it to be sent.'

Locked up, I thought. Heavens, what a situation.

'The girl is the oldest?'

'No, her brother is. But she writes better. Nico is slow – but a sweet, good boy,' she added hastily.

'And the little one – the youngest?'

'Why, here we are!' she exclaimed. 'How quickly Tomas has driven us.'

It had been hard, in the dusk and the rain, to see which way we went. We had circled round the outskirts of the town, avoiding the centre. Conchita's parents must reside somewhere out in the suburbs; I caught dim glimpses of what seemed a large new villa, set among flowering trees and shrubs. I was led through a lobby and a courtyard into a large salon filled with very handsome furniture. Compared with this place, I thought idly, my grandfather's rooms at Villaverde would seem sadly shabby. Everything here was new, glossy, heavy, and shining with gilt, varnish, or beadwork. At the end of the large chamber sat two old crumpled creatures like fat toads. Like toads' eyes, theirs did not blink as Conchita led me to them.

'Mama, Papa, here is Senor Brooke, who was so good to Juana – or, as he is called in England, Lord St Winnow.'

I bowed, they inclined their heads without speaking.

Dona de la Trava, meanwhile, laid aside her veil. Turning towards her, as she gestured me to a seat, I had a view of her face for the first time and was hard put to it not to gape like a clown. For she was the most beautiful person I had ever encountered, with perfect features, large dazzling black eyes, her face a faultless oval, and, above all, a skin of such pink-and-white velvety fineness and delicacy that one could only compare it, tritely, to the petals of flowers, white jasmine or geraniums.

'Do, please, be seated, Senor Brooke,' she was repeating graciously.

Feeling curiously ill at ease, between her startling beauty on the one hand and the two old toads on the other – how could she possibly be their daughter? – I perched myself nervously on a gilt and satin chair. Servants offered coffee, small dishes of cakes and confectionery, and flasks of hollands, sirops, and cordials. I took a cup of coffee. I noticed that the old parents were helped to liberal drams of schnapps.

'Well, Conchita – can the young senor get your children back from that devil in human form?' croaked Senor Escaroz.

'I pray that God will help me to do so, senor,' I said. 'But until I know where he has taken them, it is not easy to make a plan.'

'Conchita – show the young gentleman little Luisa's letter.'

'It is in my bedroom. Excuse me.' And she slipped from the room.

At first after she had gone, the two old creatures sat silent, sipping their schnapps. Then Senor Escaroz demanded, 'And you are the grandson of the Conde de Cabezada?'

'I have that honour, senor.'

'Your grandfather is still alive?' asked the old lady.

'Yes, senora, God be thanked.'

'He holds very scandalous political opinions, so I have been told,' she remarked acidly.

'If he does, senora, he can harm no one by them, for he is severely crippled and confined to his chair.'

'Hum!' she snapped, as if to say, that is just as well.

'How do you come to have an English title?' said her husband in a suspicious tone.

'My father was an English officer, serving in the French wars. And *his* father – who is still alive in England – bears an English title.'

Plainly they were about to ask what this was, when Conchita returned. She had a rose in her hair, I noticed. Had it been there all the time, under the veil? The hair was amazingly plentiful, thick, lustrous and soft-looking, swept up into a great black coil over her temples.

'See,' she said, 'here is my poor little Luisa's letter.'

It had plainly been written in haste on a crumpled, stained sheet of coarse paper.

Dear Mama

Do not be anxious about us. But we are rather sad. Papa keeps us locked up, in case somebody tries to take us. And he says he will kill you if you come or send Uncle Amador. Or he will kill himself and us as well. He says he will take us into the mountains where there are bears. Nico sends you a kiss.

Luisa

While I was reading this, I heard Senor Escaroz say to his wife in a low tone, 'What about the book? Do not let Conchita forget about the book,' and she made some mumbling reply.

'See, here are the children's portraits,' Conchita said to me, and she showed me three gilded and heart-shaped ornamental frames, in which were three angelic little faces with pink cheeks and rosy lips. The girl was like her mother, though without Dona Conchita's dazzling beauty; the boy quite different. Like his father, perhaps. He had a bony, heavy-browed face. The smallest one was merely a round-faced baby.

'Pretty children,' I said politely, handing the pictures back. 'You must miss them very badly, senora.'

She nodded several times without speaking, and I wondered how old she was. Not, surely, more than twenty-six? Without her veil, she did not look even that. If Nico, the eldest, was nine – if she had been married at seventeen—?

'When shall we set out?' I said. 'Tomorrow?'

'First we must see the Reverend Mother again. So that she can give permission for my cousin and her companion, Sister Belen, to ride with us.'

I did not at all see why the Reverend Mother could not have done that today; but there was no sense in finding fault. I felt much pity for Conchita, though, who must have been desperate to start in search of her children.

'I will bid you good evening now, senora,' I told her, 'and, perhaps, see you tomorrow again at the convent? And then I hope we shall be able to start on our journey without further delay.'

She looked doubtful.

'It will be too late to start tomorrow. We could not hope to go very far—'

'How far is it to where your husband's brother lives?'

'Berdun? At least forty leagues.'

Two days' riding, I supposed; with three females in the party we could not go as fast as Pedro and I had done on our own.

Old Senor Escaroz croaked out something about the

need for provisions for the journey, and an armed escort. I thought Dona Conchita looked at him with impatience – almost with dislike. But her voice, as she answered, was calm.

'All that will be taken care of, Papa.'

'Very well,' I said. 'Until tomorrow. *Buenos tardes. Adios*—' to the two old toads, who again silently inclined their heads. 'We will start the following day at dawn – all being well.' And I went out into the damp and chilly night. There had been no suggestion that I should stay to dinner; for which I was greatly relieved. I thought the Escaroz parents seemed decidedly hostile towards me. But perhaps they were opposed to the whole scheme.

Having asked the porter which road led back into town, I struck off downhill. The rain had somewhat abated, but still the way was long, and I was damp and ravenously hungry by the time I reached our inn. I found Pedro in the public room brooding over a glass of wine; from his morose expression it did not seem that he had had any success with the girls of Bilbao; and so it proved; he said they all turned up their noses at him and laughed at his Gallegan accent.

'But you?' he said eagerly. 'How did you fare? Did you see your young lady?'

'Only a brief glimpse, if that,' I told him. 'But her

cousin was there. The one whose children have been stolen.'

'So: where do we go next? And when do we start?'

Having received such a snub from the girls at the paseo, Pedro had no wish to stay any longer in Bilbao; it was a dismal dank place, he said, crammed in its valley, and he was sorry to hear that we were not to set out until the morning after tomorrow. Over supper (some excellent fish) he cheered up a little and asked a great many questions about Conchita and her parents.

'Did they receive you kindly? Civilly?'

'She, yes; her parents, no.'

'The Devil fly away with them, then! Although you have travelled all the way from Salamanca to rescue their grandchildren!'

'Well, they were not *un*civil, precisely – perhaps they don't want their grandchildren rescued.'

Of what had the old people's manner reminded me? They seemed unsure how to deal with me – as if I were some piece of unfamiliar material, as to whose utility they were unsure. I had felt them wondering – could I be moulded? Shaped? Made into something that might serve them?

After we had eaten we retired to our bedchamber, for the public room was noisy and full of smoke. Pedro soon slept, but I lay awake, hour after hour, looking at the square of sky that formed the window. Juana can see that same sky from the window of her cell, I thought, only a mile away. Do nuns sleep in cells, or in dormitories? There would be so many questions to ask her, if she was of a mind to answer.

The bells slowly tolled the hours of night, and I thought, she can hear those same bells. I remembered the last night we had spent together, in the forest of Iraty, up in the Pyrenees, not so far distant from here. We had both been exhausted, quite at the end of our strength, after a terrifying encounter with a man who seemed to be possessed by a devil. And then, when I woke up, the following morning, Juana was gone . . .

At all events, I thought, nothing can, ever again, be so bad as that time. And Manuel de la Trava cannot possibly be either as evil or as frightening as *that* man was.

Just the same, I felt desperately uncertain and lonely. And Pedro's company did nothing to lessen that loneliness.

Silently, inside my head, I said a prayer to God to be with us in our enterprise; and then, at long last, I fell asleep. Just before drifting off, I saw again the face of Conchita de la Trava – so beautiful, so sad, so full of piteous appeal. Oddly, it reminded me of some other face that I had recently seen – where, whose could it have been? Not beautiful, by no means sad or appealing, but *similar* – why could I not remember the owner of it?

Next day the procedure at the convent was as before. Except that Dona Conchita was not there. Nor, so far as I could see, was Juana. The Reverend Mother received me, just a fraction more graciously than she had on the previous day, and told me that my proposals had been favourably received, and it was permitted that I should rescue the de la Trava children.

I did not remind her that I had been invited to come and that all had been arranged already; I stood silent and polite, waiting.

'So you may set forward at dawn tomorrow,' the elderly nun said. 'Sister Belen and Sister Felicita will be ready for you, waiting at the main gate.'

'May – may I not see her – them – beforehand, so as to give them advice – instructions—?'

'That will not be necessary.'

I said, 'Will the sisters be supplied with warm clothing? Heavy footwear? We shall probably have to go into the high mountains' (thinking of the child's letter) 'where it may be very cold. And perhaps they should be armed – able to defend themselves from wild beasts, or brigands?'

The Reverend Mother drew herself up.

'Young man, when the blessed St Teresa travelled all over Spain with her nuns, they would have *scorned* to provide themselves with weapons. They were protected by the hand of God. No brigand would dare to lay a finger on them.'

'Brigands might not – but what about bears?' I objected.

(Secretly, I was not so sure about the brigands either. The ones *I* had encountered would have made little distinction, I thought, between saints and ordinary people.)

'Remember St Jerome,' said the Reverend Mother curtly. 'The sisters will need no protection, apart from the holy habit of their Order.

I was far from satisfied – and she had said nothing about the warm clothes – but saw that it would be useless to argue. Inwardly resolving to equip the expedition if need be from my own purse – for my grandfather had seen me handsomely supplied with money – I bade farewell to the sour-faced Mother Superior and said that I hoped to return her sisters to her in safety before too long a period had elapsed. Of course I hoped nothing of the kind; I hoped – what did I hope? I hardly knew.

As I took my way to the visitors' parlour earlier I

had been accosted by a small, pale-faced nun who, glancing about her nervously, had whispered that Sister Milagros would like a word with me after I had seen the Reverend Mother.

On my way out, therefore, recalling this, I asked at the portress's lodge if a message could be dispatched to Sister Milagros, saying that I was now at her service. But the portress told me that Sister Milagros had been sent on an errand to the other side of Bilbao and would not be back for some considerable time.

'Oh well, I do not imagine it can have been of great importance,' I said, 'since I do not know the sister. She left no message?'

'No, senor. But the sister did know you. She was transferred here from a House in Santander where she had met you, she said.'

One of the kind nuns who looked after my parrot while I travelled to England.

'Tell her, then, that I am very sorry indeed to miss her, but shall hope to see her on my return. I suppose she wanted to talk over old times and ask after the parrot.'

'No: she had something she wished to give you,' said the portress. 'But, as you say, it will have to wait.'

Pedro and I spent that day in purchasing various stores and tools, also arms, that we thought might be of use. Senor Escaroz had said that he would furnish transport for his daughter and the two nuns. Pedro and I had provided ourselves with mules, as before.

'For if we must go into the mountains,' Pedro said, 'horses would only be an encumbrance.'

We were not a little dismayed, therefore, next morning, arriving at the Escaroz mansion (for it had been arranged that we should escort Dona de la Trava from there to the convent) to discover that she proposed to make the journey in a great top-heavy carriage, drawn by four fat horses, and provided with two smart but knavish-looking outriders, likewise mounted on horses.

I tried to be polite about it.

'Is this well thought of, senora? We may have to make our way along wild mountain roads – they may be narrow and steep – would not a smaller conveyance be more practical?'

'But I have to take Juana, and that other sister,' objected Conchita, widening her great dark eyes. 'And we shall have the children, don't forget, on our return. And there is all my baggage—'

'Baggage?'

She had brought, we discovered, three portmanteaus, two hat boxes, and a great wooden case. I supposed that it contained clothes for the children who probably, poor things, had not a stitch to their backs.

Pedro and I looked at each other and shrugged. Perhaps we would find a pretext to leave a part of this inconvenient load somewhere along the way. There was only just room for the provisions that we had brought to be squeezed into the trunk – the coachman, meanwhile, compressing his lips and hoisting his shoulders as if we had insisted on thrusting in a most unreasonable quantity of useless gear.

'We had best hope the poor sisters are not cumbered with too much luggage,' Pedro muttered in my ear.

In fact, when we halted at the convent gate, we saw two white-robed sisters waiting outside, neither of them laden with any baggage whatsoever. The coach-man opened the door, they mounted swiftly into the carriage, and we were away in a flash, without any word said, and without my having been granted a single glimpse of their faces.

4

Conversations with Dona Conchita; Juana and Sister Belen speak in Latin; a night at Irurzun

Soon, leaving the valley of the Nervion, our road started to climb, up and up, over the steep, north facing slopes of forested mountains. The forests were of tall, slender trees, ilex, acacia, beech, and pine; wonderful gusts of damp fragrance came from them, on the rainy wind, for the acacia trees were all in clouds of white blossom. And, among the grass around their feet, tall white orchids bloomed. I hoped the carriage windows were open so that Juana could see and smell the flowers; she had been exceedingly fond of flowers, I remembered.

After a while, when the road became very steep

indeed, the coachman brought his lumbering, top-heavy conveyance to a halt, grumbling that the horses must have a rest.

'No wonder, with all that load of carved gilt the poor beasts are obliged to drag,' muttered Pedro. 'At this rate it will take a week to get to Berdun.'

On the next steep slope, the coachman decreed that his passengers must get out and walk. The two white-robed sisters did so without argument, swinging along ahead on their sandalled feet, with heads bent, talking together in low voices. I still could not decide which of them was Juana, for their hoods almost covered their faces, their loose robes concealed their build, and they were about the same height. Stupid shyness overcame me, and I was reluctant to break in on their conversation.

Meanwhile, Dona Conchita was not at all prepared to be put out on the roadway and required to proceed on foot. She apologized repeatedly in her soft musical voice – but, she said, she had not expected to be obliged to walk, the shoes she wore were wholly unsuitable, such an indignity was quite, quite out of the question.

By good luck, one of the outriders' horses was a quiet, docile beast, and so the man dismounted and led it along while she rode on it, sitting sideways with remarkable grace, considering that she was mounted on a man's saddle. I noticed that her feet were indeed tiny, and that the little silver-buckled, black velvet slippers she wore would certainly have been cut to pieces after a hundred yards' walking on this rough, stony road. Had she not, I wondered, thought to bring any more practical footwear?

By now a fine drenching mountain rain had begun to fall.

'Those poor sisters will be soaked to the skin,' Pedro said perturbedly, looking after them. 'That skimpy white calico they wear will not protect them at all.'

'Give them our cloaks,' said I, passing him mine, which had been rolled and strapped to my saddle. 'Our jackets are thick enough to keep us dry.'

Pedro threw me a puzzled glance, evidently wondering why I myself did not take this opportunity of speaking to the two sisters; however he rode on ahead and soon caught them up. At first I saw them shake their heads, as if declining the offer; but at length, evidently, he managed to persuade them that it would be foolish to let themselves be drenched to the skin so early in the journey, and they shrouded themselves in our warm riding capes.

Dona Conchita rode up on my right side.

She, I saw, was now all wrapped in a voluminous

grey fur cloak with a fur scarf over her head, so that nothing could be seen but her beautiful pink-and-white face and those large velvety eyes.

'Senor Felix?' she called softly.

'Yes, senora? How can I help you?'

'You have travelled to England, I believe?'

You know perfectly well that I have, lady, I thought, for you heard me tell the Reverend Mother so.

'Yes, senora,' I agreed politely.

'Oh, do please, then, tell me about it. I have such a curiosity to hear about England!'

'Why, truly, senora, I have seen but little of the country – only the part between my grandfather's estates and the sea-coast. And the town of Bath. I have not been to London or the university towns.'

'Describe the city of Bath to me. Is it as large as Bilbao? And tell me about your grandfather.'

Rather reluctantly, I did so. Part of me was wildly eager to hurry on ahead, to talk to the pair of sandalled sisters (Pedro, I noticed. had dismounted from his mule and was now walking beside them, discussing something with great animation and waving his arms about). Yet part of me still hesitated, nervous, touchy, and reluctant. Why, I wondered, I kept wondering, why had Juana not greeted me in any way, not by so much as the smallest gesture? Did she not wish to renew our old acquaintance? Yet, in that case, why had she sent for me? Now that she saw me again, was she ashamed of me? Or (this was a horrible thought) was neither of those two nuns Juana? Were they two total strangers? I felt dreadfully uneasy and cast down.

My answers to Dona Conchita's questions must, I am sure, have seemed lame and random indeed, yet she appeared delighted and deeply interested, laughed merrily at various of the things I told her, and asked many questions.

When I had told her all that I could remember of Bath (a most displeasing city, bitterly cold and dank, where it rains without ceasing all winter long, and all summer too, those who lived there told me), Dona Conchita demanded of me, in a careless manner, 'And pray tell me, is it not true, Senor Felix, that it was somewhere on your grandfather's land – the Spanish grandfather I mean – that all the pay-chests of General Baird's English army were cast away? Twenty-five thousand pounds' worth of silver dollars, is it not said – all thrown down the mountain-side when Bonaparte was chasing the English out of Spain? Did your grandfather's people never find those trunks of silver dollars?'

'Never, senora,' I replied calmly. 'And I am quite surprised that you should pay such heed to an idle tale.'

She opened her beautiful dark eyes very wide.

'But the pay-load *was* lost – everybody knows that story is true. And *somebody* had to find it. In fact there are many tales floating about; one of them has it that an English deserter named Smith knew where the treasure lay, and that he is now living like a lord in Tangier and calls himself Don Juan Forjador; other versions tell that your canny grandfather had the silver removed, little by little, and stored away secretly.'

'Well, you can inform whoever told you those tales, senora, that both are baseless. My grandfather certainly does not have the silver – if he did, he would long since have taken steps to return it to its proper owners. And as for poor Smith, he died, five or six years back, of the lung-rot.'

'How do you know that?' she asked quickly.

'Because I made inquiries.'

'Ah! Then you *had* met Smith?'

'Very briefly, once, yes, when I was on my way to England. And then when, by coincidence, he was taken into custody, along with a band of highway robbers, and held overnight in my grandfather's stables, he wrote a letter to me, saying that he was dying.'

'Why should he write to you?' demanded Dona Conchita.

'I had undertaken to deliver a letter from him, to his

niece. He was grateful.' And he also wrote to warn me that my great-aunt was making evil plans against me, I thought, but did not say. I was not flattered by Dona Conchita's interest in my family – which seemed nourished on vulgar tales – and saw no reason to gratify it further.

She smiled at me mischievously. 'You are certainly a cool young man, Senor Felix. If I thought there might be all those chests of silver dollars on my land, lying there for the taking, I would be out searching under every juniper-bush! But perhaps you have done that very thing and are, of course, far too shrewd to tell any inquisitive female who comes asking you about it.'

'If you choose to imagine such a thing, senora, that is your privilege.'

She laughed musically, and changed to questions about Salamanca and my studies there.

'How long will they continue?'

'To be a barrister – which was my intention – I must learn logic and physics for three years; then mathematics and Roman law; then Spanish and ecclesiastical law—'

'*Ay, Dios mio!* You will be an old, grey-bearded man by the time you qualify,' she said, throwing up her hands. 'How many years is the course, in heaven's name?'

'Thirteen for a fully qualified barrister. But, as I had good Latin, I might get through in a shorter time: all the teaching is in that language.'

'*Now* I can be quite certain that neither you nor your grandfather found that treasure; who would put himself through such a training if he could afford to live at home?'

'A man might choose to serve his country,' I said rather stiffly.

Again she gave her silvery laugh. 'Oh, pray! I heard enough of *that* kind of talk from my husband.' And she began to talk about the city of Salamanca, where she had been herself, she told me.

'I have friends there ... I know it a little,' and she mentioned some of the sights of the town, especially the famous Casa de las Conchas, a house with its facade all adorned with stone cockle-shells. 'When my little daughter Pilar first saw those cockles, she wanted every one of them for herself,' Dona Conchita told me gaily. 'Oh, how she wanted them! She cried and cried—'

'Pilar is the youngest – how old is she?'

'Hardly more than a baby. Oh, how I keep wondering and wondering what that atrocious monster is doing to my poor darlings,' she suddenly broke off to lament in a tremulous tone, very different from that she had been using.

I was trying to summon some phrases of comfort when she suddenly exclaimed, in a different tone again, 'No, really, this is *too much*!'

For, as we climbed ever higher, the fine mountain rain had changed to a fine, sleety snow, blowing and stinging in our eyes and nostrils.

'I refuse to ride on horseback any longer in this abominable blizzard!' exclaimed Dona Conchita, and she insisted on Tomas the coachman stopping and letting her seat herself in the carriage once more. 'The horses must have had sufficient rest by now – here we are, nearly at the top of the mountain!'

Tomas grumbled and objected a good deal, but she told him in the softest and gentlest manner that Senor Escaroz would dismiss him as soon as he returned home unless she had her way.

So, with downturned mouth and out-thrust jaw, he let down the step and she got back into the coach.

'What about the holy sisters?'

'Oh – they seem well enough, with the cloaks these gentlemen have been kind enough to give them. They are used to walking about in all weathers.'

Now that Esteban the outrider had his horse back, he and his companion and Pedro rode on ahead into the snowy gloom, to make sure that the road was clear.

I seized this chance to overtake the two sisters and

dismount beside them, removing my hat politely as I did so, and greeting them. As I rode up behind them I had caught a snatch of their talk, and was surprised to find that this was neither in Spanish nor in Basque nor in French, but in Latin; so I greeted them in that language.

'*Salve, mei Sorori!*'

'Aha!' said Juana's voice – her own, unmistakable voice, rather low-pitched but quick and clear – 'so you have kept up with your Latin at Salamanca, have you, Felix? But do you still remember the Basque word for sister, I wonder?'

'*Ahizpa,*' I said, dredging the word up from some deep well of memory.

'There! I wouldn't have believed it!' She laughed – the old, familiar chuckle. 'Sister Belen, we shall have him speaking fluent Euskara yet; in a hundred years, perhaps.'

Sister Belen also chuckled – a fat, deep, comfortable sound. All I could see of her, inside the deep, flapping white hood, was a round brown cheek, but her voice was friendly as the sound of a brook.

'In that case we had better, perhaps, speak Spanish.'

'Why do you converse in Latin, my sisters?' I asked.

'Oh,' Juana replied lightly, 'for good practice. And –

just in case the mountain eagles are listening to our chat.'

I caught a gleam of her copper-dark eye and remembered that one of the first things she had ever said to me was, 'I have learned to trust *nobody*.'

She was still exactly the same Juana – even if dressed up in a nun's robe; and, as the snow stung and slashed against our faces, I walked on beside her in deep content.

Next moment, round a corner of cliff, the weather changed; as so often in Spain, coming over the top of the escarpment we found a completely different climate waiting on the other side of the mountain: warm sun and a mild, grassy landscape.

Pedro and the outriders now trotted back to suggest that we should rest the horses for a short space of time and take a *merienda*.

Tomas, the coachman, very willing, quickly produced a feast from one of the large baskets in the baggage compartment: white rolls, ham, cheese, wine, fruit. A cloth was spread, the ladies perched on rocks, we all ate and drank.

The sisters put back their hoods. Sister Belen, I saw, was a round-faced, red-cheeked countrywoman as her voice had suggested, smiling and comfortable. And Juana? Juana was herself – pale, thin, her dark eyes full of fire and resolution; her hair, cropped in a short, monastic fashion, was much as I remembered it during our journey together when she had been disguised as a boy.

Pedro gave me his gap-toothed grin and murmured, 'Hey! More like a fiesta than a rescue mission?'

I had been thinking the same thing myself; it was hard to believe that this large party, drinking wine in the cheerful sunshine, had any connection with three terrified children being held captive against their will by a madman in some mountain fastness. The three children ought to be here with us, I thought – eating grapes, tumbling off rocks, and probably making thorough nuisances of themselves; I recalled the spoiled little girl in Zamora screaming at her father that she wished to ride in a carriage.

'We certainly can't drag all this circus with us wherever we go,' Pedro murmured, 'or those poor children won't be rescued by the *Ana Nuevo*.'

'You are right, of course. I have been thinking the same thing. But how are we to rid ourselves of all this company?'

'It's not going to be easy. The Dona de la Trava is a lady with a will of her own.'

I nodded, with gloom.

'Well – we shall have to find a way somehow,' Pedro

said in an undertone, as the lady herself came smilingly towards us.

'Will you not take more wine, Senor Felix, and another leg of chicken?'

'No, I thank you, senora, I think we should continue on our way, or we shall never reach Pamplona by dusk. I will just ask the sisters if they have had sufficient refreshment.'

The two sisters, as seemed to be their habit, had placed themselves somewhat apart from the rest of the group, had eaten and drunk very sparingly, and were now sitting in silence and contentment looking at the great view outspread to the south. How different it must be for them, I thought, travelling freely like this, from being shut behind that black wall in Bilbao.

They were looking away from me, had not heard my approach and I was able to look at Juana fully. I remembered Grandfather's warning: 'You must be prepared to find great changes in her. Young ladies grow up much faster than their male counterparts.' But, it seemed to me, she had not changed at all! The gleam in her eye was just as I recalled it; there was mockery in it, and merriment, but a spark of the Devil's own temper as well; at any affront, real or fancied, she was capable of firing up into a fury. Had convent discipline, I wondered, cured her of this habit? Somehow it seemed unlikely.

'Have you had sufficient, my sisters?' I asked. 'You have not taken very much?'

'Yes, thank you, we have done excellently,' Sister Belen assured me. She was plainly some years older than Juana and looked, from her outdoor complexion, as if she must be in charge of the convent's garden or livestock. She had a sensible, good-humoured face and I thought, if our expedition had to be lumbered with so many females, that she, at least, would give us little trouble. 'Come, Sister Felicita,' she said, 'the young senor wants us back in the carriage.'

I did not, of course; I wanted to walk beside Juana and recall old times. But there was no chance of that; Dona Conchita had come up and was asking how many more leagues it was to Pamplona and whether I had travelled this way before; the sisters climbed into the carriage and were shut up in it before I could exchange any more words with them.

We did not reach Pamplona that night; Dona Conchita insisted on yet another impromptu stop along the way, and dusk found us at a small village called Irurzun, where, fortunately, there was an inn simple but commodious enough to accommodate the whole party.

As soon as we halted, Juana and Sister Belen disappeared into the village church, presumably to pray for the success of the enterprise. I would have liked to follow their example, but was intercepted by Dona Conchita who asked me, with pretty civility, to take a glass of wine with her and tell her how I planned to rescue her babies.

'Well, senora, can you tell me a little about the children? It is not really possible to make any plan until we discover where they are being kept; but in the meantime, any description of their habits and dispositions may prove useful.'

This, however, she seemed to find it impossible to provide. Whether it was because the children had been reared by nurses and servants and had spent little time with their mother, or because she was the kind of person who has no gift for making a picture in words, I could not decide.

'Nico is a little angel – so good, so sweet! And Luisa is a perfect wonder at embroidery – already she has stitched two altar-cloths for the Carmelite nuns—'

'How old are they?'

'Nico is nine – the poor darling has had a birthday since that monster abducted them – and Luisa just eight—'

'And the baby?'

'Oh, little Pilar? She is four. But now, give me your own history, Senor Felix? How did your parents chance to meet? Do, pray, tell me all about yourself.'

This I had no great wish to do. Beautiful as Dona de la Trava was, kind and full of interest as she appeared, yet her company somehow made me fidgety. And the story of my parents, a very sad one, was not of a kind to be related idly, by way of passing the time, in the ale-room of a posada, no matter how cordial the audience. I jumped up and said I would hurry the cook with our dinner, so that we might make an early start the next day.

On my way back from the kitchen I encountered the two sisters returning from their devotions, and offered them a glass of wine. This they declined, but came into the ale-room to sit (indeed there was nowhere else) and placed themselves on a wooden bench. Then I remembered that Juana had met her cousin's children, they were fond of her – that, in fact, was why Dona Conchita had appealed to her for help in the first place. So I asked her if she could supply me with information as to any of their particular likes or dislikes, habits or skills or fears that she might call to mind.

'Yes, of course,' she said readily. 'Nico is very good at drawing – he loves animals and has great skill in making pictures of them. And he has a natural way with all beasts – dogs and horses trust him, and wild creatures too – he had a pet owl that he tamed, and a snake. Whereas Luisa is rather frightened of many animals – she is a nervous child, prone to nightmares. I remember she used to wake screaming, "Father! Father!"'

'Ah, the poor angel,' murmured Dona Conchita, who had been listening to this with slightly knitted brows – 'Even then, when you met them three years ago, they were terrified of their father, he cast such a shadow over the whole household—'

'And Pilar?' I asked Juana, who was frowning and looking thoughtful. 'Do you recall anything special about her? Or was she too small then to have developed any special characteristics?'

'Indeed no,' said Juana laughing. 'She was a perfect little devil. Even at the age of one it could be seen that all her ways derived straight from the Evil One.'

'Oh, come, my love, how can you be so hard on the poor child?' said Conchita, smiling, but I could see that she was not pleased. '*Poor* little Pilar, how can you say such things about her at an age when she could hardly walk or talk. And she your own cousin!'

'I remember the dance that she led her nurse, poor old Guillermina. And how she used to plague the two elder ones, scrambling after them and snatching their toys from them. Yet they were remarkably patient with her. Nico and Luisa spoke a special language to each other that they had made up themselves,' Juana told me, 'and little Pilar was wild to learn it too, though she could hardly speak Spanish then; but she used to scream with rage if they talked their own language in her presence; she would rush at them and hit them with her tiny fists. Truly, Conchita, I am sorry for her father if he has her somewhere shut up, he is the one who will suffer.'

'How can you say such things?' repeated Conchita with a hurt, smiling face.

'Because I can remember very clearly the rages Pilar used to fall into when something was not given her that she wanted – my books about flowers and birds, for instance, that Nico used to look at. He was so careful with books always, but Pilar could not be trusted; she would tear and crumple the pages. And, *Dios mio*, the passions she fell into when she saw them put up out of reach on a high shelf. If she is the same now—'

'Of course not, she is much older and wiser,' protested Conchita in her soft musical voice. 'You are giving Senor Felix quite a wrong impression. What in the world will he be thinking?'

Juana looked at me calmly.

'He won't worry. Felix has some experience in

dealing with wilful children. Yes, and with evil spirits also.' Momentarily, a grave expression passed over her face; I guessed she might be remembering, as I did, how we had been hunted over the mountains by a demon inhabiting the body of a brigand, and how we had to drive out the wicked spirit. Juana, too, I thought, has had experience in dealing with evil. Our eyes met, briefly, and I felt a closeness, as if we had clasped hands.

I said, hoping to ease the moment with Conchita, 'Well, if the little Pilar has such an unquenchable spirit in her, I hope that we can turn it to good account when it comes to the children's rescue.'

Dona Conchita smiled, just a curve of the lips and a widening of the dark velvety eyes as she thanked me.

Pedro came to tell us that our meal was ready, on a trestle table at the other end of the dim-lit room. There were four places laid, for me, Conchita, and the two sisters.

'What about you, Pedro?' I said, surprised. 'Are you not eating with us?' For, hitherto, he and I had eaten together as a matter of course.

But with a wholly expressionless tone and countenance he said he preferred to take his meal in the kitchen with Tomas and the postilions. 'Servants' gossip,' he hissed in my ear. 'You never know what you may pick up.'

From the cool glance Dona Conchita cast at him, raising her fine brows, I could see she considered the kitchen was properly his place. And as it was, the meal proved a little constrained; Juana and Sister Belen ate quietly and very sparingly of the excellent bean soup, omelette, and chicken with artichokes, Dona Conchita picked at each dish and murmured in her soft cooing voice that the soup was too salty, the omelette leathery, the chicken disgracefully overcooked, and the wine and bread horribly rough. I thought it fortunate indeed that Pedro was taking his supper elsewhere, for, nephew and great-nephew of two superb cooks, he was a very fair judge of food and might not have agreed with Conchita.

While we ate, Dona Conchita was gently, sweetly arch and mischievous about the former journey that Juana and I had taken in each other's company.

'What an intrepid pair of babies you were to travel so far, and through such dangers together. Did you ever stay in a posada such as this?'

'No indeed, we had no money for such entertainment,' said I. 'We slept in the bracken and I caught our dinner out of brooks.'

'*Ay, de mi*, what austerities! It is a wonder you survived.'

But Sister Belen said sturdily that trout fresh from

the brook was the best supper there was, and bracken made the finest bed of all. I noticed Juana throw her a grateful glance; I fancied that she was embarrassed and annoyed by Conchita's gentle raillery.

After we had eaten the two nuns went off immediately to the attic room where they had been quartered. Dona Conchita asked me if I would escort her to a very pretty waterfall that we had noticed not far from the village as we came along; it would, she said, look even prettier by moonlight. But I, with a sad lack of gallantry, replied that it would be best to retire early so that we could make an early start, since we were by no means as far advanced on our way as we should be. Observing her look of disappointment I added, however, that no doubt Pedro would be glad to escort her to the waterfall (though I knew he would not be) if she wished an escort, though, I thought, in such a rural spot, she would be perfectly safe by herself.

But she, sighing, said, no, it had been just an idle whim; and she took herself off to bed. I did likewise and found Pedro there already, casting a critical eye over the rude and scanty bedding.

'If the Dona de la Trava has done no better, we shall hear about it in the morning!' he said with a grin, as we shared out the threadbare covers between the two primitive cots.

'Well? Did you hear any servants' gossip?'

'Less than I hoped,' he said. 'Pepe and Esteban are merely hired for the journey and have no knowledge about the family. And old Tomas, even when full of wine, has little to say. He did give as his opinion, though, that the Senor de la Trava was *not* mad; or, at least, not mad at the time when he was sent to prison. But, poor devil, he was in the dungeons of Montjuich for two years – *ay, Dios!* – they say nobody comes out of that place in his right mind.'

'I wonder how he ever escaped?'

'He must have had good friends. By the way,' Pedro said, cautiously glancing about us, 'Tomas told me – speaking of friends – that Mother Agnese, the old Mother Superior of the convent where your Senora Juana was, in Bilbao – Tomas says that she is a cousin of the king's own confessor, Archbishop Saez. And also an old friend of Dona Conchita's mother, Senora Escaroz.'

'Is she indeed?' I said thoughtfully.

The king's confessor had been responsible for so much savage persecution of the Liberals that even the Russians and French had protested about him and he had, in the end, been relieved of his position as King Ferdinand's adviser, but, instead, as a consolation, made an archbishop. If he was the cousin of the gimlet-eyed Mother Agnese, it might account for her being so well-informed about my grandfather. And if she was also a close friend of the pair of old toads, Conchita's parents, what did this betoken? I resolved to be doubly discreet in all that I did and said.

I wondered if Pedro would say anything about Juana – with whom, I had observed, during the day, he had grown to be on very easy, friendly terms; she accepted his services when they were offered, or amiably declined them, without any of the prickliness of former times; and he had held various chaffing conversations with her and Sister Belen; indeed the pair seemed more comfortable with Pedro than any other members of the party. Remembering Grandfather's insistence that Pedro should come along, and my own first opposition to the plan, I thought, not for the first time, what a very shrewd old fellow Grandfather is!

'She's a proper lady, your Senora Juana,' Pedro observed pensively, blowing out the candle. 'What my great-aunt Bernie would have called one of the old school – not jumped-up nobodies but real old-fashioned aristocracy.'

'Good heavens, Pedro!' I was amused and astonished to find that Pedro's views were so identical to those of my grandfather.

'No, I mean it,' he said seriously. 'She's the sort that

will do their duty through thick and thin – if it means walking over burning coals. And yet no fine airs about her; easy and jokey as you please. Whereas—'

Whatever else he had been about to add he providently decided to withhold.

'Well, I am glad you think so well of her. Although—' Here, like Pedro, I was overtaken by second thoughts and closed my mouth.

'While as for that Sister Belen—' Now there was a broad smile in his voice. 'I wouldn't mind being washed up with *her* on a desert island.'

'*Pedro!*'

'Too bad she's a nun,' he said.

Then we slept.

5

We pass through Pamplona; the fat man again; I ask God for a sign; arrival at Berdun; the unaccountable scream; the mysterious creature in Don Ignacio's chimney; I receive my sign from God; and hold a moonlit conversation with Juana

Irurzun was only six leagues this side of Pamplona, so we reached that city early in the morning and made no long stop there. I had been there once before, with Juana, shortly before our last parting, and I remembered it with sadness, though it is a handsome place, raised upon a bluff and ringed about by mountains with the mighty snow-capped Pyrenees to northward. If Dona Conchita had not said she wished to make some purchases there, I would have suggested that we ride straight through without stopping, but since she wished to pause, I thought the time might usefully be employed in buying one or two more pieces of equipment. I suggested, therefore, that we might all meet in forty minutes' time close to the gate in the town wall that opens north-eastwards near the River Arga.

Just as I was about to take my leave of the party, Juana jumped down from the carriage and approached me.

'Felix,' she said quietly, 'would you do me a kindness?'

'Of course! You know that. Anything in the world.' My tone was no louder than hers but I tried to put my heart into it.

'Nothing difficult,' she said with a faint smile. 'If I might ask a little money from you? We have none, of course, and I would like to buy a gift or two for the children – only trifles for the poor little beings – to remind them that we used to be friends—'

'Take what you wish.' I handed her my purse, and she selected a few coins. 'It is a good thought. Poor little wretches, they will be in need of all the comfort they can get.'

I thought of the tiny box, with the four coloured stones in it, that Juana had once given me, and how, in many lonely moments, I had taken comfort from it. Would I ever be able to remind her of it? 'Can I help you in any way – shall I escort you?' I suggested.

'Oh no, no, thank you. Belen and I can look after

one another—' and she slipped away into the crowd, walking fast and quietly in her hempen sandals.

I thought about Juana's money. She had been a wealthy heiress. I remembered the letter from Auteuil Freres, the lawyers, stating that her inheritance of 30,000 reales had been paid to the convent as her dower. And now she had not even a few pesetas to buy toys. What would happen if she should ever decide to leave the Order? Would her dower have to be paid back?

Pedro and I had decided to equip ourselves with more arms. At last night's posada we had heard much talk of the lawlessness in Aragon, whither we were bound; there were said to be bands of brigands in the mountains; robbery of the mail was a frequent event in the province; merchants, when they travelled, were advised to have with them at least eight companions and eleven shotguns.

Pedro and I considered that we were equal to three bandits apiece, so, with Tomas and the two outriders, we should be a strong enough party, but there was no sense in being underarmed, and Pamplona was the last large town through which we would pass.

Besides the money given me by Grandfather, I had a sum which had recently been sent me by my English trustees. It had taken them an immensely long time to come to the decision that I should be paid an allowance, and even longer to conclude what this should be, but a figure had finally been agreed on and sent with a note to the effect that this was my stipend for a quarter of a year. It seemed to me a princely amount and I felt rich. Without hesitation, therefore, I laid out substantially on shotguns, ammunition, ropes, and rock-climbing equipment, in case Don Manuel had retreated to some giddy crag.

When we returned to the meeting-place, Pedro and I laden with our heavy bundles, we saw that Juana and Sister Belen were there before us with smaller bundles. But we had waited for many minutes before Dona Conchita arrived in a flurry of apologies.

'The folk in this town are so slow! Many of them, in the stores, seem downright simple,' she murmured placatingly in her pretty voice. 'They hardly seem to understand what one says to them.'

Tomas, who came behind her with a great load of purchases, quickly helped her into the carriage and, with expressive looks and a whispered commentary from Pedro, we were on our way again. We rode along a broad valley, through cultivated land, with here and there a tiny village. Mountains rose in the distance on either side, those to the north snow-capped and shaggy. There was no suggestion today of stopping for a picnic; possibly Dona Conchita felt contrite over having delayed us in Pamplona; or perhaps she was engaged in inspecting her purchases.

'She looked as if she had bought enough apparel for a brigade,' muttered Pedro. 'Let us hope that it included some warm stockings for those poor barefoot sisters.'

With the coming of dusk we reached a small town called Tiermas, because of the hot springs that are there. Sister Belen told me that it was once a Roman town; General Pompey (from whom Pamplona takes its name) used to bathe his gouty feet in the hot mineral waters. Since no inn there had room for us all, Pedro and I put up at a very small albergue while the ladies were housed in a more comfortable establishment.

'Felix,' said Pedro, when we had eaten our modest supper and were settling into our flock beds, 'I saw something very odd in Pamplona. It was after we had bought the guns, and while you were talking to the old crone behind the shoe-stall. I could hardly believe my eyes.'

'Well – what did you see?' I asked. 'Don't keep me in suspense.'

'You remember in Zamora – at the saddler's shop – the fat man who was asking for a saddle with a pillion seat – do you remember him?'

'Yes indeed, very well; what of him?'

'Well, there he was again in Pamplona – buying a pack of cards at a tobacco shop! The very same man! Do you think it can possibly be accident – or coincidence?'

'Hardly. Did he see you?'

'I am not sure. But could he have followed us – all the way from Zamora?'

'He would not have needed to,' I said, thinking it over.

'What do you mean, Felix?'

'Why – if he knew our destination; if he knew that we were going in search of the madman who has taken refuge somewhere in the mountains near Berdun; then he would know that we must pass through Pamplona, and he could get there much more directly than we have been obliged to do, travelling by way of Bilbao and waiting three days for the Reverend Mother's leave to depart.'

'But that,' said Pedro indignantly, 'sounds as if we are walking into a trap. And if there is one thing that annoys me, it is being taken for a fool. Especially by a fat fellow like that one.'

'Well—' I yawned and wriggled myself more comfortably into the flock, 'at least we *know* that we are walking into a trap, and that gives us some small advantage.'

'But who is setting this plaguey trap?'

'I only wish I knew!'

The following day brought us to Berdun, where Manuel de la Trava's brother, Don Ignacio, lived. By now we were in late spring or early summer; but it was a cool year; although the sun shone brightly enough, up here in Aragon, with the snow-capped Pyrenees so close, the sun's rays had little heat in them yet, and a brisk wind, coming off the snows, kept us from wishing to leave off our warm jackets. The new green corn rippled in silky waves, the willows and poplars along the well-filled watercourses bowed under the breeze and flashed their young leaves; everything was green and flowing, larks and nightingales sang, and thousands of small bright flowers spangled the grassy banks of the roads.

By all rights I ought to have been happy. Six months ago, if I had known that I would be travelling through the Aragon valley in company with Juana, I would hardly have believed that such a piece of good fortune lay ahead of me; yet now I rode along beside Pedro, troubled, anxious, and perplexed; because of this I felt quite ashamed of myself, and as if I ought to be apologising to God for my bad manners.

When I was younger – at that time, five years ago,

when I made the journey through the mountains with Juana – I used, now and then, to hold conversations with God, often finding comfort, and sometimes wisdom, in the answers He gave me. But with the addition of years, and the worldly kind of wisdom that is picked up from friends and professors, I had, little by little and without being aware of it, grown less adept at picking out the voice of God from all the other sounds of every day.

There were so many of those, and they were so loud.

Now, riding beside Pedro, between two orchards of flowering almond trees, I addressed God internally, trying to find the old ease and freedom of question and answer.

'My dear Father in heaven,' I said to Him, 'please forgive my ingratitude – for such I fear it must seem to you – that I am not simply bubbling over with joy at being permitted to make this journey in Juana's company. I am unbelievably glad to see her again – don't mistake me there – and to find that she has not changed in the least, but it is so difficult and un-comfortable and baffling to be able to talk to her only in the presence of other people – people like Dona Conchita—' Then I stopped, feeling how uncivil it was to whine and grumble at God in this manner; besides, I was sure He was not interested in my opinion of

Conchita. 'Listen, my dear Father,' I began again. 'I am quite sure You have some clear purpose in sending us on this expedition – just as You had in helping Juana and me drive away the demon from that man who had taken over the robber band. So, won't You please tell me *what* Your purpose is this time? Or at least, dear God, just give me a hint? For, to tell You the truth, I feel very troubled and worried – I feel there is something badly wrong, and I don't know what it is—' I glanced at Pedro, who rode beside me with brows knit and lips compressed; he had just the same feelings about our errand, I was sure.

'Of course, dear Father, if you think it's best for me to remain in ignorance, I will try to accept that,' I ended, as we began riding up the steep hill into Berdun.

Berdun, like Pamplona, sits on a bluff in the middle of the valley. But it is a tiny town – the whole of it would fit into one of my grandfather's large orchards. In the old days, men banded together on this little hilltop to defend themselves from the Goths, the Vandals, the Moors – its houses have been sacked and burned over and over, hundreds of times, but always doggedly built up again. Now the town seems old and quiet – the last time it was pillaged was 400 years back; like a peaceful cat, paws curled, tail tucked, it drowsed above us on its sunny hill as we rode upward.

'Ay, *Dios*!' remarked Pedro, grinning, 'the Escaroz carriage is never going to get through *there*!'

The only way into the town was under an exceedingly low and narrow arch, through which the road, which had already twisted in several sharp bends as it climbed the bluff, now angled its way round yet another hairpin corner.

'What is the trouble, Tomas? Why do you not continue?' called Conchita's soft voice, and her head came out of the carriage window.

'This place was built for pygmies, not men,' grumbled Tomas, getting down to open the carriage door. 'The senora will have to walk – it is not at all dignified.'

Pedro and I had already dismounted and tethered our mules to stanchions in the outer wall; now, with Conchita and the two sisters, we walked through the arched gateway into Berdun. We found the Calle Mayor, where Don Ignacio lived, without the least trouble, since there were only two streets in the town, running parallel, neither of them as wide as a cart track. But the houses, built of stone, were tall and handsome, and that of Don Ignacio de la Trava had a great ancient coat-of-arms carved over its door.

Pedro had acquired a good deal of information about the de la Trava brothers from Tomas the coachman, and had passed it on to me. They came of an exceedingly ancient family, he said, and claimed descent from the *ricos hombres*, or great lords of medieval times, and, before that, from the Romans and the Moorish kings. Formerly they had been very rich, owned great tracts of land, villages, churches, towns; they had complete powers over the people who lived on their estates, and many ancient privileges, such as freedom from taxation. Their incomes had once been counted in hundreds of thousands of ducats. But, during the last century, the family had fallen into debt, spent much too much at the king's court in Madrid, on travel and luxury, and on lavish dowries for their daughters. Lands had had to be sold. Now little remained, save a ruined castle in the mountains, a vine-yard or two in the region of Zaragoza, a house in Madrid, and the estates round Berdun. There were two brothers left: Manuel, the elder, the Marquis of Urraca, who, since he inherited no money, had joined the army as a young man, fought in the Royal Corps of Spanish Artillery under the French, become a colonel, and lost an eye at the battle of Vitoria. When the French wars ended, he was denounced as a Bonapartist and a Liberal, obliged to live under police supervision. For a time he was banished to Santiago de Compostela, but, after his marriage, permitted to return to Madrid.

Then, having been so rash as to write pamphlets criticising the state of the country, he had been thrown into prison.

The younger brother, Don Ignacio, was quite a different character. Originally destined for the church, he had been unable, because of some illness, to become a priest, and so took a minor position at Court when King Ferdinand was restored to the throne, for he was an ardent royalist. At first successful and popular, for he had been a very handsome fellow and knew how to make himself agreeable, he fell on hard times, and, when his illness worsened and he lost his looks and good spirits, retired to Berdun, where he lived on his share of what was left of the family estates.

What, I wondered, did the two brothers feel for one another? Were they attached? Devoted? After such very different lives and histories?

Now the front door – on which Pedro had been, all this while, methodically tapping with an ancient iron door-knocker shaped like a serpent – suddenly flew open. Within stood a massive woman in black dress and voluminous apron, who looked at us with great ill-temper.

'No need to batter the house down!' she said. 'I heard you. I was coming. It is a long way from the kitchen.'

In her hand she held – oddly enough – a pair of black silk shoe-laces. I supposed that she had been, perhaps, washing or ironing them when we disturbed her. But it was odd that she had not taken the time to lay them down somewhere.

'Dona Conchita de la Trava is here,' I said. 'I think her brother-in-law is expecting her.'

'Ay, ay,' the woman answered shortly. 'The senor is out just at present – how did *we* know what time of day to expect the lady? He will be back in due course.'

'I hope it will be convenient for us to come in and rest,' Dona Conchita said in her soft pretty voice. 'We have been travelling all day . . .'

With visible reluctance, the housekeeper let us in, along a dark hallway floored with shiny red tiles, and up a steep, highly polished stair to a long chamber with several windows that commanded a wide view, southward, across the valley. Its furnishings had once been handsome but were now shabby and worn. Conchita sank into an armchair, the two sisters stood by the window, I waited by the door.

'I will inform His Excellency of your arrival when he returns,' the housekeeper said shortly, and was going away, when Conchita halted her by asking for a little refreshment.

'A cup of chocolate, perhaps . . .'

Sourly, compressing her lips, the woman retreated, and presently reappeared, carrying a tray. To my silent amusement she had taken the request literally and brought *one* very small cup of chocolate, which she presented to Dona Conchita; nothing was offered to the sisters or myself. I met Juana's eye; she shrugged her shoulders with a slight twitch of the lips.

The housekeeper was again retiring when a most hideous and startling scream rent the silence of the house – followed by a series of others each seeming louder and more hysterical than the last. They came from downstairs.

'*Madre de Dios* – what has that monster done now—?' hissed the housekeeper and ran from the room.

'Sister Felicita – I believe we should see if we can be of use,' said Belen, and the two nuns followed swiftly. So, after a moment's hesitation, did Dona Conchita. So, more slowly, did I; but by the time I had reached the foot of the stair, the others had vanished from view. I moved a few paces through the shadows of the downstairs hall – with the front door closed, it was almost entirely dark – and was waiting for some sound to guide me towards the source of the trouble, when I heard a slight movement to my rear. Something small and exceedingly swift – a dog, a cat, a monkey?

– had whipped past, scampered up the stairs behind me, and was now out of sight in the upper storey. Instinctively I turned and bounded back up the stair in pursuit, pausing at the top. Now which way? A faint breeze of movement came from the chamber we had just quitted, and I re-entered it. But all seemed in order – the faded satin chairs, the well-polished side-tables, the glass cabinets – nothing moved. There was, however, an alcove at the end of the room, to the left; into this I could not see, and I moved that way. Again, I heard a sound, a furtive scrambling. At the same moment, from downstairs, there came the slam of a door and the sound of men's voices. Ignoring these, I walked into the alcove – which was, in fact, an L-shaped end to the room, containing an enormous fireplace in which, at present, no fire burned.

A huge cone-shaped chimney, like a dunce's cap, pierced upward through the ceiling. Part of its outer surface was visible. It was like a house within a house. The ashes on the hearth had been disturbed; their dust and a smell of woodsmoke still lingered in the air.

Stepping forward under the massive rim of the chimney-funnel, I looked up, and saw something small and black scrambling above me, mounting towards the tiny circle of light at the top. But how in the world had whatever it was achieved the upward leap needful to get into the chimney – the bottom edge of which came two feet above my head? A survey of the rim showed me two pairs of iron bars cutting across the curve of masonry – no doubt they were for the purpose of smoking meat or drying herbs – I reached up both hands, caught hold of a bar, and, without too much trouble, swung myself up. Now that I was contained within the gloom of the chimney, I could see stones protruding here and there from the inner surface of the chimney wall, set out like steps, probably to allow sweeps to climb up with their brushes and clean away the soot.

At this moment the chimney became wholly dark; my quarry, climbing above me, had blocked the hole at the top by squeezing through; then light shone down again, but, looking up, I realised that my pursuit was vain; though I might climb to the top and get my head through the hole, I could by no possible means push my shoulders after it; the opening was far too small.

Feeling foolish and thwarted, I was about to begin the descent when the sound of voices in the room below brought me to a sudden stop.

They were men's voices; they seemed to be standing in the alcove and the sound came up very clearly.

'If your brother is found to be lunatic, then what

becomes of the property? Quick – this I must know before we see them—'

'If Manuel is mad – and dies in his madness – then the family estates are mine by inheritance. While such money as there may be goes to his wife.'

'Ah! But if he is sane?'

'If he is judged to be sane – *then* he is an enemy of the state, and *all* his property will be forfeit.'

Suddenly in a flash I recalled my two aunts Josefina and Visitacion twittering by my bed: 'If your grand-father's estates are confiscated – we and your grandmother will be forced to beg in the streets!'

'So,' continued the second voice – and a cold thrill ran through my bones at its soft and deadly emphasis, 'so therefore he must be mad, and die in his madness.'

'Agreed.'

God in heaven, I thought, now what do I do? If I dare to make my presence known—

Merciful Father, what a predicament!

And I remembered, as if in a dream, how, not half an hour since, riding idly along the road from Tiermas, I had prayed, dear Father, won't you just give me a hint?

Here was my hint, with a vengeance.

By immense good fortune there came, at this moment, some commotion downstairs, audible apparently to the two men, though not to me in my chimney, which caused the second one to say, 'Hark, I hear voices. That must be them arriving; though it is strange I heard no knock at the front door.'

Footsteps retreated; in two seconds I was down on the floor, brushing myself over as best I could. Fortunately my breeches and jacket were of a dark colour so that smears of soot would not be too conspicuous; I smoothed my hair and scrubbed my face with my handkerchief, hoping that I did not have the appearance of a chimney-boy. Feeling myself still in grave danger of discovery here – for if the two men returned into the room they must know that I had heard what they said – I crept to the door and peered out. Fortunately they were descending the stair and did not look back so, on silent feet, I stole in the other direction along a dark hallway that led I knew not where, and opened a door at random. It gave into a bedchamber – disused, it could be guessed from its musty smell and lack of furnishings; the bed was the only object in the room.

Light from the door I had opened showed another stair from the hallway, leading upwards; I ran up this, and then came down again, making a great noise and clatter, and so on down to the ground floor where, in the long hall, there had now assembled a whole group of people: Dona Conchita, the two sisters, the hard-faced housekeeper, and two men. A lamp had been placed on a table, so that faces could be seen.

'*Bueno*, here is Senor Brooke,' said Conchita in her gentle voice. 'Don Ignacio, allow me to present him to you – he is the young *caballero* who was of such signal assistance to my cousin—'

'Ah, senor,' said my host, bowing slightly but making no attempt to take my hand. In fact he looked at me with considerable suspicion, evidently wondering where the devil I had just come from.

'Your pardon, senor,' said I, bowing likewise. 'You must wonder at my making so free of your house. But, after the outcry just now – what caused it, by the way? – something, some creature dashed past me up the stairs, and I chased it, thinking it must be an animal. It fled to the upper floor but there, I fear, it escaped me.'

'No matter, no matter,' said Don Ignacio irritably. 'Doubtless it was a cat or a rat – some small vermin.' His tone on the word *vermin* was exceedingly acid. I noticed that the housekeeper, who was frowning, frowned even more.

'Dona Callixta, will you prepare dinner at once, please, for these gentry,' Don Ignacio continued, in the same irritable tone. 'I fear I cannot accommodate your party in my house,' he said, turning to Conchita, 'for it is many years since I have been accustomed to receive guests and my resources are scanty. But you will dine with me, and I daresay you can find beds at the posada.'

'I will send my coachman to inquire,' she told him sweetly, though she looked rather put out. 'Of course we must not discommode you, dear Don Ignacio.'

'Until dinner is ready, pray consider my house at your disposal.' His voice was dry and cold, depriving this statement of any trace of hospitality. 'Would you wish to step upstairs and – and take a little refreshment?'

We all returned up the stairs into the room with the chimney where, by and by, a thin, ill-favoured man-servant brought a bottle of wine and some little plates of dry biscuits. Conchita and our host meanwhile kept up a somewhat stilted conversation about affairs and people in Madrid, the two sisters remained silent, and so did I, looking vigilantly about me.

What, I wondered, had become of the other man who had been there briefly downstairs? He had not been introduced, and when we came up he did not accompany us, but melted away somewhere into the gloom. He, I assumed, was the second voice I had heard from the chimney; the first was certainly that of Don Ignacio, whose tones I recognised at once. He it was who had said, 'He must be mad, and die in his madness.'

What a blood-curdling thing to say about one's own brother!

As may be imagined, I studied Don Ignacio with great attention.

He was a big man, with a kind of ruined good looks. Once he must have been handsome indeed, large-boned and strong-featured. Now his hair had receded until it was no more than a greasy straggle behind his ears. The skin of his face and neck was red, flaky and unhealthy-looking, with a glisten of sweat over the forehead and bald crown. His eyes were lashless and their brows mere ragged tufts. His teeth were discoloured and rotted, his hands, like his face, red and puffy; they trembled continuously. I would have hated to touch them and was glad he had not offered to shake hands. Indeed, the whole appearance of Don Ignacio de la Trava would have made me distrust him, even if I had not heard him make that cold-blooded remark about his brother. It was plain, however, that he was a man of breeding and education; he conversed civilly enough with Dona Conchita. He was carefully groomed, his linen snowy white and I could detect the odour of some sweet-smelling essence coming from him. At one point he remembered to make a polite inquiry about my grandfather.

He took no notice at all of the two sisters, but I observed Juana eyeing him very intently, and wondered what opinion she was forming. In remarkable contrast to him was a portrait that hung behind him on the wall: this was of a man in military uniform with a long, narrow, exceedingly handsome face, square-chinned, large-eyed, with well-cut lips, high cheekbones, a straight nose, a resolute expression, and a large black patch over the right eye. This dashing figure could hardly have been more different from Don Ignacio; yet there was a faint, lurking resemblance between the two. I noticed that Conchita had given a start when she first saw the portrait and then deliberately kept her eyes away from it. Could that, I wondered, be her husband, the elder brother Don Manuel? The man that we had come so far to seek?

I thought it surprising that Don Ignacio should keep in his house a portrait that was in such contrast to his own ruined looks. (Afterwards I learned from Juana that it was by the famous painter Francisco de Goya; that was why he kept it, waiting for its value to increase.)

When, presently, we were summoned to dinner I asked Juana in an undertone if the portrait was of Don Manuel, and she answered by a quick nod.

'What was all that commotion and shrieking down-stairs?' I demanded, for we had lagged behind the others in descending the stair.

It seemed to me strange that no one had referred to the incident.

'Oh, it was nothing – a servant girl, going to get onions from a basket in the back kitchen, found a viper curled up among them. She has a horror of snakes, it seems . . .'

'Odd, though, that one should make its way into the house? Especially in a town.'

'There is a tiny garden behind the house, in which snakes have been seen, the housekeeper said. Though she did seem uncommonly put out.'

Then we both fell silent. I was remembering how, on our former adventure, I had been bitten by a viper which curled round my arm while I slept; the bite inflamed, making me deathly sick, and Juana had to coax me along for miles, feverish and half delirious, leading my pony and reciting poetry to me. I smiled, remembering, and she smiled too.

'Do you still—?' I was beginning, but she shook her head, for Don Ignacio had begun a long Latin grace, evidently a relic from the days when he had trained for the priesthood.

The dining-room, on the ground floor, was dark and

shabby, with a great scratched walnut table and side-boards, the china chipped and cracked and the plate not of the best; on the walls hung the inevitable still-life paintings of dead hares, water melon, and slices of hake. But the meal presently served was sumptuous; it was plain to see where Don Ignacio's real interest lay, as course followed course: scallops, a great fish soup, omelettes, roast goose, almond tarts, and syllabub. Our host gobbled with such speed and greed that he hardly spared attention to see how his guests fared. The rest of us ate rather scantily; the sisters from habit; Conchita, seeming a little downcast, merely picked at what was on her plate; I felt disgusted by the sight of my host and had no wish to imitate his example.

After the meal Pedro appeared at the front door to say that bedrooms had been bespoken at the two small inns in the town. Conchita and the sisters went with him at once, but Don Ignacio beckoned me, with a nod, to follow him into another ground-floor room, a kind of study, furnished with half a dozen books and a few fowling-pieces which seemed in an equally poor state of preservation, either mildewy or rusty.

'This business of despatching my brother—' he began, having signed me to a chair. 'I hope it can be dealt with speedily.'

'Of course we wish to rescue the three children from

him as soon as we can,' I said. 'The poor things may be suffering from dreadful hardship—' Don Ignacio stared at me, thoroughly startled. His lashless eyes widened, then flickered. Plainly he had not been thinking about the children at all.

'It is the children that I was summoned to rescue, Don Ignacio,' I said firmly. 'They are my only concern.'

'But my brother is a dangerous lunatic – a traitor to the state—'

'What he is, or has done, is no concern of mine, Don Ignacio. I am not a hired assassin.'

'Certainly not – of course not—' Now he was flustered. 'But I do not see how – how they are to be removed from his clutches – unless—'

'Have you any idea where he has taken them?'

Now I could see that Don Ignacio was thinking hard – calculating.

'When he left here – when I refused to give him shelter – he spoke of going to the Monastery of San Juan de la Pena,' he said slowly.

'A monastery? He would take them to a monastery?'

'Oh, it is only a ruin, with an old church. No monks live there now – or only a couple. But there is a cave – and various underground rooms; I suppose Manuel thought it would make a shelter for them.'

'We will go there tomorrow. Is it far?'

'Not far – five leagues. But a very steep ascent, on the side of a mountain.'

'I will bid you good night then, senor.'

As I left him I could hear a hurried scampering upstairs, then a thud, then a series of angry shrieks, quite different from those of the maid who had been frightened by the snake. A parrot? A monkey? The house was plainly very large; I had noticed half a dozen doors in the ball above, and as many again on the top storey when I ran up the second stair; if all the rooms were the size of the empty bedroom, Don Ignacio could house a platoon without the least difficulty. Still, I was glad that he was too stingy to invite us; I would have hated to sleep under his roof.

I walked across the tiny plaza towards the albergue where Pedro and I were to sleep, which was on the north side of the little town. Greatly to my surprise, as I passed the church, Juana moved out from the shadow of its doorway and indicated, with a finger at her lips and a summoning gesture, that she wished to speak, but elsewhere, and in a place where we would not be overheard. We walked around the church to a little garden, containing a few graves and a couple of cypress trees, bounded by an outer wall that looked over the valley.

When we were at the far end of the enclosure, where nobody could steal up close without being seen, Juana said bluntly, 'What did that man want you to do?'

And I answered as bluntly, 'He wanted me to kill his brother.'

'And you said no.'

'Of course.'

'I do not trust him at all,' Juana said. 'How can two brothers be so different?'

'Your brother wanted to kill you,' I reminded her. 'And for the same reason – inheritance.'

She shivered. 'What an ugly world, Felix! In many ways I am glad to be out of it.'

I wondered if I dared suggest that this was rather a cowardly attitude; then decided that I did not dare. I remembered how Juana could flash out! Besides, if she chose to be a nun, it was entirely her own concern.

She went on, 'I am most anxious about this affair, Felix. It seems to me that there is something very wrong about it.'

'I think so too.'

'Do you?' She turned and stared at me. In the moonlight I could see her face very distinctly under its hood. I was reminded of so many nights when we had talked and argued, in the forest, in the mountains.

'I am very troubled now, in my mind, that I ever

brought you into it. I hope it will not lead to harm.'

'*I* am not sorry,' I said roundly. 'How could I be? For at least it has meant that we met again.'

She frowned. 'Yes; that is why – why I was so willing – when Conchita wrote to me asking for my help – asking for *your* help too – to rescue her children—'

I felt an almost physical pain in my heart. Juana had not, then, thought of summoning me herself? It had been at Conchita's suggestion?

'But why should she ask for *me*?' I said, gulping down this bitterness. 'When did Conchita de la Trava ever hear about me?'

'Oh, from me. When she came and stayed at my father's house in France while I was disposing of his estates. I told Conchita about you. It was a stupid thing to do,' said Juana angrily. 'It was childish – boastful. I just wanted to tell our story to somebody—'

'Oh Juana . . .'

Now the pain was different: like the fierce tingle when frozen fingers first begin to thaw. Looking at her face, so anxious and vulnerable in the moonlight, I thought, I love this girl. I know her far better than I shall ever know anybody else in the whole world, and I love her. Even if she goes back into her convent and we never meet again, I shall love her all my life.

'I wanted to *see* you again, do you see?' she was

saying gruffly and awkwardly. 'So, when Conchita suggested that you might rescue her children, I – I agreed to the plan. I thought, perhaps, if I *saw* you – that you might have changed. Or not be as I remembered you. And that – that would help me to make up my mind, one way or the other.'

From a kind of precarious happiness I was plunged again into fear. I did not dare ask if she had indeed found me changed. Nor how, if this was so, it would help her make up her mind. I could not bear to imagine the words in which she might reply.

Instead – and in some surprise at myself, for it was not in the least what I had intended to say – I remarked, ponderingly, 'Do you know that we are speaking English?'

'Yes, of course I know!' said Juana. 'That way, no one will be able to understand us, even if they overhear.'

'But when did you learn to speak English?'

'At the convent in Bayonne. There was an English nun, Sister Rose, I used to talk to her every day. I – it helped, when I first entered.'

'You speak it so well – what a clever girl you are, Juana! I remember how you always wished to read Pope and Dryden and Shakespeare.'

'Well,' she said, 'now I have read them.'

'And do you still write your own poetry, Juana?'

'No,' she said. 'That is not allowed.'

I wanted to exclaim at such an arbitrary prohibition, but a knifelike quality in her tone and glance held me back; instead I made some lame comment about her proficiency in the English tongue.

'Well,' she said, 'I knew it was no use waiting for you to learn Euskara, Felix!'

She looked up at me with her old teasing smile.

I was, at the same time, so happy and so very unhappy that I thought my heart would split in two. I would have liked to remain with her, talking all night, leaning on the churchyard wall, with the milky plain stretching away below, a belt of mist over the Aragon river, and the mountains beyond. But I said, 'We had better go to our beds, Juana. Tomorrow we must make a search at the ruined monastery of San Juan. Maybe, after all, there will be some simple way to rescue those children.'

'Somehow I cannot believe that,' said Juana.

Before retiring, in the albergue, I emptied my pockets, as was my custom, and puzzled over a tangle of black string that had found its way into one of them. Where could I have picked it up? Then, looking closer, I saw that it was not string, but two black silk shoe-laces, somehow plaited together, with a horn button strung on them in the middle. The housekeeper, I then recalled, had held a similar pair of laces when she came to answer Don Ignacio's door; but her pair had been smoothly ironed. These were in a sorry tangle, and smeared with ash . . . Vaguely, now, I thought I remembered picking them up off the hearth, before starting up the chimney in pursuit of that elusive creature, whatever it was.

Something the housekeeper had said floated back into my head: '*Madre de Dios*, what has that monster done now?'

Did Don Ignacio keep a tame chimpanzee? With a fondness for shoe-laces?

But soon my thoughts went back to Juana. And I thanked God, very humbly, for having created her in the first place, for having permitted me to see her again, and for having been so patient with me when I grumbled at Him.

Very faintly, as it might have been from the top of the chimney, I heard His voice answer, 'Be vigilant, Felix. I have troubles in store for you yet . . .'

Then I slept.

6

Trouble with the Escaroz horses; Pedro and I go to the monastery of San Juan; there we meet 'Figaro'; I return to Berdun; am surprised at the municipal arrangements for refuse; Dona Conchita objects to being carried in a lobster-pot; more news of the fat man

Drinking our lumpy chocolate next morning in the albergue, Pedro and I were startled by the voice of Tomas the coachman, aroused in fury and denunciation.

'What is the matter?' I asked, walking out into the narrow street to join him.

'*Matter?* What is the *matter?* The matter is that somebody has poisoned Senor Escaroz's horses – they are all sick and dying – *Valgame Dios!* Better horses never came out of Andalusia, and now they are sweating and frothing and near their end, how shall I ever be able to face my master?'

'Where are the horses?'

They were, it seemed, stabled in the valley below the town, so Pedro and I walked down a steep footpath which dropped from corner to corner of the zigzag road leading to the main gate. On the level ground stood groups of barns and farm buildings where the townspeople kept their mules and goats, cattle and poultry, for which there was no space among the houses tightly crammed together up on the bluff.

Sure enough, Senor Escaroz's four handsome Andalou horses were all lying down in their straw, eyes closed, sweating and gasping, with great ropes of spittle streaming from their nostrils and mouths.

'Ay, ay, *Madre mia*, this looks bad,' said Pedro, who knew a great deal about horses. 'You are right, Senor Tomas; somebody has given them some venomous dose.'

'If I could catch whoever it was I would throttle him with my bare hands,' yelled Tomas, in a passion. 'My beautiful horses – that they should die like this, so far from home!'

'*Do* you think they will die, Pedro?' said I.

He gave me a solemn look; then knelt by each in turn, inspected their eyes, their nostrils, their mouths, listened to their breathing.

'No,' he said then, 'I do not think they will die. But

they will be very sick for several days, not fit for the road for at least a week. You must give them a warm mash, Senor Tomas, with wine and bran, keep them well blanketed, with warm water to drink administered every hour of the day. And, at first, dose them with laudanum and turpentine, mixed in linseed oil, and apply hot fomentations to the belly. If the symptoms do not abate after that, try a laxative of Barbados aloes with one scruple of croton bean and one drachm of calomel. Give them no corn at all; only dry bran with cut hay. Would you like me to help you give the first dose?'

'Why, thank you, Senor Pedro, I shall be very much obliged,' said Tomas, greatly impressed by this expert knowledge, and so Pedro remained there to physic the horses while I went, first to inspect our humble mules – who were, fortunately, well and frisky; no one, it seemed, had attempted to tamper with *them* – and then back to the town to find Dona Conchita and tell her about this misfortune.

She was still breakfasting at her posada and was aghast at the news.

'*Por Dios!* What shall we do? My father's horses! This is terrible! I will ask Don Ignacio if he has any horses he can lend us.'

Don Ignacio, needless to say, had no horses to spare

for such a purpose; he regretted, infinitely, but he had only the one riding-horse, kept no carriage himself, and knew for a fact that there was neither a carriage nor draught-horse to be had in all the town. 'We are poor people hereabouts, Dona Conchita,' he said with a thin smile, 'and have learned to make do with mules and mule-carts.'

Ride in a mule-cart! Dona Conchita looked appalled at such a suggestion.

However it seemed that there was not, immediately even a mule-cart to be had in Berdun. Don Ignacio said that he would send off to Anso, the next town, where he thought there might be a tilbury for hire. 'But for today I fear you must be content to rest at your posada; no doubt you will be glad to do so after the fatigues of your journey,' he ended, making it plain that he did not intend to offer any more hospitality.

She shrugged, raising her beautiful brows. 'What else can I do, indeed? But you, Senor Felix—' with a pleading look, 'you need not be bound by my misfortune—'

'By no means, senora,' I said. 'With your permission, Pedro and I will set off for San Juan de la Pena directly he has finished helping Tomas dose the horses.'

Her face cleared. 'So, too much time will not be lost.'

I was sorry not to see Juana just then, but sure that she would understand. And, truth to tell, when Pedro and I rode off eastward, along the road that led towards Jaca, we felt decidedly light of heart. It was a great relief not to have to limit our pace to that of the carriage; Tomas was a surly, self-willed old man, and the two outriders, Pepe and Esteban, were lazy and disobliging; we were delighted to be rid of them all.

Conchita had asked if we wished the outriders to accompany us, but we said no; supposing that Manuel de la Trava had really taken refuge in the ruined monastery, there would be more chance of discovering his hiding-place if just two of us went there quietly than if a large group rode up with noise and clatter.

'The sickness of those horses was a great piece of luck for us,' I said. 'I wonder who did it?'

'Doubtless we shall never discover,' said Pedro, his face and tone blandly expressionless.

After an hour or so's riding we came to the little mountain village of Santa Cruz de la Seros. There we left our beasts in the shed of an obliging farmer and continued on foot up the back-breaking forest track.

'How did those ancient monks ever bring their supplies up here?' I panted, as we stopped to catch our breath on a shoulder of hill.

We had been told that a holy settlement had stood here since very ancient times. Indeed the church, some eight or nine centuries old, contained the tombs of the first kings of Aragon.

'Up here I daresay they had a better chance of keeping their heads safe on their shoulders while the Moors were pillaging down below – or the Goths,' said Pedro, mopping his forehead.

The place when we reached it certainly inspired awe. A huge curving cheek of reddish rock soared upward towards the mountain top. Below it was a great split, like a mouth running sideways across the hillside. And tucked into this mouthlike crack was a whole church, and a cloister alongside; both church and cloister were roofed by the overhang of the bulging mountain.

As we neared the church we heard the faint sound of chanting. And, looking with caution through the door, which was half open, we found two exceedingly old monks conducting the service of Sext. Removing our hats we joined them, and I again took the opportunity of thanking God for his interesting and unexpected kindnesses.

When the service was done, I asked the holy fathers if any stranger had lately visited this ancient place – but thinking, as I did so, that if Manuel de la Trava had taken refuge here, not even the President of the Military Commission in Madrid would have power to dislodge him, for he would surely be in sanctuary. To my slight surprise, one of the monks nodded his head.

'Yes, my son. There is a person here now at this very time. He told us that he was a scholar, pursuing researches into the Early Church, and asked leave to examine the tombs of the kings of Aragon and the other curiosities to be seen here. You will find him somewhere about the place.'

No word of three children.

So we began to explore and hunt about, finding more and more dark rock chambers, nooks and vaults and chapels cut out from the overhanging cliff, with steps going down into darkness, and water dripping, and a cold smell of dust and rock and loneliness. But there was no sign of Manuel de la Trava or his three children; if three children had ever been there, I thought, surely the monks must have seen them? Somehow I began to feel certain that the man we sought was not here.

However my certainty was shaken when we heard a footstep and a cough in one of the very lowest chambers – a small dark vault or crypt which I thought must be very ancient indeed.

'*Quien vive?*' called Pedro sharply. Both of us instinctively put our hands on our pistols – though I felt rather ashamed of doing so in a holy place, and the more so next moment when an astonished voice exclaimed, 'And who under the sun are *you?*'

Out of the darkness at the far end of the chapel emerged a short, slight man – nothing but his size could be seen in the dim light. But even before my eyes grew accustomed I could be sure that he was not Manuel de la Trava – he was nothing like tall enough and had no black patch over his eye.

'Your pardon, senor – we did not intend to disturb you – we were looking for a – a person,' I said rather lamely.

'A person? And what person might that be?'

He began to climb the stair, so we followed; plainly there was nobody else down here.

In the big vaulted hall above he was revealed as a man of rather less than average height with tawny, badger-coloured hair, a keen shrewd face, and such eyes! They glowed like those of a wild cat, full of intelligence and fire in his pale face.

I might have remained silent, but Pedro said bluntly, 'We are searching for Senor Manuel de la Trava, who has absconded with his three children.'

'Oh, *are* you indeed?' said the pale-faced man,

looking at us very sharply. 'And what do you propose to do with Senor de la Trava when you find him?'

'Senor,' I said, 'our business is not with him at all, but with the children; I have been engaged by their mother to search for them. It is not right that they should be carried off into the wilderness, and she is most deeply distressed about them.'

The man nodded his head once or twice. 'So who are *you*?' he asked at length.

I might have been rather affronted at his assuming the right to interrogate me like this, if there had not been such an air of authority about him – instinctively I felt that he was to be respected. And trusted.

'My name is Felix de Cabezada y Brooke,' I said, and he nodded again, frowning.

'I have heard of your grandfather; and of you, a little,' he said. 'Your grandfather the Conde is a good man—'

'Oh yes, senor, he is—'

'I hope that you resemble him. I hope that you are telling the truth.'

Pedro looked offended, but I said, 'Senor, I am telling the entire truth. I mean no harm whatsoever to Manuel de la Trava.'

He accepted this with a thoughtful look, and said, after a moment, 'My name is Jose de Larra—'

'Oh,' I exclaimed, 'senor, I have heard of you, naturally!' and I looked at him with great interest. 'I have read some of your writings.'

'You are lucky not to have been thrown into jail for doing so,' he remarked drily.

Hardly older than I – though he looked it; his face was weary and careworn – Jose de Larra was already one of the best-known political writers in Spain; I had heard it said that he was better paid than any other journalist. Under the pen-name of Figaro he had written many essays attacking government corruption, false patriotism, and our national indolence and backwardness.

'I am honoured to meet you, senor,' I said. 'But greatly surprised, I must confess, to encounter you here. I thought that you lived in Madrid.'

'So I do. But – like you – I am here searching for my friend Manuel de la Trava. I received a message that he had escaped from Montjuich.' He looked at me narrowly; it was plain that he was still not prepared to give us entire trust. He said, 'Where is Dona Conchita? Is she here too?'

'She is in Berdun.' I explained about the carriage horses.

'Is she staying with her brother-in-law? Do not trust that man,' de Larra said quickly. 'He is a rat – a snake

– he would not give asylum to his brother when asked, and I am quite sure he immediately informed the authorities that Manuel was in this region.'

I thought of the second man whose voice I had heard from the chimney. Very likely he was some official from the Military Commission.

'Yes, I believe you, senor.'

He reflected, then said, 'If you plan to take charge of the children – I confess that *would* relieve me – for I hope to help my friend Manuel, but two children as well would make the task far more difficult.'

Plainly he was not disposed to give me any more information. I guessed that he might have plans to smuggle Manuel out of the country, perhaps help him take ship for Mexico or another of the Spanish American provinces that had rebelled and freed themselves from Spanish rule.

'The three children are best with their mother, no doubt,' I said.

'Three? You said three? I had thought there were only two. Manuel spoke of two – I was able to visit him, once, in jail, before he was sent to Barcelona—'

'No, there are certainly three: Nico and Luisa and Pilar.'

'Odd – most odd. Can I have been mistaken?' He shook his head. 'Still, it is of no importance.'

Then there came a pause. We looked at one another warily, like card players each wondering what was in the other's hand. Did I trust him? Did he trust me?

'Come into the church,' he said abruptly, so we followed him in there. The old brothers had gone to their living-quarters in some cranny of the cliff, leaving a candle burning on the altar.

'Lay your hand on that altar and swear that you mean no harm to Manuel de la Trava,' said Jose de Larra.

'Very gladly, if you will too, senor.'

So we all three swore. Then de Larra said, 'What will you do next?'

'I suppose I must report back to Dona Conchita. For I promised to do so today.' I regretted this promise but she had begged me in such a trembling voice, with tears in her eyes.

De Larra said, 'I would prefer that you did not tell her about my presence here. She does not like or trust me.'

Something in his voice told me that he did not trust her either. Well, I thought, recalling Juana, he was probably right to trust as few people as possible.

'Very well, senor, I promise.'

He went on, 'There's a place called the Mouth of Hell, Boca del Infierno. High up in the mountains near the source of the Aragon river. The de la Travas own land in that region; there is a ruined castle. I think Manuel may be there.'

This did sound probable, and hope rose in my heart.

'I shall go there today without delay,' said de Larra. 'How far is it from here?'

'Seven or eight leagues, perhaps. But it is among the high mountains, to the north – 6,000 feet up, twice as high as we are here. And a most wild and rugged road. It is a hard place to reach.'

'You have been there before?'

'Yes – before – with Manuel – when we were both boys.'

'Is it a place to which I could take Dona Conchita?'

He looked horrified.

'*Por Dios*, no! On no account. Why should she want to go?'

'I – I suppose to beg – to plead for the restoration of her children.'

I thought of Dona Conchita's silk dresses; of her feet in their tiny velvet slippers; Boca del Infierno certainly did not sound like the kind of place that it would be suitable for her to visit.

'It will be much, *much* better if you do not bring her,' said de Larra positively. 'She and her husband did not agree. It was a foolish marriage – he was bewitched by her black eyes and white skin. But they had nothing in common. By the time he was imprisoned they had come to disagree most bitterly. Indeed they had already parted. The sight of her would do nothing but harm.'

'Well, I will try to dissuade her. But she is a lady with a very strong will.'

Pedro said diffidently, 'Senor Felix, do you think it would be a good thing if I went with Senor de Larra now, to find out the way to this place? Then I could return to Berdun and guide you – or meet you somewhere along the way tomorrow?'

'Yes, I do think that a good plan – if Senor de Larra agrees?'

After some thought, Jose de Larra did agree. Pedro was visibly a good and simple fellow and also a tough and well-muscled fighter, if fighting should be required. It would have been folly to refuse his offer.

As we all walked down the hill – de Larra's mule, he told us, was stabled like ours in the village below – Pedro said to me privily, 'I've a notion that it will be a good thing to get to this Boca del Infierno as soon as possible, just in case somebody tries to steal a march on us.'

'You are thinking of our fat friend?'

He nodded.

'We didn't see him in Berdun.'

'That's not to say he wasn't there.'

In fact, I had wondered: could the other voice, talking to Don Ignacio, have been the fat man's? I tried to remember him in Zamora saying to the child, 'Do not scold poor papa! You shall have all the treats you want at the end of the journey.' Could it have been the same voice? And what *was* the end of his journey?

We all rode a short way together along the carretera, and then, at a hamlet called Puenta de la Reina, where there is a bridge over the brawling Aragon river, Pedro and Jose de Larra turned northward towards the mountains. Pedro promised to meet me, or to leave word for me tomorrow, at a village called San Quilez, about five leagues into the foothills. And I rode back to Berdun at a brisk pace.

Leaving my beast, as before, stabled in a barn at the foot of the hill, I made my way up the steep zigzag track into the town and inquired at the posada for the ladies. Sister Belen was within, I heard, tending various sick people who had come to her for help; the other two ladies had walked out and I should easily find them somewhere about.

Accordingly I turned along the Calle Mayor to its end, then emerged through a narrow doorway in the town wall and followed a footpath that girdled it on the outer side. This path commanded a handsome view over the plain below, and a little rocky river, the Veral, that wound around Berdun and ran down to join the Aragon.

And there, leaning on a low wall by a flowering acacia, were my two ladies, one in white, the other black-veiled in her fur cloak, for the evening was cool and breezy. They were talking together and did not at first notice my approach.

Juana was saying, 'But why in the world did you not bring the old nurse, Guillermina? I'd have thought you would need her badly once they are found – after all, you have never had to care for them entirely by yourself—'

'Oh, my dear! Where would we have put her? On the floor?'

'Belen or I could have sat on the box.'

'Unthinkable! Besides – in fact – I had to dismiss old Guillermina. She was becoming quite incapable of dealing with little Pilar – couldn't discipline her at all—'

She seemed to have forgotten how affronted she was when Juana said the same thing.

'Well,' Juana was saying doubtfully, 'I hope that I shall be—'

Then she turned and saw me and fell silent.

Dona Conchita was all smiles and welcome.

'Felix! Our good friend! I am so rejoiced to see you back! What fortune have you had?'

I explained that we had had no luck at San Juan but that somebody we saw there – I contrived to make it sound as if it were one of the old priests – had advised us to try la Boca del Infierno. She listened, nodding gravely.

'Then it is there that we must certainly go tomorrow. This time I will accompany you. I feel in my bones that is the place where Manuel has my poor darlings confined; if only he does not have them chained up and half starved! Oh, it is too horrible to contemplate! We must start directly breakfast is over. Don Ignacio has managed to find us some kind of equipage and a couple of animals to pull it.'

'From the sound of the road, senora,' I said, 'I don't know if even that will take you all the way. It may be necessary to walk. I should certainly advise you to wear some stout shoes.'

'Walk!' she said distastefully.

All this while Juana had remained silent. The dusk was now so thick that I could not see her face, shadowed under the white hood. But I felt an emanation of anger coming from her. Could I in some way have displeased her, I wondered?

We turned back towards the posada, Conchita

chatting gaily about the deficiencies of the town.

'Only think! There is just the one baker. And no doctor at all. If you fall sick, you say a prayer in the church – or ride twelve leagues into Jaca and seek help there. And, just see what they do with their waste—'

She pointed to a structure we just passed, a massive wooden trough, supported on props, the top end of which rested on the low wall by which the ladies had stood. The trough ran down the steep rocky precipice which dropped away on the north side of the town, and disappeared into the darkness below; where it ended one could not see.

'That is how they dispose of their refuse,' Conchita said laughing. 'Is it not ingenious? They just toss down there anything that is not wanted. Though I fear that in summer, townsfolk who have windows facing this way may have to keep them closed!'

I made appropriate comments, wondering what could be the matter with Juana.

Conchita noticed her silence too, and became solicitous.

'Are you tired, my love? It is such a change for you, from convent life, all this travel, all this to-and-fro; I feel that I am imposing on you shamefully, you and your good, kind companion; how you must long for your peaceful cells! Poor dear Juana! Never mind, let us hope that it may not be many more days. If only our clever Felix can, perhaps tomorrow, find my hateful husband and remove the children from him – then we can all be at rest . . .'

So she rattled on until they reached the door of the posada.

'Will you not come in, dear Senor Felix, and dine with us?'

No, I said, I was tired and would take the opportunity of an early night; that way we could start at cockcrow tomorrow.

'Cockcrow?' said Conchita with a little shriek. 'Oh, not quite at cockcrow, dearest Senor Felix. Say, half-past eight?'

In the end the hour of eight o'clock was fixed on.

All this time Juana had not uttered a word, and she disappeared into the posada without bidding me good night.

Feeling sore and puzzled and ill-used, I made my way to my own albergue.

Next morning, long before cockcrow, I was up and inspecting the open carriage that Don Ignacio had procured for his sister-in-law. It seemed sound enough, though shabby and of rustic design. Old Tomas, who had spent the night with his suffering horses and was up early fomenting them, agreed dourly that he supposed it would do well enough to carry the Dona on a mountain road where nobody could see them. 'Though what Senor Escaroz would say!' The mules that had been found to draw the equipage were lean, haggard animals not much larger than ponies, but clean-legged and bright-eyed. I wished Pedro were there to inspect them, but concluded they would do their work sufficiently well. Having surveyed the whole turn-out I went back to the albergue, loaded a pack for myself, and then walked round to the ladies' posada and asked the waiting-girl for Sister Belen.

The good sister came down directly, thinking, I daresay, that some sick person was asking for her. When she saw me she smiled and said, 'Why, it is our young Senor Amarillo!' which she had taken to calling me, I suppose because of my yellow hair.

'Good morning, Sister Belen. I want you to do me a kindness.'

'With all my heart. What is it?'

'I want you to accept, and persuade Sister Felicita to accept, these things, which I bought in Pamplona. You are going today into high mountains and the weather has worsened—' which was true, a sharp wind blew, combined with a fine, penetrating rain – 'your habits are not warm enough to protect you here.'

She took the bundles, which consisted of a dark blue

baize riding-habit and a hooded cape of the same warm material for each of the nuns, and two pairs of riding boots made from supple Cordoba leather.

'*Vaya, vaya!*' she exclaimed in astonishment. 'What forethought! What good sense! You will make a fine, considering husband some day. But how in the world did you guess the size of our feet—?' trying one of the boots against her own sandalled foot, which was broad and sturdy, almost as wide as it was long.

'Oh, that was easy. Do you remember the muddy road outside the posada at Irurzun? I measured your footprints after you had each walked out to the carriage.'

At that she laughed immensely. 'Wicked boy – what a planner, what a plotter! I do not know what Sister Felicita will say.'

'You will persuade her to accept them, won't you, Sister Belen?' I asked anxiously. 'Pray do! For I fear she is displeased with me, and indeed I don't know why.'

To my surprise Sister Belen gave me five or six quick little pats on the shoulder.

'I am sure it is no fault of yours at all. It is some idle thing Dona Conchita said to her. Don't let yourself be troubled about it. Whatever it is can be of but slight importance.'

Then she bustled off with the bundles.

When we finally assembled outside the main town gate – Dona Conchita late as usual – and she turned to survey the conveyance that had been procured for the ladies, the whole excursion nearly came to a halt then and there.

'Ride in *that*?' she shrieked. 'Why not simply carry us in a lobster-pot?'

It did bear a certain resemblance to a lobster-pot, being a *tartana*, a kind of country vehicle often used in Aragon. We had seen them along the way. It was a two-wheeled, oblong conveyance, not large, drawn by two mules, the main feature of it being that the floor is woven from a rope network. This makes it light for hilly country, and also easily repaired.

'I am *not* going to sit with my legs dangling through that net,' objected Conchita. 'Why, it almost touches the ground. We should be scraped to death.'

I noticed that, today, she had left off her velvet slippers and wore a pair of neat little buttoned boots which peeped demurely out from below her black silk skirts; but they looked hardly more suitable for mountain walking than the slippers had been.

'Why, then,' calmly said Juana, who was going to do the driving – Tomas had insisted on remaining with his master's horses – 'why, then, you will have to sit with me on the box.'

'Must I? Oh – very well. What papa would say if he knew. Those are certainly the sorriest, scraggiest beasts I ever did see—'

'Where is Sister Belen?' I asked in surprise, as they seemed preparing to set off without her.

'Our good Sister Belen is not coming today,' Conchita told me, settling herself with her many wraps and cushions, and clucks of distaste for her situation, as she took her seat alongside Juana. 'Belen finds there are such a great number of sick persons in Berdun that she says her day will be better spent there – and who would argue with her choice in such horrible weather? Brrr!'

She contrived to make it sound as if Sister Belen were taking the day's holiday out of laziness because she did not want the discomfort of a trip into the mountains, which I felt very sure was not the case.

Juana quietly climbed to the driver's seat and took the reins. To my joy she was wearing the clothes I had bought; they fitted her well. Conchita was jocose about them.

'You are a most gallant caballero, Senor Felix, to have bought our friends those elegant habits. Ay, *de mi*! Our little Juana looks like a princess today, does she not? What would the Reverend Mother say, I wonder?'

Juana's eye met mine. She was red with anger. I could see that for two pins she would return to the posada, tear off the new warm clothes, and put on her old white habit. I rolled my eyes imploringly, looking like a clown, I daresay; she gave a small reluctant shrug, flicked the mules sharply with the reins, and set them in motion. Pepe and Esteban were astride their beasts already; I sprang on mine and followed the cavalcade along the straight road eastward.

For many miles we rode in silence. The mountains to north and south were veiled in mist. Juana and Conchita had nothing to say to one another, and, wishing to avoid being drawn into idle conversation by the latter, I took care to stay twenty paces to the rear of the tartana, allowing Pepe and Esteban to lead the way. In this formation we proceeded to Puenta de la Reina, and there turned north, up into the foothills. All the way we met with very few passers-by, apart from an occasional shepherd and flock of goats.

About an hour after noon we reached the small mountain village of San Quilez, where Pedro had promised to meet us. It was no more than a handful of rough stone houses, clustered about a church. A small, swift rocky brook divided the houses; a high arched bridge joined the two sections. Perched on a spur of the northern foothills, San Quilez should have commanded a great view of the Aragon valley, but the mist cloaked everything; the houses were no more than grey shapes, and only a kind of shadowy darkness up above indicated the near presence of craggy mountains towering over the slate roofs and granite chimneys (each with a carved beast perched on top).

'Those are to prevent demons coming down the chimney,' Juana coldly informed me. She had hopped out of the tartana and tethered the mules to a holly tree. I was glad to see that her anger was abating, or forgotten, or set on one side. She seemed calm, remote, and unapproachable.

'I'd have expected devils to go *up* chimneys, not down them,' I said, thinking of the creature that escaped me up the chimney of Don Ignacio's house.

Conchita joined us, a faint cloud on her exquisite brow.

'Was not Pedro supposed to meet us here?'

Her tone suggested that it was remiss of us to be standing about making foolish conversation while her affairs were neglected.

'He was, senora, but I see no sign of him. That place over there might be an albergue – shall we see if they can provide us with any food while we wait?'

A house by the church, rather larger than the others, seemed to combine the function of inn and bakery;

women came and went from it with trays of loaves, baked and unbaked; I walked inside and found a stone-floored room with a fire, also a great barrel of red wine from which all customers were served in wooden cups.

'The senora says that she can make you an omelette,' I reported, returning to Conchita. With a faint moue of distaste at the darkness and discomfort of the place she entered and sat on a stool. Pepe and Esteban followed and were served with mugs of wine.

'Pay the score and keep Conchita contented,' I murmured to Juana, pushing a fistful of coins into her hand. 'I'll be back as soon as I can—' and I slipped away through a back door. For, while gazing at the chimneys and their carved guardians, I had caught a glimpse of bright red up on the hillside, among the misty trees by the brook. Pedro had a red hand-kerchief; I had seen it a hundred times.

Sure enough, when I had crossed over the bridge and followed a goat-trodden footpath along the stream, up into the wood, I found Pedro, leaning against a tree.

'Took you long enough to get here,' he said.

'Well! What is all this hide-and-seek about?'

'Matters are complicated.'

'As if I hadn't guessed that. Did you find—?'

'Hush! Trees have ears.'

Pedro looked about. A dozen yards upstream there was a four-foot waterfall in the brook, with a flat-topped rock above it in the middle of the water. 'Let us sit on there,' said Pedro. So we perched on the rock, where the sound of rushing water would drown our voices.

Then he said, 'Yes! We found him! Jose de Larra was right in his guess. Don Manuel has taken refuge in the ruined castle up there. Castillo de Acher, it is called.' He nodded backward towards where the mountains ought to have been.

'Did you see him? Speak to him?'

'I saw him. You can't speak, it is too high. De Larra sent him up a note.'

'Sent? Who took the note?'

'He has a rope. He lowers it, with a basket.'

'Ay, *Dios*! Where is he, then, in an eagle's eyrie?'

'Not unlike.' Pedro described the Castillo de Acher. 'It is up on top of a crag, two hundred feet above the forest.'

'But there must be a road up.'

'Not any more. Don Manuel dynamited it.'

'How did he come by dynamite, in heaven's name?'

Don Manuel had known of a supply of arms hidden there, left over from the French wars, Pedro said. The *castillo* had once been strongly fortified; but the French had, as it happened, never advanced that way, so the stores of arms were never used.

'Now, in consequence, he is well armed. And having blown a great hole out of the road, all he has to do is sit up in his turret and pick off anybody foolhardy enough to go up and try to bridge the gap.'

'How did de Larra know about the place?'

'It seems when they were boys together they used to explore the ruins, and once planned such a scheme. They had even arranged a signal: when two shots were fired at the foot of the crag, a basket would be lowered. De Larra remembered it, and so did Manuel.'

'So you went there and de Larra fired two shots?'

'We did; and presently, sure enough, down came a basket on the end of a cord. De Larra put in his seal, and a note he had written. Then, by and by, up there looking over the battlements, we see our fine gentleman; and the two little ones.'

'Two? Where was the third?'

Pedro shrugged. 'Maybe not tall enough to see over. But no – now I recall – when Senor de Larra had made his offer, of help and escort into France, and then on to Mexico or Ecuador – he explained that other provision would be made for the three little ones, in Spain; and then Don Manuel told him that there were only two.'

'How very strange! What can have become of the third?'

'Fell over the cliff, maybe,' said Pedro indifferently.

Putting aside this problem for later consideration, I said, 'But did Don Manuel agree to his friend's plan? What was the outcome?'

'It all had to be carried on slowly and laboriously by notes. You cannot hold a conversation up and down two hundred feet of cliff. Back and forth went the basket, and in the end the rope broke – it was only a villainous old ravelled bit of hempen cord which had probably been lying about in the damp ruins for twenty years – so de Larra said he would go off and procure more rope, also some food, for they were running short—'

'We have rope—'

'Well, I know, but I thought it would do no harm. And by the time he returned, Don Manuel promised to have reached a decision on the matter.'

'But if he decides not to accept his friend's offer? What then?'

Pedro said, 'He will never, never allow himself to be recaptured. He said so. He said, sooner than that, he will jump off the battlements and take the children with him.'

'Heaven forbid! Did he seem mad, Pedro?'

'Not in the least mad,' answered Pedro, shaking his head. 'Of course one could not see his features at such a distance; but what he wrote to his friend was perfectly sensible.'

'It is as I thought . . .'

I sat frowning down at the clear hurrying water and twisted a twig in my fingers until it snapped. 'So de Larra is now engaged in fetching rope and provisions. Where from?'

'Not from this village,' Pedro said. 'There is a monastery on the other side of the gorge, to the north-west, in the forest. If you will take my advice, Senor Felix, we will wait here comfortably until de Larra has spirited away his friend; then, without the least difficulty, we can remove the children.'

'I have two objections to that plan.'

'Which are?'

'First, there seems to be a child missing. In order to know what has happened to that one, it is needful for me to meet Manuel de la Trava, so that I can give an account of the matter to Dona Conchita.'

'Two children or three,' said Pedro impatiently, 'what difference can that make? If one got lost some-where, it is not our fault. Well? What is your other difficulty?'

'Such a simple solution is no part of Don Ignacio's

plan. *He* wants Don Manuel dead – and before his death he must be pronounced mad, so that his heirs may inherit his estate. That would not happen if he escapes to the Americas. So Don Ignacio is sure to try to prevent his escape.'

Pedro chewed his thumb thoughtfully.

Then he said, 'But Don Ignacio does not seem to be active in the matter.'

'I am not so certain. How do we know what secret moves he may have made?'

For instance, I thought, where is the second man who was in the hall? Where is the fat man? What part does he play in this affair?

'Then,' said Pedro, '*we* had better move without delay.'

'That is what I think. How far to the castillo?'

'Oh, as the crow flies, not far. A couple of leagues, perhaps a little more. But—' Pedro's grin was not without malice – 'if the Dona thinks she is going to get there in her carriage, even in a mule-trap, she is due for a rude awakening. Firstly, the cart road comes to a stop where there is a rope bridge—'

'A rope bridge!'

'A rope bridge,' said Pedro with satisfaction, 'over a deep ravine. How our fine lady is to get across that, I leave to your brilliant wits.'

'Is there no other way to approach the castillo?'

'I asked de Larra. He said, possibly, if one were to travel south from here, for several leagues, and take a small road that winds eastward up another valley, round the other side of the mountain. But then you would finish up on the wrong side of the ridge and might find there was no track over the top. He was not certain. Or, you can go on up the valley, a league or so, cross a footbridge, and come back on the other side of the river – but then you have to cross two ridges, and it is only a goat track through the forest.'

'Well,' I said, 'it looks as if the lady will not be able to reach her husband's hide-away.'

'If you ask me,' said Pedro, 'that is just as well. One of the first questions he asked de Larra was, had he seen Conchita, did he come from her? He hates her, it is plain. Only when de Larra swore he had had no dealings with the lady would Don Manuel even consider his offer.'

I thought.

'Is there somewhere close to this rope bridge – a farm, cottage, barn – where the Dona could wait in shelter while I go on and try to see her husband?'

'Yes, there is. A foresters' hut.' Pedro's sniff said, not what she is used to.

'Good, then let us collect the women and set out.'

We jumped across to the bank and had started back towards the houses, along the brookside, when, ten paces from the bridge, I heard a familiar voice.

'No, *hija*! I said, come back! I said, we must go into the house. Be a good girl now. You can do that another time. Do as Papa says – please, *querida*!'

And a shrill, angry little voice, replying, 'But I *want* to do this. I want it very much!'

'But, *hija*! You promised that you would be a good girl. You promised. And we *must* go inside!'

'Why?'

'Otherwise we might be seen.'

Pedro's eye met mine. Then, curious to discover what would happen next, I walked along to the bridge, and up on to it. The speakers had been beyond, out of sight, down by the water's edge on the far side. As we briskly and loudly walked on to the arch of the bridge, they moved under it, remaining out of sight.

When we had crossed the brook and passed the corner of a house that stood nearby, Pedro said in a low voice, 'Why did you not accost him?'

'Because, now, he still thinks himself undiscovered.'

He nodded, slowly.

'And perhaps the fat fellow will betray himself. Very good. But it passes wonder why he should saddle himself in the wilderness with that spoiled pest of a child.'

'No,' I said, 'don't you see—'

'See what, in mercy's name?'

'Where are your mathematics, Pedro? You who are so good at calculating? The child is the missing factor to the question. On one side there is a child too few – on the other—'

'But why?'

'Hush!'

Dona Conchita was standing in the doorway of the bakery looking impatiently in our direction, tapping the doorpost with her black ostrich-feather fan.

'*There* you are! The omelette is quite ready!' she called. 'Eat it without delay so that we can be on our way.' And she almost pushed us inside, then demanded urgently of Pedro, 'Well? Well? Did you see my husband? Is he there, in that castillo?'

While she interrogated him, I thought I caught the sound of hoofs outside. Then I noticed that Juana seemed eager to catch my eye. Her glance was full of meaning, and I made a cautious movement of my head, indicating that I would speak to her elsewhere when occasion presented.

Pedro was bolting bites of omelette between replies to Conchita.

'Yes, senora, yes – I saw your husband – he is in the castillo. Yes, with the children – I saw them also, high, high up on the ramparts.'

'Oh, then let us go to them at once – at once!' cried Conchita. 'Poor little darlings – they are probably starved to death.'

Yet then, in spite of her declared impatience to be off, she wasted a good half-hour buying bread from the baker; she would not make do with the few loaves left over in his tray from the last baking, but insisted on waiting until the new batch came out from the big wall-oven, hot and fragrant.

'It will be so much nicer for the poor children like that,' she said; though Pedro muttered in my ear that the loaves would be chilly enough by the time they had reached the children, if he knew anything of the matter.

While Conchita was making her wishes known in the bakehouse, I contrived to step out of doors for a moment with Juana. The mist had thickened; we had only to move a few feet away from the building to be out of sight.

'What is it?' I asked quietly.

She was frowning; I could see that she was troubled, embarrassed, angry even; could her anger be directed against me?

'Felix . . . you will think me a spiteful busybody, I daresay—'

'Why should I do so? You are no such thing.'

She had a rosary of wooden beads attached to her belt; these she twisted unhappily, looking down at her hands, not at me.

'I know that you like Conchita very much. And it will seem as if I am trying to spoil that liking – in a mean, petty way—'

She looked so like the troubled, sulky boy whom I had believed her to be on our former journey that words came from me of their own accord, 'Come, Juan, how can you misjudge me so? I know that you could never in your life be mean or petty.' And I added in the old teasing manner, 'Fierce and savage, yes; I remember when you called me a hateful, infamous, tyrannical *pig*—'

At that she did turn startled eyes up to me. 'Never! I am sure I never did.'

'I can remember the very place. It was behind the blacksmith's forge in Licq-Athérey.'

'Oh, well—' she blushed, remembering, 'That was different! And I was much younger then. No, but listen. I *hate* myself for telling this – I would not do it – only I feel that, as I brought you into this affair – and it may be dangerous—'

'My friend, stop beating about the bush, and just tell me.'

She drew a quick breath.

'Well then – the baker's wife knew that I was a sister – news of that kind travels quickly all over the country – and she asked me to come upstairs to look at her baby, who is sick. While I was in her upstairs room I saw, through the window, that Conchita went out of doors and into the church.'

'To say a prayer for her children,' I suggested.

'No doubt.' There was an indefinable inflection in Juana's voice, as if she were doing her utmost to be scrupulously fair, against considerable difficulty. 'Presently Conchita came out of the church again and went quickly away; then, several minutes later – I was walking back and forth by the window, you understand, hushing the child in my arms all this while – a few minutes later, out came a fat man and a child. Out of the church.'

'Ah. You knew the man?'

'No, I did not,' said Juana firmly. 'I had never laid eyes on him in my life. But the child I knew – very well indeed. I could not mistake – despite the fact that she had grown since I saw her last—'

'Yes?' I said encouragingly.

'It was that little demon, Pilar – Conchita's youngest. Nobody who had once met her could forget her.'

'Can you describe her?'

'Thin – with her hair plaited up on top of her head – a little pointed face, full of self-will and petulance—'

'You need say no more. I, too, have met her. She resembles her mother, in fact, does she not? But,' I said, 'you are perfectly sure that you have never met the fat man who was with her?'

'No,' said Juana, with reluctance and discomfort, 'but I think I know who he is. When Conchita came to visit me with the children in France, the elder ones, Nico and Luisa, often spoke of a friend of their mother's, Don Amador de Castanos. He was very fat, they said – they made jokes about him as children will. Nico drew a picture of him like a balloon. Then Conchita became angry and forbade them to mention him.'

'But you think that might be he? The fat man in the church.'

'It might be,' she said, troubled, with a crease between her brows. I guessed that there might be more which she scrupled to tell me; gossip, hearsay from the children's nurse, perhaps. 'The other two children said that he was very fond of Pilar – especially attached to her.'

'Who or what is this Don Amador, do you know?'

'Guillermina the nurse told me that Don Amador was a cousin of Calomarde, the Minister of Justice, and that he himself held a government position in Madrid. That was where he met Conchita.'

'In that case, it certainly is very odd to see him in a little mountain hamlet such as San Quilez.'

'So I think also.'

'You did not see him *with* Dona Conchita – speaking to her?'

'No.' Juana sounded relieved that this was the case. 'No I did not. They came separately from the church – they might not even have noticed one another. It is dark in there. But it was so strange that he – that he was with—'

'Conchita's youngest child; who is assumed by everybody to be shut up with the others in the castillo.'

'Yes!' she said, turning on me her clear dark-brown eyes with their coppery lights. 'That is strange, is it not, Felix?'

'Oh well – I daresay there will turn out to be some very simple explanation,' I suggested robustly. '*All* explanations are simple when you hear them.'

'Do you think I should tell Conchita that I have seen Pilar?'

'Why not? It would be the natural thing to do.'

Her face cleared. 'Then I will do so. I hate deception. Bless you, Felix! You have relieved my mind of a weight.' She spun on her heel and walked back inside the albergue.

Nearby I noticed one of the villagers, a man in a high conical Aragonese hat.

'Senor,' I said to him, 'have you by any chance seen a rather stout gentleman, well-dressed, with a little girl?'

He looked me straight in the eye, spat deliberately, then replied, 'No, senor. I have seen no such persons. No such persons have been in this place.'

Then he walked away, not slow, not fast.

Humph, I thought, someone has greased *your* palm well, my friend.

7

Arrival at the rope bridge; the bear; Pedro stunned; I encounter little Pilar on a cliff; Don Manuel and his children; the book; I carry a letter to Juana

When we were on our way again, with the females driving in the tartana, Pepe and Esteban in attendance, and Pedro and myself riding ahead, I noticed two things. One was that Conchita and Juana seemed to be on even more distant terms than they had been during the morning ride. Juana attended diligently to her driving, coaxing the mules along over the bad road with firmly set lips and knitted brow; while, beside her, Conchita sat bolt upright, looked straight ahead, and flicked her fan about in a displeased manner; neither of them seemed to address a single word to the other.

Conchita does not believe that little Pilar was in San Quilez, I thought. Or chooses to pretend disbelief. Which?

I noticed, also, that Pedro had some news that he wished to communicate; his eyes were huge with it, and he could hardly contain himself until we had drawn away from the others along a couple of turns of the track, which here, as we penetrated and climbed higher into the mountains, became increasingly narrow and rocky. The mist was too thick for any view in front, but the vast and cold presence of the High Pyrenees could be felt invisibly and forbiddingly around and ahead of us, like an army of huge granite ghosts. Dear Father in heaven, I thought – somehow it came more naturally to converse with God in such a place – dear Father, I presume You had some excellent reason for causing Manuel de la Trava to come and hide himself in these tremendous mountains. And I shall be greatly obliged if in due course You will divulge it to me.

Naturally I had a good reason, Felix, you ninny, came the chiding voice of God. From here, as the eagle flies, it is now hardly more than five leagues to the French frontier. The truth, my son, is always simple.

Overhead the faint shrill cry of an eagle impressed on me the force of God's words. I looked up and saw the mighty bird, balancing in the mist on his wings, six cubits across, wider in their span than the height of the tallest man. I saw him drop a great haunch-bone from his talons and then swoop after it into some distant gully, to peck out the marrow from the smashed bone.

'We need to be on the watch for wild boar hereabouts,' remarked Pedro. 'I saw half a dozen of them on my ride back to San Quilez. Singly they may be no great danger, but meet a group of them – or even one savage old tusker—'

'Bears too, I suppose,' I said, as a branch snapped among the trees, which cloaked the steep slopes of the mountain and came down close to the track.

'Yes, bears; de Larra told me he had seen a big brown brute.'

'Well? What is it you wanted to tell me?' I asked, when several turns of the track lay between us and the mule-cart.

Pedro grinned widely. 'You don't miss much, do you, Felix? Why, it is this: those two precious postilions are part of the business too. While the lady was buying bread I went into the shed where I had left my mule, for I noticed that he had been walking tender on one hoof. I was sitting on the floor, picking out a splinter of stone, when I heard their voices. They did not know I was there. 'Whatever you do,' said one of them, 'don't kill him before we have what we want from him. His Excellency would have our tongues for pen-wipers if his death came about before—' And then the other one said, 'Quiet, you fool. I know that as well as you do,' and they walked out into the plaza. I heard them as plain as I can hear you.'

'Did you indeed?' said I. 'Well, I am not particularly surprised. I always thought they were a pair of untrustworthy-looking scoundrels. I wonder who His Excellency is.'

'Don Ignacio, perhaps. Or Dona Conchita's father. Or the fat man.'

'His name is Don Amador de Castanos,' I said, and told Pedro what Juana had told me.

He whistled. 'And Don Amador is travelling with the Dona's third child. Well! What do you make of that?'

'What do you?'

'*Calla boca!* It is quite plain. The child is his and the lady Conchita's, and none of de la Trava's at all. I am sorry if this spoils your notion of her, Felix – I know you seemed to find her a very gracious and perfect young lady at first—'

'Not quite as perfect as all that,' I said shortly. 'But I had to be civil to her; it is on her errand that we are employed, after all.'

Pedro eyed me sideways.

'Well, *I* thought you seemed mightily taken with her. And I could see the Dona Juana wasn't best pleased with that. However, that's none of my affair! My own opinion, from the very start, is that Dona de la Trava is one of those sweet-spoken smilers who would be very happy to drive their carriage right over you, if you should chance to fill a hole in the road—'

'Suppose you are right; what is the purpose of Don Amador flitting all over the landscape with little Pilar?'

Pedro considered. 'As I see it: the fact that little Pilar isn't de la Trava's child at all, that he didn't choose to abduct her with the others, rather spoils the picture of Dona Conchita as a poor bereaved mother and a wronged wife. Does it not? If she hopes to inherit de la Trava's money – and there's somebody important that she has to enlist on her side – the Minister of Justice, perhaps, or that Reverend Mother you saw—'

'—who is the cousin of the king's confessor,' I remembered. 'Yes; I expect you are right, Pedro. Conchita needs little Pilar to be at hand when the other two are rescued—'

'So that she can be fitted neatly into the pattern.'

Pedro laughed.

'From the way she was carrying on in that saddler's in Zamora, I doubt if that one will fit neatly into anybody's pattern!'

Except God's, perhaps, I thought.

'I suppose she was the cause of all that commotion in Berdun.'

'What commotion?' said Pedro.

'I forgot; you'd gone to stable the mules.' I told Pedro about the servant who had found a viper among the onions, and the small sprite or demon who had scampered ahead of me up the stairs and climbed the big conical chimney. 'I'd be ready to wager that was little Pilar. Yes, and in fact I know it was.' For now I remembered the sooty little necklet I had picked up in Don Ignacio's fireplace – a shoe-lace threaded with buttons and plaited. At the time it had reminded me of something, but I could not think what the something was. Now I knew: it was the plaited thongs and blue bead I dropped over Pilar's head in the saddler's shop.

Pilar had copied my model, as children will, using other materials.

'But, Felix,' Pedro went on, after we had ridden in silence for another hundred paces, 'it seems to me that this errand is a nasty, dirty business! And if your grandfather knew the true rights of it, he would never have allowed you to take part in it.'

'As if he could have stopped me!' I exclaimed indignantly.

Still, in my heart, I agreed with Pedro. Grandfather

would feel nothing but loathing and scorn for the plots and plans of Don Ignacio, of Conchita, of Amador de Castanos. Did Don Amador hope to marry Conchita, once her husband was disposed of? Did *she* plan to marry *him*? Or had she other plans in mind?

Pedro smiled and shrugged, as much as to say, I know you and your grandfather better than you know yourselves. After a minute, he observed, 'Well, it is lucky that we ran into Senor de Larra. There is *one* honest man, at least. And with God's help he will get de la Trava out of Spain and out of the clutches of all these griffin vultures. And that will be a good end to the business.'

'We had better keep those two *picaros* under sharp observation, if they have been hired to kill Don Manuel.'

'I have a suggestion to make,' said Pedro, ' Another league will bring us to the rope bridge. We shall be obliged to leave the females there. And Dona Conchita certainly won't want to remain unprotected. So Pepe and Esteban can be told to stay and guard her.'

This seemed a practical arrangement, though I feared that Juana would not be best pleased at being left behind again with Conchita and the outriders.

In a quarter of an hour we all reached the bridge, and halted.

It was a gloomy place. For some time the valley had been growing narrower as we rode northward. The sides were so steep that it was a wonder the forest trees could cling to them; below us in its gorge the Aragon river was almost out of sight, but its voice could be heard roaring between vertical rocky banks.

To the left of the track a quarry had long ago been hacked out, leaving a semi-circle of flat ground with rock walls rising behind; in the quarry stood a cheerless-looking stone building, what is known as a *korta*, or foresters' summer hut. The windows were holes, the door split logs nailed roughly together. A pile of firewood lay nearby.

And the bridge? That was simply two strands of rope stretched across the gorge, one above the other. Knotted to them at equal intervals and lacing them together, another rope ran zigzag between.

'*Madre de Dios*,' said Conchita shivering. 'Are men expected to go across that?'

'Why, it is nothing, senora,' said Pedro cheerfully. 'You just do it like this!' And he demonstrated, moving sideways nimbly on the rope.

'Nobody is going to get me on that flimsy affair. Surely there must be some other road to the castillo? How did they take in their supplies?' she demanded.

'There was another road,' I told her. 'But it has been blown up.'

'What about the road that we are on? Where does it go? Is there no other bridge across the river, farther along?'

'There is a footbridge, yes, where the river narrows, but no road back to the castillo. Only a footpath. There are cliffs in between, very high.'

'Trust Manuel to hide himself in such a barbarous spot!' she exclaimed in a fury.

'So what do you propose, Senor Felix?' calmly inquired Juana.

Conchita and the two outriders gazed at her in surprise; she had dismounted, tied the mules to a hasp on the wall of the hut, and was surveying the bridge with critical interest. She raised her brows at me with a slight smile. When she was younger, I remembered, she had been terrified of heights; was she recalling one of our adventures when we had hidden halfway up a cliff, and been caught there by a thunderstorm?

'I propose,' said I carefully, 'that you ladies remain here, with Pepe and Esteban to guard you from bears and brigands, while Pedro and I go on to the castillo, which is less than a third of a league farther, on the other side of the river; Pedro says that you could see it from just up there, if the mist were not so thick.'

We all peered hopefully upward; nothing was visible, however, but damp foliage, veiled in mist, rising up the sides of the gorge, and nothing to be heard save the roar of the river and some creature, izard perhaps, or mountain deer, crunching among the trees.

'Are you quite *sure* that this road does not lead on to some place where we might rest more comfortably?' persisted Conchita.

'I assure you, senora, it does not.'

In fact, as I knew, having carefully studied a map at the albergue, the road, becoming a track, then dwindling to a path, then hardly even that, followed the curve of the Aragon north-eastward, round to the right, almost as far as the river's source, then took a northerly direction, climbing up to the ridge that formed the frontier and crossing into France at a point called Les Forges d'Abel. If Don Manuel took that path, he could strike downward into the valley of the Aspe, and so make his way to Oloron.

'There is absolutely no village, hamlet, or even a house beyond this point, senora,' I told Conchita. 'Only mountains.'

'Oh!' she said with a discontented shiver. 'Well, in that case I suppose we must do as you suggest. I had not supposed *at all* that matters would turn out like this.' And she glanced round with displeasure, as if we had all personally brought about the inconveniences that she was obliged to suffer. Again, I was reminded of little Pilar; she was her mother's own child. 'Esteban,' she went on, 'light a fire in that hideous hut. At least we need not die of cold while we wait. Pepe, put the mules somewhere, so they are not devoured by wild beasts.'

A distant howl in the forest underlined the good sense of her words. Pepe led the beasts round to the back of the hut, where there was an open stable.

'Juana,' ordered Conchita in exactly the same tone that she had used to the menservants, 'you had best write a letter for Senor Felix to carry to Manuel.'

'I have no writing materials.'

'I brought some.' And, from among the various bundles in the tartana, Conchita produced a pen, ink, and a writing tablet.

'What do you expect me to write?' Juana's tone was dry as she surveyed this evidence of forethought.

Conchita raised her fine brows. 'Why? Nothing but the truth, of course. That you are waiting here, ready to receive and cherish the children; that you will be with them and care for them as long as is necessary.'

'I can't give such a promise,' Juana said.

'Why not?'

'It would not be true. I will put only that I am here, and will escort them to their grandparents.'

Conchita started to say something; changed her mind. 'Very well,' she said.

Juana sat on a rock and, dipping the pen in the ink, began to write.

'You had better,' said Conchita, 'put in a message in that ridiculous language that you and the children used to speak together; so that they will know it is really you, here, waiting for them.'

Juana laid down the quill.

'Don't you think, Conchita, that it would be better if I accompanied Felix? Then the children could see me for themselves. And so could Manuel.'

She cast a look of dread, mixed with resolution, at the bridge; I noticed the trembling of her hands and my heart applauded her courage.

Conchita visibly wavered. But, I thought, she was not wishful to be left alone with the two outriders whose looks, now I came to consider them in the light of what Pedro had heard, did nothing to recommend them: Pepe was little, sharp, and weaselly, Esteban big, lowering, and loutish.

Conchita said, 'What, and leave me alone in this wilderness? I thank you, no! Finish the letter.'

Juana shrugged, nodded, and continued to write.

She finished by drawing something at the foot of the paper, then folded and gave it to me.

She said, 'It's an owl. Luisa will remember. I always used to draw owls for her.'

A thread of smoke was now rising from the hut's crude chimney.

'You had best be off, Felix,' urged Conchita.

'Should I not take some of that bread you brought?' I suggested.

'*Por favor*, no! My husband would be sure to think it poisoned. They may have it when they come here, tell them. Now, Senor Felix, you *will* bring my little ones back to me – won't you? You know how entirely I depend on you?'

Suddenly Conchita quite shed her former cold, brisk manner, and was all melting tenderness; her eyes swam with real tears, she clasped her hands together in pitiful appeal as she gazed up at me.

Of course I promised to do all that lay within my power. Pedro, unimpressed by this affecting scene, had already begun working his way across the rope bridge, first a hand, then a foot, then the other hand, then the other foot. His progress was slow; traversing the gorge took him about five minutes. I waited to start until he had reached the farther bank, in case I might shake the ropes too much and loosen his hold. Then, when he

211

was safely over, I began my own crossing. For somebody used, as I was, to climbing rocks and trusting to the strength of my arms, it was not difficult; but to look down into the gorge far below was not advisable. It gave a horrible hollow feeling in the pit of the stomach. The water ran so white, dashing among jagged rocks. And I must confess that I suffered from a considerable dread that the rope might break; I wondered how often it was renewed, and by whom? Not very often, judging by its grey and frayed appearance. Then, too, supposing that an enemy came by while one was halfway over! How easy to sever the strand with one slice of a knife. Or loose off a bullet at somebody helplessly spread-eagled, halfway along . . .

While these thoughts came and went in my mind, I was methodically working my way along, and had gone well past the halfway point when a shout from Esteban made me turn my head cautiously towards the bank that I had left. There I saw a sight that shook me badly. A smallish brown beast had come out from the bushes on the bank and was standing, sniffing and pawing inquisitively at the vibrating ropes and the stone pier to which they were tethered. It was a bear cub; not big, perhaps eight weeks old; activated, as bear cubs often are, by foolhardy curiosity, not in the least afraid of the humans near at hand.

I heard Conchita cry, 'Shoot it, shoot the beast! Shoot it, Esteban!'

And I heard his answering cry, '*Bueno, bueno*, senora!'

'*No*, you fool, leave it alone!' I yelled at the top of my lungs, and set the bridge oscillating wildly by my sudden movement. Pedro likewise shouted, '*Don't shoot!* Don't shoot it!' but to no avail. Esteban, delighted to have some action required of him at last, snatched up his gun and discharged it at the cub, which was still standing on hind legs and sniffing at the rope. It tumbled down, dead, and the two postilions ran eagerly to pick it up.

'Its fur will make a jacket,' I heard Conchita say.

'Idiots!' yelled Pedro with all his strength. 'Watch out for the *mother*!'

And indeed, next moment, the mother appeared out of the undergrowth. She was taller than a tall man, heavy as a cart-horse; with a high yelling cry, something like that of a pig, she launched herself at the two men who were handling her dead cub. Aghast, they dropped the corpse and ran in different directions, shouting with terror and shock; Conchita flew into the hut and barricaded herself inside it; which left Juana standing unprotected on the bank, where she had stationed herself to watch my crossing of the rope bridge.

My heart seemed to fall clean out of my body into the gorge below. There she was, defenceless, in deadly danger, and here *I* was, strung on two ropes over the gulf, with my gun strapped out of reach, useless on my back; however fast I moved, I would never be able to get back in time to save her if the bear flew at her.

'Juana! Keep very still!' I called hoarsely.

The massive bear turned, at the sound of my voice, and eyed me intently. I joggled frantically on the rope, to hold its attention, and shouted, 'Ho! Ho! Hilloo! Yah! Bah!'

Juana remained still as a stone, but the wind was rising, and blew the folds of her blue hood about her face. The movement caught the bear's eye, and it turned again slowly in her direction.

'Bear! Bear!' I yelled. 'Look at me! Look at me on the bridge. Come and get me, bear! Here I am!'

The bear considered. Then it moved towards the pier that supported the two ropes, sniffed at them, and tested them with its massive paw, armed with huge sickle claws.

'Jesu Maria!' I heard Pedro whisper. The bear must weigh all of 1,000 pounds; if it climbed on to those ropes they would snap like pack-thread. Glancing sideways out of the corner of my eye I could see that Pedro, quite close on my left, had unstrapped his gun and was taking careful aim.

'Please, dear Father,' I heard myself muttering, 'oh, please don't let Juana—' and then the report of Pedro's gun echoed sharply in the gorge and a ball whistled close to my cheek. Looking the other way I saw the great bulk of the bear turn and totter, then fall majestically into the gorge, bouncing and crashing among branches of small trees that grew down the face of the cliff.

With arms and legs grown weak as melted wax I completed the crossing, stepped on to firm ground, swayed, and had to support myself by grabbing at the ropes again. I turned at once to see what was happening on the other bank.

Juana was crouching as if her legs, like mine, would hardly hold her up; she steadied herself by holding on to a sapling tree. The two outriders had returned, shambling and sheepish, from wherever they had fled to, and tiptoed to peer over the edge of the cliff and see what had become of the bear. Its body was visible to me, lodged in a tree fork about thirty feet down; I was not sure whether they could see it.

'It is dead!' I yelled angrily across the gorge. 'Small thanks to you!'

Then I turned to Pedro and embraced him.

'Pedro, I am in debt to you for the rest of my life. That was a superb shot.'

'Ah, *vaya, vaya*,' he said, embarrassed. 'It was nothing. Yours would have been just as good, if you had been able to shoot. But I am very sorry for the poor old mother-bear. Why should she lose her cub, and her life? As for that *bruja*, that female crocodile, that she-devil—' he went on for some minutes, using the most wicked language.

'Pedro, Pedro! It is a good thing she can't hear you!'

'It is a good thing she is not here, close enough for me to get my hands on her throat. Saving herself! Leaving the lady Juana in such danger—'

I saw, over his shoulder, that Esteban was tapping on the hut door, obviously informing Conchita that the danger was now past. She put her head out, he said something, and she emerged, looked about her carefully, walked to the cliff edge and waved a hand.

'It is quite safe,' she called. 'Esteban has shot the bear. You can go on your way.'

'*Oh—!*' exploded Pedro.

Laughing – all of a sudden I felt wonderfully light-hearted – I took his arm and said, 'Come along, come along, *amigo*. She is right. We had better proceed with dispatch. After all, the day is more than half done. And I think there is a storm gathering.'

As we walked away from the bridge, I thought, Grandfather was right. I suppose he is always right, the old wretch. What in the world should I have done on this excursion without Pedro?

The rope bridge crossed the Aragon river just beyond the point where another, smaller tributary river joined it from the east, deep in its own narrow gorge. We now stood on the triangle of land where the two streams met; ahead of us, a great corner of mountain, all shrouded in trees, came down to the confluence.

'Which way now?' I asked Pedro.

'Along here.' He led the way on a barely discernible track, still following the course of the Aragon; then he stopped to examine some broken twigs. 'Hey, hey, somebody else has been this way.'

'Well, it was probably de Larra, coming with fresh supplies. Or it could have been Don Amador. I noticed fresh horse-droppings behind the foresters' hut. Amador is not very careful about concealing his tracks.'

'I wonder where he put the horse itself?'

'Hobbled it in the forest, perhaps.'

'Let us hope the bear ate it,' said Pedro.

We rounded a corner of cliff, and, suddenly, there was the Castillo de Acher, in full view, high above the forest.

I have seen many castles, some ruined, some still inhabited, during my journeyings across Spain, but none so large or so dramatically situated as this one.

For a start, it was perched right over our heads on top of a 200-foot crag. To the rear of the castle, where the slope was not so steep, an encircling wall ran down to a fortified gatehouse; but it could be seen that there was no possibility of approaching on that route, for the road to the gatehouse, which cut to and fro in zigzags across the hillside, had been blown out in two places.

Although many centuries old, the castle looked amazingly new, for it was squarely built of pale-brown stone, all the towers and turrets and angles sharp and clear as if each stone had only just been laid in position by the mason.

'What a place!' I breathed. 'You would think Don Ignacio would prefer living there to the house in Berdun.'

'Too steep a climb every time you want to go fishing,' said Pedro.

'So where was the rope that Don Manuel let down?'

'Over this way.'

Pedro led the way to a point at the very foot of the cliff, which was not quite sheer, but ran down into a wild meadow, sloping like the side of a steeple – seamed, scarred grey rock, with here and there a gnarled tree growing out of it. At a point near the top there was an overhang, and above this a wooden arm had been built into a block of masonry. There was a wheel and a pulley, but no rope.

'Humph,' I said. 'It looks as if de Larra's not back yet with his new rope and stock of provisions. What do we do now? I doubt there'd be any purpose in our firing off two shots—'

'De Larra did speak of another way into the castle,' Pedro said doubtfully. 'A tunnel running up through the rock. But if he knew where it was, he kept that knowledge to himself.'

'He didn't wholly trust us, and who's to blame him?'

'I'd give a month's pay to know where that fat fellow has got to—' Pedro was beginning, when a slight noise above made me glance up.

'*Look out!*' I threw Pedro to one side and ducked myself, but had moved just too late; a cascade of stones and larger lumps of rock came splattering and bouncing down the cliff, and a great block about the size of a leg of mutton caught Pedro a blow on the side of the head and knocked him to the ground.

I flung myself on my knees by him and reached for his pulse; thank heaven it beat strongly; he was only half stunned, and indeed in a moment or two he murmured, 'Ay, *diablo!* What was that? Here, let me up—'

219

'No, no, lie still; you had a sharp knock there.' Carefully, I felt his skull; thank God, it seemed undamaged, due in part to the stout leather hat that he wore. I dragged him away from the cliff foot and laid him under a thick pine tree with drooping branches which ought to protect him from any more such hazards. 'Stay there quietly, Pedro – I'll be back soon.'

Then, scanning the face of the cliff above me again, I found what I was seeking.

A small voice called, 'You must come and help me! I can't get any farther.'

'Come down then!' I snapped.

'I don't wish to!'

'Then stay where you are.'

I took off my jacket and wrapped it round Pedro.

'I do not *wish* to do that. I wish to go on!'

I almost laughed. Even stuck halfway up a cliff, little Pilar was unchangeably herself.

If she inherited no other virtues from her knavish parents, she did possess tenacity of purpose. And courage too, I thought, starting up the beetling cliff after her.

Among the things we had purchased in Pamplona were a number of cramping-irons for just such an operation as this. From the beginning it had been in my mind that Don Manuel might have chosen some such eyrie by way of a refuge; fortunately I had carried a bag of these irons with me. By jamming them into cracks I was able to swarm up the rock face at a fair speed, making use of all the notches, ledges, lumps, and tree-roots that came within reach. In due course I found little Pilar, somewhat hazardously perched on a fairly wide ledge that underran an overhang, about two-thirds of the way up.

'Why didn't you come faster?' she complained.

'You little wretch! You should be thankful that I came at all. Where in the world is your papa? How could he permit you to do such a crazy thing?'

'Oh,' she said discontentedly, 'he went off to search for a tunnel. And he took so long about it that I thought I had better go up this way. I like to climb. I am a good climber.'

'So I have observed.'

'But now I can't see which way to go.' She squinted up disapprovingly at the overhang. 'That big bulge is a *nuisance*.'

I smiled to myself; her intonations were so like those of Conchita.

'Now,' I suggested, 'You just have to come down again.'

'No – no – *no*!'

I thought she was going to have a tantrum, like the

one in the saddler's shop. 'I will not, will *not* go down again. I am going up, up, up, to see Nico and Weeza, and my other papa, whom I love a great deal better than fat old Dor-Dor.'

'Oh indeed?'

'And you must help me.'

On consideration, that did not seem such a bad notion. After all, we were more than hallway up already. I had my letter from Juana as a passport, and possibly this little imp of Satan would not cause any harm to my mission.

Is this Your plan for me? I asked God, and, receiving no sign of dissent, I told little Pilar, 'You stay there a moment while I work my way past you and see what lies at the far end of this ledge.'

Accommodatingly, she packed herself into a kind of chimney comer while I wriggled past. To my great relief, at the narrow end of the shelf I discovered a useful crack in the rock, leading upward. And above that was an outcrop with several good hand-holds, and above that . . .

'Come along,' I said, returning to Pilar. 'I have managed to stick some irons into the rock which will make it easier to climb; you can go on ahead and I will give you a lift upward when it is needful.'

'Don't you dare touch me unless I ask for it,' she

ordered sharply. 'I can manage very well by myself.'

Indeed she could. Sure-footed as a monkey she clambered upward; I could well understand how she had managed to negotiate the conical chimney in Don Ignacio's house.

Twenty minutes' more scrambling brought us to a grassy dip at the top of the cliff; here we stopped to get our breath and survey our injuries; little Pilar's blue cloth dress was in shreds and her hands, elbows, and knees were badly scraped, but she bore these injuries with fortitude; I had various abrasions and a cut on the forehead from a falling rock. Pilar was ready in a moment to continue exploring.

'Look, there's some steps—' she began.

'Hush!'

'Why must I hush?' she demanded.

'Because Don Manuel – your other papa, if that is what you call him – is not expecting visitors. For all I know, he has a loaded musket pointed in this direction, ready to blow our heads off. So we must tiptoe along very quietly.'

Fortunately this plan appealed to her.

'Yes! We will creep so quietly that we take them quite by surprise!'

We ascended the steps, of which there were a great many, and made our way softly about the great labyrinthine place. There were ruined chambers, open to the sky, arches, corridors, a donjon, a bailey, a keep, a well, there were stables, a chapel, with beautifully carved pillars, a banqueting-hall, roofless and crumbling; there were galleries, cloisters, and arcades. The place seemed, at various times, in its long history, to have combined the function of both castle and monastery. All empty now, ruined and desolate, with full-sized trees growing in some of its courts and huge holes gaping in its walls. And a great view out over the clouds in all directions. Huge snow-capped peaks hemmed us in to northward.

Pilar began to look very dejected; her underlip protruded farther and farther as we wandered about finding nobody. And I began to grow anxious. The clouds were turning blacker and blacker; the way down was going to be far more difficult than the ascent had been; and where were Don Manuel and the other children? Had they left the place?

'I don't see—' Pilar began, when I said, 'Hush!' again.

Most of the castle ruins ended not far above ground level; but one portion of the central keep had a second, even a third storey. From a window of the second floor I believed I had heard the sound of a voice; most improbably, it seemed, somebody was singing.

I discovered a wooden door that led into this portion of the castle; but it was closed. Softly I tried it, and found it barred. Pilar's underlip stuck out even farther. Scowling, she looked as if she intended to hammer on the door. Laying my forefinger warningly on her lip, I pointed to a tree that had thrust its way up to a considerable height alongside the building. Its branches were thick and tangled; there would be no difficulty in climbing up them.

Pilar nodded her delighted comprehension, ran at once to the tree, and flung herself confidently into the branches. I followed close behind, and we were soon high enough to be able to see without difficulty into the windows of the second-floor chamber.

The scene that met our eyes was unexpected, to say the least.

On an open hearth blazed a fire of pine-branches, giving a ruddy illumination to the room, which was not large and contained no furniture at all.

In the middle of the room, a man was dancing. He held a child in his arms. He danced very slowly, gravely, and correctly. As he danced, he sang an air; and the child – she was a girl – sang softly with him. Nearby a boy, standing, solemnly clapped his hands in time to the beat.

I found this tableau inexpressibly sad.

The man's dignity, his absorption in what he was doing, the attentive and fond looks directed at him by both children, the visible trust and love that they felt for him, and he for them, so totally contradicted the picture Conchita had painted of a ruffianly madman and two terrified prisoners that I wondered how I could ever have swallowed her version for so much as a moment.

But of course I had not known Conchita when I first heard the tale.

Now everything fell into place.

Don Manuel had taken his children because he loved them and wished to see them. He had left little Pilar behind because he knew she was none of his.

And Conchita, afraid that this damaging fact would come to light, had instructed her lover, Don Amador, to keep Pilar out of sight until a rescue could be arranged and the children all presented together, while her unsatisfactory husband was somehow disposed of.

As these thoughts slipped rapidly through my head, Pilar, characteristically, made her own dispositions.

Agile as a squirrel, she climbed to a higher bough, which bent under her weight and carried her within a hand's breadth of the stone windowsill; then, with great intrepidity she flung herself across the gap and tumbled into the room, shouting exultantly.

'Weeza! Nico! I found you, I found you! I *found* you!' she clamoured, and ran to hug the boy, who looked startled out of his wits, but stooped to embrace her affectionately enough; to my relief I saw (following Pilar with less agility but as quickly as I could) that she was accepted with affection and good nature by her siblings, they did not exclude her as, it seemed, Don Manuel had done.

Indeed he did not, now, greet her with unkindness, though I could see that he was shocked, astonished, and not at all happy at her arrival.

'*Madre de Dios!* Pilar! How in the world did you get here, child?'

'I climbed! I climbed up all by myself!'

Then Don Manuel turned and saw me and his face stiffened.

When he was younger, I thought, he must have resembled a god. Even now, thin, worn, dusty, his clothes in tatters, his hair untrimmed, blind in one eye, a stubble of several days' growth on his chin, he was the most handsome and imposing man I had ever seen, and looked as if he might well be descended from the ancient kings of Aragon. Over the blind eye he wore a black patch, held in place by a black silk ribbon; the other eye was large, deep-set, sparkling, and formidable. His finely chiselled lips were set strongly together;

he did not scowl, but regarded me with ferocious intensity as if, should he think it necessary, he would toss me out of the window without the least hesitation. And he could probably have done so; he was at least a head taller than I, and seemed built of nothing but bone and muscle.

'*Vaya!* We have another guest, it seems. And who may you be, my young senor?'

'My name is Felix Brooke,' I said quickly. 'I – I am acquainted with your friend Don Mariano Jose de Larra. I am working with him, indeed. And I have a letter, concerning the children, from Senorita Juana Esparza – or Sister Felicita, as she is now called. May I give it to you?'

With – I must acknowledge – a slightly shaking hand, I pulled the letter from my pouch and extended it.

Don Manuel still bent on me that deep, dark, penetrating and mistrustful eye.

'You do not come from my wife – from Dona Conchita?'

I hesitated, then said, 'Senor, I was called in by her at the start. I admit it. But I am not – I am not of her party. Please read the letter. I am sure Senorita Esparza puts the whole story much more clearly than I can. *She* is my real friend in this matter.'

I said this, I suppose, proudly, and Don Manuel's

look became a fraction less hostile and suspicious.

He said, 'Anybody befriended by Dona Juana has a friend indeed. I have met that young lady once or twice and have a high opinion of her goodness and integrity.'

'Is the letter really from Cousin Juana, Papa?' demanded the little girl he had been carrying. He had put the child down to receive the paper. She was, I judged, three or four years older than Pilar, a round-faced child, not pretty, but with a look of great simplicity and sweetness. The boy, aged about nine, was thin, dark, haunted-looking, with a strong resemblance to his father but lacking his beauty. Both children eyed me warily, mirroring their father's mistrust.

'So it seems, Luisa. Quiet, now, while I read it.' He unfolded the paper and gave it his attention. I noticed that his hands were terribly scarred, as if they had been burned with hot irons. Tales of the fearsome fortress of Montjuich, where he had been imprisoned, came back to me, of how prisoners there had put an end to their lives, rather than endure the cruelties practised by the jailors. Escapes were almost unknown.

Yet, having got away from that dread place, Don Manuel had not made his way out of Spain and into freedom and safety; he had gone to see his children.

'Is the letter truly from Cousin Juana?' repeated Luisa when he had read it.

'Judge for yourself, *querida*. She has drawn you an owl.'

'Oh yes, yes, that is one of Juana's owls!' exclaimed the boy, looking over his sister's shoulder. 'And she has put in a verse of that song we used to sing with her:

> Zankhoua mehe eta
> Buria pelatu;
> Hori duzu senale
> Zirela Zahartu.
> Zahartu izan eta
> Ezorano conzatu
> Oficiotto hori
> Beharduzu kitatu.

And a line of our secret language.'

'What does it say?' inquired Don Manuel.

'It says, "You can trust this friend, he is a good man."'

'I am happy to hear it.' Don Manuel did not look at all happy, however. He continued to regard me with fixed gravity. 'So,' he demanded, 'what is your proposal, Senor Brooke? Why are you here?'

'Well, senor,' said I with diffidence, 'I have had a

little conversation with Senor Jose de Larra. He, I understand, has plans to convey you to other lands where you may continue to work for the Liberal cause in freedom and safety. After all, you cannot stay in this refuge for ever. But—' I glanced at Nico and Luisa – 'what I have to say is perhaps better said between ourselves, senor.'

'Anything you have to say can be said in front of these children,' he answered quickly and calmly.

The boy looked up at him at once in deep anxiety.

'You are not going away – are you, Papa? If you go, can we go too?'

Don Manuel's look met mine over Nico's head.

'I hope so, indeed, my son. We shall have to see.'

Little Pilar at once began to dance around her brother and sister and Don Manuel, frantically clamouring, 'Do not go away from us, dear Papa, do *not*! I love you much better than Mama and Guillermina and Abuelo Escaroz and Uncle Dor-Dor, who says he is my papa; but *I* think that *you* are my *real* papa. I do not *wish* you to go away, I do not, I do not!'

'Hush, *chiquita*,' said Luisa, seeing that Pilar was starting to work herself up into a frenzy. 'Tell me about where you have been, all these weeks?' Luisa seemed to have much greater skill in managing her little sister

231

than did fat Don Amador. Pilar quieted down at once and began a long excited rigmarole about horses, carriages, and posadas.

'I regret that I cannot offer you any refreshment, Senor Brooke,' said Don Manuel, with great courtesy. 'But I fear that we have not a scrap of food or drink about the place. My friend de Larra was to have brought us further supplies – I wonder what can have become of him, by the way? I expected him here by now.'

A shade of anxiety crossed his brow.

'Pray do not trouble yourself, senor. In fact – now I come to think of it – *I* have a loaf of bread about me, to which the children are more than welcome—'

I had bought a small loaf myself, at the baker's, thinking we might be glad of it, along the way. Now I pulled it out of my pouch and offered it to Luisa, whose eyes lit up. Her father, however, said quickly, 'Thank the young senor, Luisa, but we have a little ritual here that we always perform before eating. We share our rations with the birds.'

He took a morsel of the bread, crumbled it, and spread the crumbs on the sill of one of the several large unglazed windows, through which swallows, mountain doves, and other small birds had, from time to time, been flitting in and out. On the western side of the room the windows looked directly over the cliff; the drop from them was formidable.

I saw the children's eyes widen, as if they were surprised by what their father did. His 'little ritual' then, was *not* always performed, but was new to them? After a cluster of birds had found the crumbs, pecked at them, and quickly demolished them, he relaxed, smiled, and said, '*Vaya!* Enjoy your dinner, children.'

Did he, perhaps, suspect poison? Knowing Conchita, I supposed, he might not consider that possibility wholly out of the question. It was a bad thought.

While the children ate, sharing out the bread with scrupulous fairness, I said in a low voice, 'Don Manuel: I believe that Senor Jose de Larra told you it might not be practicable for you to take the children with you on this present journey? Later on, perhaps, when you are established safely overseas, it may be that you can send for them—?'

He answered quickly and firmly.

'Understand this, Senor Brooke. In *no* circumstances will I consent to leave my children in the care of that – that viperess and her fat slug of a lover. Are you aware that it was *they* who denounced me – that it was they who, on a set of false charges, had me consigned to Montjuich prison? Do you think that I would leave these good, innocent children with such a pair as that? Do you think Conchita Escaroz is a proper person to have the care of young ones? Why, she has never looked after them for a single day in her life. She is lazy, spoiled, self-absorbed, malicious, and a liar. Would you leave a child of yours with her?'

I thought about it. The news that it was Conchita herself who had denounced her husband did not, by now, entirely surprise me; it bore out various observations I had made myself. I could imagine her perfectly capable of such an act, if she had good reason for wishing to rid herself of an inconvenient tie. As for taking care of the children – no, I could not imagine that she had ever felt that responsibility very deeply. After all, she had cast off little Pilar into the care of fat Don Amador negligently enough. Despite her tears and occasional exclamations about her 'little ones' she had not, in general, displayed any particular anxiety about them; had eaten well, slept well, judging by her looks, and devoted rather more attention to her own comfort than to anything else.

'No,' I answered slowly, 'I must confess that I would not . . .'

The children having eaten, Luisa, in a motherly way, was attempting to put her little sister to rights. With a comb from her own hair she had laboriously straightened Pilar's tangled locks, had gently and carefully cleaned her numerous grazes with a handkerchief dipped in a cup of water, and was now doing her best to brush and straighten the tattered blue dress.

'But what is this, *hija*? What is this packet here, in your petticoat pocket – you have brought us some candy, perhaps, some *turron*?'

'Oh, no; it is only a book. I forgot about it. It is a book that Mama said I might bring to Papa – the one he was asking for when he was in prison,' Pilar said carelessly. 'Sing me "Tragala, tragala," Nico!'

'Hush! We must sing that only when there is nobody to hear.'

'Well, there is no one here but Papa and Yellow-hair. And *he* is not bad. He made me a necklace.'

To my surprise she pulled from under her collar the circlet of plaited thongs with a blue bead that I had light-heartedly dropped over her head when we were in Zamora; which, it seemed, she had worn ever since.

Very softly Nico and Luisa began singing. I recognised the words: they were the battle-hymn of those who wished to re-establish the Constitution.

Si los curas ye frailes supieran
La paliza que los vamos a dar
Se pondrian en coro gritando:
Libertad! Libertad! Libertad!

Tragala, tragala, tragala,
Cara de morron
Ne queremos reina bruja
Ni queremos rey follon.*

Don Manuel was walking up and down, up and down the long room, with his hands behind his back and brows compressed.

I sat on the windowsill and waited. At one point he came up to me and said in a low voice, but with terrific

*If the priests and friars only knew
what a beating we are going to give them
they would huddle together shouting
Liberty, Liberty, Liberty!

Swallow it, swallow it, swallow it
old long-face diehard
we don't want a witch for a queen
or a sluggard for a king.

(Riego's hymn became the National Anthem of the Spanish Republic in 1931.)

236

emphasis, 'I tell you, senor, rather than leave these good, simple children in the clutches of that harpy, I would take them with me and jump off the cliff, out there!' He nodded to the window.

'I fancy that Dona Conchita would probably leave the children in the custody of her parents for most of the time,' I suggested doubtfully.

'The old Escaroz? And what sort of care would *that* be? They are Carlists, dyed-in-the-wool reactionaries.'

Have you no kin of your own, I was on the point of asking, who might undertake the maintenance of the children, then remembered Don Ignacio, who had refused to shelter his brother, and had, it was thought, reported him to the Military Commission. And not a reliable-looking man . . .

'Well, I would leave them only on one condition,' Don Manuel said suddenly. 'If Dona Juana would undertake to have them—'

'But, senor, how could I possibly promise for her? After all, she is a nun, devoting her life to God – and, in any case, why would Dona Conchita ever consent to such an arrangement?'

His suggestion seemed to me hopelessly impracticable and set about with difficulties; indeed, now that I came to think of it, Juana herself had raised some objection, when she was writing the letter, when Conchita suggested—

'*Luisa!* What have you got there?' suddenly exclaimed Don Manuel, in a sharp, strange, frightening voice.

'Why, it is nothing but a little book, Papa – it is your little book of birds, remember? – that Mama has sent to you. I have been showing the pictures to Pilar. See, Pilar, here is an eagle, we saw one just like that earlier today. I have been unsticking the pages because the book must have got damp – they are all stuck together—'

'Give it here! At *once*!' His voice and face were both terrible; the children, trembling, gazed at him petrified, and I, all at once, began to remember the stories of his madness, the fits of frenzy and ungovernability – though, now that I came to think of it, most of those stories had issued from Conchita . . .

Violently he snatched the book from Luisa's hands. I had a momentary glimpse of it: a tiny leather-bound volume, about the size of a pack of cards, but thicker; on every second page was a highly-tinted picture of a bird, with text opposite.

'It is your dear little bird book that you had when you were a boy,' Luisa said reproachfully. 'You promised that Nico should have it one day as he loved it so. I remember when you wrote from prison and asked Mama to send it—'

'Yes! And she never did. But now she sends it – why, I wonder? As a reminder of past kindness between us? I think not! I'll take nothing – nothing from that harpy!' The book spun from his fingers, out through the window – one of those windows that looked over the cliff. He turned on his heel and swooped towards me.

'Did you know about this book?' The terrible eye bored into mine.

'Indeed I did not, senor! – I – I only encountered your daughter Pilar when she was halfway up the cliff – previously she was in the care of Don Amador—'

'Yellow-hair came climbing up and helped me,' corroborated Pilar. 'But I wouldn't have been stuck for very long on my own,' she added quickly.

'How did you come to be by the cliff, then, child?'

'Uncle Dor-Dor left me there. He said he was going to look for a tunnel.'

'He did, did he?' Don Manuel said grimly. Again he turned on me. 'Do you know Don Amador?'

'No, senor, I do not. He has been travelling separately from Dona Conchita – but he was in San Quilez this morning, Dona Juana had a glimpse of him—'

'That is a pity. If you were acquainted with him, you could have taken him a message from me. The tunnel he seeks is mined, as the road was. If I choose, I can destroy it, as I did the road.'

Don Manuel began his tigerish pacing again.

Oh, heavenly Father, what do I do now, I wondered? Tentatively, hesitantly, I said, 'Senor, if you were to write a letter to Dona Juana Esparza – if you were to ask her to undertake the care of your children – until you were ready for them – I do not really see how she could refuse such a request. I can see that is, perhaps, the only solution.'

And waited, without a great deal of hope, for his answer. His mood seemed so much fiercer now. 'I could take Juana the letter,' I said. 'And perhaps – perhaps in the circumstances, Dona Conchita would agree—'

Perhaps, perhaps, I thought. Too many perhaps.

The three children huddled together apprehensively, watching their father. The two elder ones loved him deeply, I could see by their expressions; but, just the same, this predicament was more than children of such an age should have to bear. They were tired and half-starved, and dreadfully frightened. Supposing troops from the Military Commission should come and bombard the castle? Suppose the assassins Pepe and Esteban made their way in, as I had, and killed Don Manuel? The murderers would no doubt say that it was sufficient evidence of madness just to have brought the children and taken refuge in such a place.

I began to be sorry that I had inserted those cramping-irons.

'Well,' said Don Manuel at last, in a milder tone, 'I will write a note to Juana Esparza. Her, I know I can trust. And you, Senor Felix Brooke, will be so kind as to deliver it. Are you, by the way—' he glanced at Juana's letter– 'a grandson of Don Francisco, the Conde de Cabezada?'

'Why yes, sir.'

'He is a fine man, your grandfather. You may give him my respects, if you please, when you next see him. Now, how can I write? I have no paper, ink, nor pen.'

It was a pity, I thought, that he had just thrown away that useful little book.

'You could write on the back of Juana's letter,' I suggested, 'and I can easily make a pen – here are hundreds of feathers—'

It was true. Pigeons had used the place extensively for nesting.

'And we can make ink from soot and water,' suggested Luisa.

'*Bueno*. You are a practical little woman, *hija*.

Would you like to be taken care of by your cousin Juana – until I have found a new home for you?'

'Oh yes!' Their faces lit up. 'Cousin Juana has a beautiful home of her own in France. We stayed there once, and she told us stories about the *laminak*. But we would rather be with you, Papa.'

I refrained from telling the poor things that Juana's home had been sold to furnish her dowry for the convent in Bayonne. One step at a time, I thought.

Don Manuel slowly wrote his note, with the pen I had trimmed, and the ink made from soot.

'There, then. Bring me back her reply, acceding to my request, and I will let you take the children to her. De Larra will see that the arrangements are faithfully carried out.'

Their faces drooped. And I could not help wondering how Conchita would ever submit to such a disposition of her children; but that, too, must wait for time to solve.

'*Vaya!*' He handed me the note. 'Now you had best climb down quickly, for the weather worsens.'

This was an understatement. A mountain storm was brewing up, the sky had gone black as a boar's hide, large drops of rain had begun to fall, and thunder growled a low, ominous warning. I was exceedingly glad that I had left Pedro lying under a thick-set pine tree, and my gun beside him, well wrapped up in my jacket.

'Senor – with your permission – I brought along a piece of rope – just in case Don Jose failed to obtain any. Rather than climb down that cliff, which in this rain would be a great deal more difficult than climbing up, I will put your pulley back into working order. I daresay Nico will help me, will you not, Nico?'

'Oh yes, senor,' the boy said readily, and, having received his father's permission, he led me down the stairs, unbarred the door at the foot, and showed me the way to the pulley. It was governed by a primitive device, like a capstan. The old rope, tattered and frayed, still dangled from the wheel; it was a comfort to recall that what I had brought was good stout new hempen cord, the best that Pamplona could provide. Even so it was with scanty enthusiasm that, having replaced the old rope by the new, tested the pulley-arm, wheel, and capstan, I finally (having discarded the rickety old basket which seemed to have been used in long ago times for hoisting up supplies) made a loop of the rope, sat myself in it, and instructed Nico to let me down slowly. This, although a slender boy, he could do easily enough, because of the ratchet mechanism which prevented the rope from running too fast.

'Will you not say goodbye to Papa and the girls?' he asked.

'No, I shall be seeing them again, soon enough, when I come back with your cousin Juana's reply.' Let the poor things have time together while they can, I thought. Besides, I was growing anxious about Pedro. 'Take care of them, Nico! I hope Senor de Larra comes soon with some more food for you.'

He will be fairly astonished to find a new rope already installed, I thought, rather smugly; I have stolen a march on you there, my friend! And then I concentrated on the disagreeable task of getting myself down, in the rain, wind, and semi-dark, without dashing out my brains on protruding jags of rock. The descent, spinning giddily round and round, seemed to take an eternity – far, far longer than the climb up the cliff.

8

We meet Don Amador; a night in the cave; reappearance of Figaro

Under the pine tree I was relieved to find Pedro still stretched out, breathing peacefully and regularly; his faint had turned to genuine slumber. When I touched him he responded drowsily. 'Hmmm?'

'*Que tal*, friend? How do you find yourself?'

'*Nada, nada.* It is a trifle – except that my head aches like the Devil,' he grumbled, rubbing it. I noticed that when he scrambled up he swayed, and had to grab a branch; which filled me with great anxiety as to how, in this shaky state, he was going to manage the crossing of the rope bridge.

'Come,' I said. 'Lean on me. This is no spot in which to loiter.'

For the rain was now cataracting down, and jagged shafts of lightning every minute weirdly irradiated the castillo perched high above us on its crag. I had a notion that lightning might strike the cliff and bring down more masses of rock tumbling upon our heads.

And what about those poor children, immured up there in such a comfortless shelter, without food or bedding? Would they not be frightened to death as the storm raged about their ears? They had a fire, it was true, and their father – and the bit of bread I had brought, to dull the worst pangs of hunger; but that was no place for children. The sooner they are out of there, I thought, the better; and I hoped that Juana would feel as I did about the matter.

'Courage, *hombre*,' I said to Pedro. 'Make what speed you can.'

'If this accursed lightning did not get in one's eyes so,' he mumbled, tripping over a root and leaning heavily on my arm. Cumbered as I was, carrying both of our guns slung over my other shoulder, and he still weak and stumbling, we made but slow progress. I did not like to hurry him, though the thought of Juana troubled me; in this storm she would be wondering what had become of us.

Suddenly, in one of the lightning flashes, I saw, a few yards ahead of us, an unmistakable figure floundering about in the darkness, much as we were ourselves. I recognised him at once from his girth.

'*Hola* there, Don Amador!' I shouted. '*Hola!*'

I saw his big face turn – wet, white, and startled – lit by the next dazzling flash.

'Who calls? *Quien es?*'

'It is us – Felix Brooke and Pedro.' For of course he must know, he couldn't help knowing perfectly well who we were, just as we knew him. It seemed foolish to keep up the pretence of ignorance any longer. 'My friend has been hurt by a falling rock,' I called. 'Can you help us along?'

'Willingly, senor.'

In fact he seemed pleased to have our company.

'Have you by any chance seen a little brat of a child?' he asked me confidentially, taking Pedro's other arm. 'I have searched for her everywhere – but everywhere! I do hope that she has not fallen into the gorge. For if so, Dona Conchita will be angry with me. I shall be in real trouble. But what could I do? I cannot be in two places at once. "Find the tunnel!" Conchita tells me. As if it would be marked with a big sign: *This way to the castillo*. High and low I looked for the cursed tunnel. Not so much as a rabbit-hole did I find. And, meanwhile, the wretched child disappears! Ten million devils, what a time I have had of it, nursemaiding that little scorpion across Spain. I would sooner be in charge of a barracuda! Conchita claims that she is mine, but that fact I take leave to doubt. No other member of my family – but *nobody* – has ever been possessed of such a temper. She is ungovernable! I think she is a child of the Evil One – heaven protect us!' He stopped to cross himself and to drink, from a flask, something that smelt like aguardiente – it was plain that he had taken a good deal of it already.

'Set your mind at rest, senor,' I said. 'Little Pilar climbed up the cliff into the castillo. She is with her brother and sister.'

'*Really?* Did she, indeed?' Don Amador seemed delighted. 'Do you know,' he confided, 'I had half a notion that, if I left her at the foot of the cliff, some such idea might light into her head. She is a devil for climbing. But what happened then, senor? Did the madman devour her?'

To my ear, he sounded hopeful, rather than anxious.

'No, he did not. And the other children greeted her kindly enough.'

'Ay, ay, they are not bad children. Though heaven forbid that I should be saddled with their upkeep,' he added hastily. 'But what of the madman? Did *you* see him, senor? *El Tuerto*? Is he raving?'

'Yes, I saw Don Manuel. And, no, I must say that he seemed to me perfectly sensible, in full command of his wits.'

'Is that so indeed?'

My information seemed to depress Don Amador.

He trudged along for a few yards in silence. Then he asked, 'Did *El Tuerto* – Don Manuel – did he and Pilar speak together at all? Did she – did she give him any message from her mother?'

'Message? No, not that I can recall. Don Manuel is very, very bitter against his wife,' I could not help saying. 'He can hardly hear her name without a curse. He believes that it was her deposition that had him flung into jail.'

Don Amador sighed. It seemed to me that he felt some little sympathy for the man up in the castle. Was he tired of being allotted all the inconvenient tasks while Conchita stayed behind and took care of herself? Did he wonder what his reward was likely to be, in the end?

'You are quite certain that little Pilar gave her father no message from Dona Conchita?' he persisted.

'Yes, positive – unless there was some note contained in the little book that she brought. Might there have been something written in that, a message? But the pages were all stuck together,' I remembered. I did not go on to inform him that Don Manuel had thrown the book out of the window; it occurred to me that I was giving Don Amador a good deal more information than he was giving me.

'What will Dona Conchita do, if he refuses to part with the children?' I asked.

'A company of armed men is being sent from Pamplona; they will very soon blow him out of his nest,' said Don Amador with satisfaction. 'They will bombard the castillo.'

'But the children!' I said in horror. 'They will be hurt too!'

'That will be Don Manuel's responsibility.'

And their mother's, also. And yours, you fat hypocrite, I thought.

'When will the soldiers arrive?'

'*Quien sabe?*' Don Amador had an abrupt late access of caution. He added gaily, 'Well, well, very likely the soldiers will not be needed – perhaps Don Manuel will have a sudden change of heart. Sudden things have been known to happen. Tra la la!' And he sang a few cheerful bars of a song, as we continued to help Pedro along the narrow path; then, with a complete change of tone, and in a polished, social manner, he observed to me chattily, 'So, then Senor Felix, I hear that you are to be a *duque*? Allow me to congratulate you. I hear that your English grandfather has died at last.'

'Oh, indeed?' said I, greatly astonished at such information coming from such a source. 'How in the world do you come to know that, Don Amador?'

'Why, from my friend Sir Thomas Jay, he is the English ambassador in Madrid, you know. Your English grandfather died last month. There was a note about it in the Diplomatic Bag. Doubtless you will find the tidings waiting for you when you return home.'

I digested this news in silence as we made our way onwards. Would this mean that I must travel to England? Must I take on a whole load of new and unwelcome duties over there in that rainswept land? If there was any means by which I could disclaim the inheritance, I resolved to do so. Surely, somewhere, there must be another English heir who would be glad to step into a dukedom?

Now, to our great relief, a light came into view, twinkling on the far side of the gorge. There was the hut, and even if it contained Conchita and the two untrustworthy postilions, it was a most welcome sight.

But at this point Pedro subsided to the ground with a groan.

'Felix, I'm not going to be able to cross that devilish contraption,' he croaked. 'My head swims; I'm as limp as a rag; my hands wouldn't hold the rope.'

I looked at him in deep concern and realised that he was quite right. He was white, and shaking badly. It would be total folly for him to attempt the crossing.

'Well then, there is nothing for it: you must stay on this side. And I will too. Don Amador can go across and explain. Sit and rest yourself against that beech tree, Pedro, while I hunt about and see if I can find some shelter where we can pass the night – all you need, now, is to be soaked and chilled, on top of having your head broken by our young friend dropping a rock on you.'

'Eh, dear, dear, what a misfortune. I suppose I had better cross the bridge, then,' said Don Amador, with a decided want of alacrity. 'I will inform the Dona that you both remain here on this side. Here –' he passed his flask to Pedro, 'take a sup of that, my dear fellow, it will do you good.'

'Thanks, senor.' Pedro tipped up the flask, in which there was only about a spoonful left. '*Salud!*' he said, wiping his mouth on his sleeve.

Poor Don Amador seemed wholly reluctant to launch himself across the rope bridge, in the teeth of the storm that was now raging. Rain fell like lances.

And the incessant flicker of lightning illuminated his fat form dangling and swinging like a fly on a spider-web as he made his painful way across.

Meanwhile I searched around as best I could, and was lucky to find a cave, or at least a cleft under an overhang in the rocky mountain-side that sloped down to the river so steeply. The ground under the overhang was reasonably dry, and the place had the merit of being within sight of the bridge. To this refuge I half dragged, half carried Pedro, then busied myself with lighting a fire in it, kindling dry grasses and dead leaves with flint and tinder, then feeding the flame with all the scraps of dry wood that I could collect. By and by it burned briskly enough, and I could add some larger, damper pieces without the risk of putting out the flame.

A mouthful of hot food would not come amiss now, I thought yearningly, and decided that, when the fire was sufficiently well established, I would cross to the hut and bring back something to eat.

'I am a shameful trouble to you, Felix,' croaked Pedro miserably. 'I could kick myself. Acting like this – like a baby – just because a pebble fell on my thick skull.'

'A pebble! It was a lump the size of a doorstep. And whose shot was it that saved Juana from the bear, pray?'

'Whose indeed?' said a voice, and into the circle of firelight stepped Juana herself with raindrops glistening on her dark-blue hood and habit. 'Well! You have got your two selves pretty snugly established here; and I can't say I blame you. But it was rather hard, leaving me on the other side with those *delinquentes*, so I have just come to join you.'

'Juana! You came across the rope? In the storm? You dared to do that?'

'Is it so brave to do something that you have both done – and Pedro three times over?'

She removed a bag from her shoulder and added, laughing, 'Well, I will admit that I kept my eyes tight shut all the way over; though with so many lightning flashes, keeping them shut made very little difference. And skirts on a contraption like that are a horrible disadvantage. Here – at least one of that pair of ruffians did something useful, he shot an izard—' and she pulled out a good-sized haunch of roasted meat and a loaf. 'Just as well. Imagine it! With all the rugs and furs she took along to keep herself warm, Conchita hadn't thought to add anything in the way of provisions, except for the bread. And that was just a pretext to let Don Amador get away from San Quilez before the rest of us. Fortunately I brought some wine and sausage from Berdun.'

She added a leather bottle. 'Here, my friend – a drink of this will do you good,' she said to Pedro.

'Dona Juana, you are a blessed angel,' he mumbled. 'And presently you will be sitting up on high, playing a golden harp!'

'Oh indeed? Well, let me tell you, my thoughts have not been very angelic today, stuck in that hut with . . . But tell me, how did you get on?' she added, in a wholly different tone. 'Tell me what *happened*?'

So I told her, and showed her the note that Don Manuel had written.

She read it in silence – not once, but half a dozen times, sitting cross-legged in the firelight, with her chin resting on her clenched fist. And I remembered many former occasions when we had sat, thus, by a woodland fire, on that other journey, five years ago.

As she seemed wholly wrapped in thought, and not at all ready to break the silence, Pedro said to me in a low voice, 'What was it that the fat fellow was saying to you, Felix, about your being a duque? My head was throbbing badly, I did not take it in. Something about your English grandfather?'

'It seems he has died. Don Amador appears to be a very well-informed character.'

'So that makes you, then, an English duke?'

'I believe so.'

'And rich?'

'Maybe.'

Well, if I am that, I thought, with a lift of the heart, I can use some of my English money to help Grandfather look after the old ladies and the people on the estate; he won't have to end his days in continual worry.

'No wonder that Dona Conchita has been setting her cap at you,' Pedro murmured thoughtfully.

'Pedro!'

'Putting the fat fellow's nose out of joint.'

'It's nothing to joke about. Anyway – I wouldn't have her if she was the last woman in the world. After that business of the bear—' And I thought of the things that Don Manuel had let fall.

When Pedro had eaten a little, and drunk a few more mouthfuls of wine, and was drowsing again by the fire, I said, 'Well, I suppose I should go across and make my report—' as Juana still had not spoken but continued to sit brooding, chin on fists. 'Would you object to staying here with him?' I asked her.

'How can you ask? He saved my life!'

I put the guns within reach, told her to use them if need be, made up the fire, and then groped my way across the rope bridge. The hut door was shut, so I knocked on it loudly. Nobody bade me enter, but

I walked in without waiting to be invited. Conchita, I saw, sat by the fire, Don Amador was talking to the two postilions.

She jumped up, came to greet me, and clasped my wrists.

'Tell me quick, Felix – how are my babies? Are they well? Did they ask for me? Has that brute ill-treated them?'

'No, he has not, senora,' I said. 'They appear to be in good health.'

Her hypocrisy sickened me. I could hardly bear to look her in the eye. To my own annoyance, the falsity seemed to be in me just as much as in her. Treating with people who are false breeds wrong thoughts in oneself. To cover my feelings I spoke quickly and loudly.

'Don Manuel says that he will not, in any circumstances, give up the children to you, senora,' I told her. 'But he has written a letter to Dona Juana, asking if she will be prepared to take charge of them. In which case he would be prepared to relinquish them.'

'To be brought up by *Juana*! What an extraordinary suggestion! He would surrender them to a mere girl – a *nun*!' Conchita laughed loudly and scornfully, but it was plain that she was shaken and perplexed, as well as very angry indeed. 'Well – that just proves that he is mad! Where *is* Juana? – oh, I recall – I sent her across with some dinner for your servant. How does she respond to this very peculiar proposal?'

'She has said nothing. She is thinking about it. She may not agree to it,' I said coldly. 'Why should she do so? They are not her children.'

'Well – I do not know what to say. I will see. I will think. You had better come back to me tomorrow and I will give you my answer then. I understand that you plan to spend the night on the other side of the river.'

She did not inquire after Pedro or ask if we were comfortable or needed anything.

Muchas gracias, senora, I thought sourly, observing the change in her manner. Two days ago she could hardly load me with sufficient civility. And I wondered, when did *she* hear that news about my English grandfather? But now she seemed to have abandoned her attempts to win my favour. Perhaps she had seen the disgust in my eye.

I heard raised voices at the other end of the hut. 'Why did you not take better care of him, idiots?' demanded Don Amador in squeaky, furious tones. 'One of the best mules out of Andalusia, and you tell me he is gone? How do you mean, gone?'

'His tether broke. Maybe the bear ate him,' said Esteban sulkily.

Then Don Amador observed me and came hastening in my direction – possibly to cut short anything approaching dalliance between me and Dona Conchita. But he need not have troubled about that.

'How is that unfortunate fellow? Did he take some food?'

'A little, I thank you, senor. And I will see you very early in the morning,' I said, halfway through the door, mindful of that troop on its way from Pamplona. 'By that time, no doubt, Dona Juana will have taken her decision.'

And I left them.

When I returned to the cave I found that Juana had built and banked up the fire with peat and beechmast so that it had a good heart and would last through the night. Pedro slept, and she still sat with her arms wrapped round her knees. She was not asleep; I could see the gleam of her eye reflecting the faint red glow of the fire.

'Are you not tired?' I said. 'Shall I help you to go back over the rope bridge?'

'Help me? How could you do that?' she answered rather snappishly. 'If that were possible, poor Pedro could have been helped across. No, I will pass the night here. To tell truth, I would prefer it. The sight of Conchita with Don Amador makes me sick.'

I felt the same, but said doubtfully, 'If you stay here with us, though, Conchita will think – she will say—'

'Why should I trouble my head about what Conchita thinks, or what she says?' Juana retorted.

I could see that she was in a very prickly mood. During our former acquaintance these bursts of ill-temper had been frequent enough on her part. Since we had met again, though, I had seen less of them; she appeared to have grown more serene. Perhaps becoming a nun had done that to her. But now all the former danger signs were present and I regarded her with caution. Leaving her to herself to simmer down was the only recourse during such states of irritation, I knew; she could not be cajoled or joked out of them.

So I replied, peaceably, 'Indeed, there is no reason why you should trouble about Conchita,' and scraped myself a kind of cushion of wet leaves to sit on. Pedro occupied the rear corner of the cleft, and in front of him the fire glimmered; on either side of the fire Juana and I sat, half in, half out of shelter. Luckily the storm had died away; the wet trees dripped but the rain no longer poured down. The air had turned a great deal colder and the warmth of the fire was a decided comfort.

'Those poor children up there—' I muttered.

'Have they bedding? Covers?'

'None that I saw.'

'But their father behaves lovingly towards them?'

'Yes, very much so. But that cannot remedy these other wants. They cannot be allowed to stay there for long.'

'He is a good man,' she said in a combative tone.

'I can see that. It is terrible that a good, sincere man, who wants to do his best for his country, should be hunted like a criminal.'

'I know nothing about politics and care less,' said Juana crossly.

I remained silent.

'Well?' she attacked me. 'Well? I suppose you think I should offer to take on the care of those children?'

'Oh, Juana. How can I possibly tell you what to do?'

'I suppose you think,' she went on stormily, 'that I should make any offer – no matter whether I intend to keep it or not – so as to make Don Manuel give them up?'

'I think nothing of the kind! Why should you expect me to be so dishonest?'

'You don't seem to have been afflicted by many scruples in your dealings with Conchita!'

'My dear girl, I had a task to perform, and was only

trying to do it as best I could – I had to be civil to her—'

And it was because of *you* that I was selected for this mission, I could have said, but wisdom kept my mouth closed.

It made no difference. All of a sudden we were quarrelling, as if we were eight years old instead of eighteen, hotly and unreasonably.

'I had a vocation from God to become a holy sister – you expect me to throw all that aside, to change my whole life – no one would expect a man to do such a thing—'

'Well? I was expected to give up my studies, or whatever I happened to be doing, and travel half across Spain, simply in order to—'

'Just because you are the grandson of an English duke you think you—'

'How dare you be so unreasonable? As if I ever – *ever*—'

I am far, far prouder of my dear grandfather the Conde than of any English duke, I thought. But Juana was storming on:

'It means nothing to you that I gave up everything I had in the world to join— the house where I was born, the . . . You never considered that. And now—'

'For that matter, you haven't displayed any

particular interest in what I—' Then I took a deep, shaky breath and said, 'Stop! Let us stop! We are both being horribly childish. It's a lucky thing nobody can hear us.' Except God, of course. 'For heaven's sake, let us leave it all till morning. Here, why don't you lie on my jacket—'

'Oh, that is just like you,' exploded Juana, 'To decide that *you* should be the one to call a stop—'

All the while we were wrangling, some humble, scullion portion of my mind had been appealing to me, fidgeting, trying urgently to attract my attention. There had been a sound in the night that was alien, different from the other sounds of forest and river – now hushed to a murmur; what was it that I had heard? A creak and then another creak, and then a thud; and now, suddenly, a branch snapped.

I sprang up, calling out sharply, '*Quien es?*' and took several paces into the darkness, cocking my pistol.

'Don't shoot, don't shoot, my friend, it is only I,' said a quiet voice, which I recognised as that of Jose de Larra. And he stepped forward into the faint glow from the fire.

'Don Jose – pardon me! I – I did not expect you—' Horribly embarrassed at having been caught in the midst of a childish wrangle, I awkwardly and stumblingly introduced him to Juana, who acknowledged the introduction with haughty composure.

He explained his arrival.

'I have been much delayed. The monks at Siresa would not help me – ill-natured bigots! – they said that Manuel was a heretic and that I myself would be in danger of hellfire if I tried to prevent his recapture. They would not give me so much as a candle.'

'You seem to have managed to persuade them somehow,' I suggested, for he carried a large leather sack over his shoulder, which seemed well-filled.

'Oh, this? No, that was sheer good fortune. I had started back in the direction of San Quilez when I met a train of *esquiladores* travelling across the mountains from Anso to Jaca and Zaragoza.'

I nodded. The esquiladores are a tribe of gypsy craftsmen who travel about the country, migrating south at this time of year; their trade is to shear horses, sheep, and cattle; in their leather pouches they carry shears, clippers and scissors of every shape and for every possible purpose. They seem to make a good living from their labours and are in general handsomely dressed and well supplied.

This band, de Larra told us, had been able to furnish him with all he asked: provisions, clothes for Don Manuel, and a piece of rope. The latter, I told him, was no longer necessary; and I gave him the story of my own entry into the castillo. He listened intently, scowling at my account of Don Amador and his part in the business.

'I do not know whether to put that one down as more knave or fool; without doubt he is the besotted slave of Conchita Escaroz. It is a frightful inconvenience that she is encamped just across the river; because of her and those hired assassins lounging about all day taking shots at all that moved, I have been obliged to wait until now to get back across the bridge. One or the other of them was always by it. Why in the world did you allow her to come so close?'

'How could I stop her coming?' I objected, but he went on without listening.

'A couple of the esquiladores have promised help; they are brave fellows, free-living as eagles, who care nothing for priests or friars or the Madrid government. If I can persuade Manuel to leave the castillo by the underground passage, they will meet him in the Sobordan valley and escort him by a secret way into France. I found a mule.' Don Jose began to laugh. 'The gypsies are taking care of it now. Manuel may as well have the use of it.'

'Don Amador's missing mount.' I laughed too.

'But the question is, will Manuel – can he be persuaded to leave his children behind?'

Involuntarily my eyes turned to Juana, who still sat motionless, looking down at her plaited fingers. 'I am on my way there now to talk to him,' de Larra said. 'I must not delay any longer. What do you think he will say?'

'I'll walk with you as far as the bottom of the cliff,' I said.

Juana looked up and said slowly, 'Senor de Larra: will you please tell Don Manuel that I am thinking deeply about his request. It is not one to be answered in haste. He has asked me to take care of his children. But that would mean that I must give up my life as a holy sister.'

'Not an easy decision,' de Larra said. But he spoke rather drily; he sounded as if he thought she was making a selfish commotion over a trifle. Suddenly I felt a great sympathy for Juana. After all, I thought, nobody is requiring Don Jose to give up his life as a political writer to look after three young children.

'You see,' said Juana, addressing de Larra still, 'Dona Conchita *is* their mother, after all. How can we have the right to decide their future or take them from her? How, indeed, could it possibly be arranged? Why would she ever agree?'

'My dear,' said de Larra more kindly, 'Dona Conchita has not spent one week under the same roof as those children in the last three years. They have been handed about here and there – to Don Manuel's parents when they were alive, to her own parents in Bilbao. It is my personal opinion that Conchita has about as much mother-love in her as this rock—' He thumped the side of the cave.

'But,' said Juana, troubled, 'the children love her. Or they did. When they were staying at my house they seemed to think her perfect. I—' her voice shook a little, 'I lost my own mother when I was twelve – I would not wish to inflict that sorrow on a child.'

'Your feelings do you credit, Dona Juana. But three years have passed since you saw the children; they may feel differently now. And your own mother, I daresay, was not such a one as Dona Conchita.' De Larra spoke patiently. But under his words I could sense an urgency to have the matter decided, which he could only just keep in check.

'Well,' said Juana with a sigh, 'tell Don Manuel that I will bring him my decision by dawn. I promise to delay no longer than that.'

'Good, senora. I will tell him.' De Larra bowed and kissed her hand, which surprised me – I had thought he was rather annoyed with her for not deciding on the spot.

Walking to the castle cliff I told de Larra about the troop of militia that were coming to bombard the castle.

'That is what I expected,' he said gloomily. 'They can sit across on the other side of the river and knock holes in the only habitable portion. And anybody going up or down the rope will be directly in their range.'

I remembered the tunnel, and told him that Don Manuel had said it was mined. 'It is as well that you did not enter by it, senor.'

'I don't remember where it comes out, or I would have. I daresay it is safe enough unless Manuel lights the fuse. The entrance is nowhere near here, though; I know that it is on the other side of the ridge. The passage runs northward into the Sobordan valley.'

That, I thought, accounts for the fact that Don Amador was unable to find it. A lucky circumstance.

My rope was still in position when we reached the foot of the castle crag.

De Larra pulled out his pistol and fired two shots.

After a longish lapse of time a hoarse voice above called 'Quien es?'

'It is Mariano,' called de Larra, and added, '*vuelva usted manana*,' which appeared to be a kind of password, for Don Manuel called '*Bienvenido*,' and I heard the ratchet begin to turn. Presently de Larra was hauled up the rock-face and I turned to walk thoughtfully back to the cave.

9

Juana's decision; return to the castillo; terrible news; Don Manuel and his wife; Conchita's downfall; departure of Manuel and Figaro

Returning to the cave, I found Pedro still sleeping and Juana still wide awake.

The stars had come out now, and blazed with great brilliancy above our heads, between the shoulders of the mountains. I could see her eyes shine, in their light.

'I have been thinking, Felix,' she began.

'And I have too. After all, Nico is nine – in ten years he will be a man, and able to look after his sisters. You could return to the convent then. It is not as if you are being asked to sacrifice your whole life—'

'Oh, *Felix*!' she burst out in a tone of utter exasperation. 'How old are you – nineteen? Eighteen? Do *you* consider yourself a man? Capable of looking after three children? Sometimes you seem to me more childish than when we were last together.'

Hurt and baffled, I was silent for a moment, swallowing the rebuff. I had only intended to help, after all.

'What were you going to say?' I asked then.

'I was wondering if the children could go to school in Bayonne – then I could see them regularly, they could visit me in my convent—'

That sounded a bleak outlook for the poor things, I thought.

'Why remove them from their own country? They could go to school in Bilbao, for that matter, and you remain in the convent there.'

'Perhaps,' she said slowly. 'I suppose so,' but she did not sound overjoyed at the suggestion.

How I longed to be able to say, 'Let the children come to Villaverde. There they can run wild and ride my grandfather's horses, and Prudencia will dote on them and feed them fritters and chocolate, as her mother Bernardina used to with me—'

But how could I make such an offer? What shadow of right had I to do so? I had no connection with these children.

Cautiously, expecting another rebuff, I inquired, 'What does God tell you to do?'

In a harassed voice, as if she had run out of patience, both with God and myself, she replied, 'If I *knew* that, don't you think I would have set about doing it?'

Another long silence fell, at the end of which Juana gave a deep sigh, stretched, and stood up. 'Well,' she said, 'I shall have to give Don Manuel the promise he wants.'

'Oh, Juana!' I jumped up, and grabbed her hands. 'I am very sure that you are right to do so. I am *sure* you will not regret it! And I – I promise that I will do my utmost to help and not hinder you.'

'Will you climb up into the castillo and tell him?'

'Yes, but first I must tell Dona Conchita. I promised that I would let her know in the morning—'

'Why must you do that? I don't see the necessity,' said Juana crossly. And I thought to myself, making this sacrifice doesn't mean that you have become perfect all in a moment, my dearest Juana. In fact, now is the time when we must look out for tempests; and I grinned to myself, thinking of little Pilar and her tantrums.

'Well, I have to keep my promise,' I said temperately, and made my way over the rope bridge.

What was my astonishment, coming to the hut, to

find it empty, nobody inside, the fire out, and the mules gone from the shelter at the rear.

Rather perturbed, I returned to Juana and told her this.

'Which way did they go? Could you see tracks?'

'No, it was too dark.'

'They must have gone very quietly,' she said. 'I don't like it.'

'Nor do I. I think we should go to Don Manuel without delay.'

Accordingly, without further discussion, we hurried along towards the castle cliff, leaving Pedro still asleep. Having arrived at the cliff foot, I fired off my pistol twice. Then we waited for a long time. At last Juana said in a low voice, 'What shall we do if no one answers?'

I had been wondering the same thing myself. But at that moment a voice called from above. It was that of Jose de Larra.

'*Quien es?*'

'It is I – Felix – and Dona Juana. She has come to give her promise to Don Manuel.'

'Ay, *Dios!* She may well have come too late.'

'Too late? What can you mean?'

'I suppose you had better come up,' he called, though not at all in a welcoming manner. There was something very strange about his voice.

'You had better go first,' I said to Juana, hearing him wind the ratchet. 'Seat yourself in the loop of rope – and hold tight. Shut your eyes – like when you crossed the bridge. Use your hands to push yourself away from the rock-face.'

Even by starlight I could see that she was as white as paper. She looked sick with dread.

'I – I don't think I—'

'My friend – you have *got* to.' I tried to sound much more forceful than I felt. What if she won't? I thought. 'Don Manuel will never believe my word alone. And think of the children up there—'

Well I knew her terror of heights. I remembered her anguish on the cliff above Bidassoa.

'You can do it – I promise you,' I said.

She managed a faint smile. 'You are too free with your promises, my friend.' Then she went aloft.

It was too dark to follow her progress. But at last I heard de Larra call '*Muy bien*,' and the rope came down again.

Me he pulled up bruisingly fast; in the course of the ascent I lost enough skin to cover an ostrich's egg, despite the fact that I kept fending myself away from the cliff-face with my feet and hands. My speed, I discovered on arriving at the top, was because Juana had been helping to wind the ratchet. She and de Larra were both panting by the time I reached the crane arm and swung myself on to the flat platform below it.

At the sight of de Larra's face – it was lighter up here – I said, 'What is it? What has happened?'

Without reply, he swung away and began walking rapidly up the steps towards the keep. Juana and I followed in silence and fear.

Once he turned and said to Juana, 'Are you skilled at nursing? Did they teach you that, in your convent?'

'I – I know a little,' she stammered. 'Why—?'

But already he was hurrying on again, up the slopes and through the roofless chambers, under arches, past ruined walls, without pausing to see if we were managing to keep pace with him.

In an undertone I asked Juana, 'You don't know what—? He didn't say?'

She shook her head, stumbling over a lump of masonry concealed among rough shrubs, and I caught her hand to help her. It felt warm and strong.

Then, in the distance, we heard a quiet, regular sound: clink, and then a thud; another clink, then another thud. A familiar sound, but unexpected here.

'Somebody *digging*?' whispered Juana, puzzled. We reached the wooden door to the keep. De Larra let us in through it, waited, and closed it behind us. At the foot of the stair, where we stood in pitch darkness, he suddenly seized my arm.

'Were you in the secret, about the book?' he hissed in my ear. 'Did you know about it? For if you did – as God is my witness – I will stick this knife through your gullet.'

I could feel the blade press against my windpipe, cold and deadly sharp. It made me cough.

'*Book?*' I spluttered. 'What book, senor? I have no idea what you are talking about.'

'The book that child brought, from her mother.'

Then I remembered the tiny volume, the handbook on birds, that Pilar had in her petticoat pocket, that Don Manuel furiously flung out of the window. A cold dread ran up my spine to the pit of my throat.

'Of all the cold, calculated acts of *villainy*—' de Larra was saying. 'Medea herself could not have equalled it. You *swear* that you knew nothing?'

'As God is my judge, senor!'

'Is that the truth?' I could feel his ferocious mind, searching mine in the dark.

Juana said strongly, 'El Senor Brooke is an honourable man, Don Jose. You do wrong to doubt him.'

At that, de Larra gave a great sigh, and the knifeblade dropped away from my neck.

'Very well – very well – forgive me. But we have been nearly mad with helplessness and horror.'

'Why, *why*?' demanded Juana. 'What has *happened*?'

Still without answering, he led the way up into the room where I had been before. The fire had gone out, but up here the large, unglazed windows gave light enough to see. We caught a faint sound of sobbing and whimpering, then perceived little Pilar, crouched by the body of another child that lay full length on the floor. Approaching more closely, I discovered this to be the boy, Nico, apparently ill or fainted; he moved and groaned a little, twisting about, and Pilar wailed, 'Nico, Nico! Please don't go, like Luisa! Don't!'

'Where is the other girl?' I asked with dread.

'Dead,' replied de Larra. Pilar sobbed again.

'*Dead?* But how?'

Juana had dropped on her knees beside the boy and was anxiously, carefully feeling his brow and his hands.

'It was that cursed book their mother sent. That hag! That vulture! Vitriol runs in her veins, not blood – that she could plan and carry out such an act!'

'The book? I don't understand?'

Then I began to recall how the pages of the little

volume were all gummed together and how Luisa had eagerly tugged them apart, licking her finger to moisten them.

'You mean the sticky pages—?'

'Poisoned,' he said. 'Manuel guessed immediately that there was some wicked trick, and threw it away. But already both the elder children—'

'Yes, now I remember. And – and the girl – she is dead? Already?'

'First she went mad,' said Don Jose curtly. 'She ran, she laughed, she danced, she screamed that angels were dancing with her. Then she said that she was a bird and could fly – before her father could stop her she leaped from that window there—'

Juana, kneeling by the boy, had one hand pressed over her mouth in horror. The other arm was clasped round the sobbing Pilar.

'Her father is out there now, digging her a grave,' said de Larra.

'And Nico – he also—?'

'He had not handled the book so much as his sister, Manuel says. But, you see—'

'Have you given him anything?' said Juana quickly. 'He should have white of egg beaten in milk, or a mustard emetic—'

De Larra laughed shortly. 'You think we have those

278

things up here? We gave him water – as much as he could drink—'

'But I don't understand,' I said slowly. 'Even Conchita – even *she* – can't have meant her children to die?'

'No, of course not. Don't you see,' impatiently interrupted Juana, 'it was her husband the book was meant for. It was Don Manuel. And she didn't mean him to die; she meant to send him mad. So that she could claim his estate.'

I remembered Don Ignacio saying, 'He must be mad, and die in his madness.'

'But what a fool!' Juana was going on furiously. 'I always thought Conchita stupid, but not as stupid as that! A plan that might so easily miscarry—'

At that moment we heard steps on the stair.

'Manuel,' said de Larra in a quick warning voice. 'Do not question him – he has been distressed beyond bearing—'

Don Manuel came in. He did indeed look beaten and ravaged, ten years older than when I had seen him last. At sight of us he checked.

'Don Felix and Dona Juana are innocent,' said de Larra at once. 'They knew nothing. They feel for you, most truly.'

Indeed Juana, getting up, walked straight to him and clasped his hands in hers.

His face still stared past her. He seemed hardly aware of his surroundings. But two slow tears found their way down his cheeks, as she continued to press his hands.

Little Pilar ran to him and seized him round the leg.

'Papa! Papa! Is Nico going to die also? *Please* don't let Nico die!'

'It is as God wills, child,' he said wearily. He looked down at Pilar with, I thought, some revulsion; and I could hardly blame him. Then, apparently taking in, for the first time, the presence of Juana, he murmured, 'You are – you are Sister Juana – who used to be Juana Esparza?'

'Yes, senor. I have come to give you—' she stopped and swallowed – 'to give you my promise about your children.'

'I remember you,' he went on slowly. 'I always thought you – a good influence. A true friend. Will you – I have dug her grave and laid her in it. Will you come and say a prayer for my daughter Luisa?'

His words came loosely as if they drifted from him without direction.

'Of course I will, Don Manuel,' Juana said in deep compassion. 'Let us all go. I will just make this poor boy a little more comfortable.' She took off the blue cloak I had given her and folded it into a wad for him to lie on. Then she made a sign of assent to Don Manuel and we went after him down the stair, little Pilar following forlornly in the rear. She seemed quite quenched with crying – very different from the other occasions on which I had seen her.

The grave he had dug for Luisa was under the tree that Pilar and I had climbed. It was an oak.

The only tools he had been able to find for digging were a rusty iron bar and an old blunt axe-blade. It must have been a formidable task, using such implements, in the hard and scanty soil; I could see that his hands were dusty and gashed and bleeding, on top of those earlier scars. He had hauled over part of a broken pillar to lie on top of the grave, in order to mark it, and keep off wild beasts.

Juana knelt down at the foot of the grave and the rest of us did likewise, wherever we happened to be placed. Dawn had come by now. A lark was singing nearby; we waited in silence for a moment or two, while its voice spiralled upward into the pale green sky, and while Juana collected her thoughts.

Then she said, 'Most pitiful Father: we need not ask you to take charge of your dear child Luisa, for she is already with You and sharing Your eternal joy. But we do ask you to comfort her brother and sister. May their lives be as guiltless and free from harm as hers was.'

I could hardly feel this was likely to be true of Pilar, but doubtless it did no harm to ask.

'Console this poor child's bereaved father and help him to see his path clear ahead,' went on Juana. Then she paused. I wondered if she was thinking about asking God to punish the ill-doers who had caused Luisa's horrible and untimely death. In the old days she would certainly have done so. Then she had a strong and passionate sense of justice and used to long for retribution against the people who had hurt her.

But she can safely leave all that to God? Surely she knows that by now? I thought.

Yes, Felix, said the voice of God in my ear. And *you* can safely leave Juana to me.

I almost smiled, the message came through so warm and clear, like a sudden blaze of sunshine in my mind.

Juana looked up over her joined hands, and met my eyes, for I was kneeling at the opposite end of the grave. She was frowning with concentration and resolve and glanced at me, just then, as if I were no more than a tree or a stone.

'And I hereby give my solemn promise that as much of my life as they may need shall be devoted to the care of Luisa's brother and sister; that I will help them to grow in grace and wisdom, and so free themselves from this wicked wrong and tragedy.

'Please give me your support in this work, my dear Lord.'

'Amen,' said Don Manuel strongly, and so did the rest of us.

Then Juana recited a prayer for the dead, in Latin, to which we made the responses. After that she stood up, without self-consciousness, and held out her hand again to Don Manuel. This time he took it between both of his.

'Thank you, child,' he said huskily. 'I do believe that you will do as you say. I pray God that my son lives to receive your care. And you restore, a little, my faith in human nature.'

'If that is so, I am glad to hear it.' Her voice was calm, quite matter-of-fact. She went on, 'And now, Don Manuel, it is a hard thing to tell you, but I think you should leave this place without delay.'

'Yes!' said de Larra in heartfelt agreement. 'Dona Juana is right, Manuel.'

'But, the boy—' His face contorted in anguish.

'The boy is in the hands of God. Your staying can make no difference. These young people will care for him as well as you can – better—'

Young people, I thought indignantly; how old are you, Senor de Larra, I should like to know? Not much older than I myself. But it was true that Don Manuel was older, was in his middle or late thirties – indeed he looked at this moment almost like an old man; there must have been a considerable gap in age between him and his wife. Perhaps that was why . . .

At that moment I saw Conchita herself coming over the grass.

She was dressed very stately, in black silk, with a black lace mantilla. She carried her great black ostrich-feather fan. True these things were a little dusty and mud-splashed, but she had plainly taken considerable pains with her appearance, and moved with great dignity, waving her fan from side to side as she approached.

Behind her came Don Amador, even more dusty and dishevelled, and panting a little as he endeavoured to keep pace with her.

I could see that Conchita was taken aback at the sight of de Larra. Myself and Juana she had perhaps expected, but Don Jose she had not, and his presence disturbed her, though she did her best to conceal the fact and came on composedly. What startled her even more was the appearance of her own husband, when he turned round and became aware of her. She drew a sharp breath and gazed at him with huge eyes.

He, for his part, turned completely white, so that his face looked like a shield, with the black eye patch and the diagonal line of its ribbon across his cheek. The good eye blazed with outrage.

'You!' he brought out harshly. 'How in the name of the fiend did *you* get here?'

Having come as close as she dared, Conchita stood still and stared at her husband, her face gradually growing as pale as his.

Of course, I thought, she expected to find him run mad and raving. That was why she came. To be a witness to his madness. And now, since he is plainly not mad at all, but sane and sober as anybody else present, she does not know what to do.

'How did I get here?' she repeated slowly. 'Why – by the tunnel, Manuel. You are not the only one who knows its location. Your brother Ignacio told me how to find it.'

She was staring at him, all the while, with a deep, distraught look, almost one of appeal. It was, I supposed, a couple of years since she had seen him; his appearance plainly shocked and disturbed her.

Dear God, I thought in astonishment, she loves him; in spite of having betrayed him and plotted his ruin and death, she does still love him in her own selfish, childish way.

'Manuel!' she exclaimed suddenly, as if they were alone together. 'Can't you forget all this wretched politics? Leave it! What is the good of it all? You will never gain your ends – whatever they are. And see what it leads to! Can't we go back? Be as we were at first – when we were happy? We *were* happy once—'

'Go back?' he repeated, in that harsh, husky voice. 'Go back? After the things you did? Do you see this?' He gestured towards the grave. 'Do you know what it is? Do you know who lies buried under there?'

She gaped at him in silence. She had not, up to that moment, taken in the fact that we were standing round a grave.

'Your daughter Luisa lies buried there!' he shouted at her. 'Poisoned by the filthy book that you sent in with that other misbegotten brat. She is dead! And you say that we can go *back*?'

'Oh – *no*!' She let out a faint, horrified cry, dropping the fan, pressing her hands against her mouth. 'No, it's not true! It can't be true! You are telling lies to frighten me – you monster!'

'You call me a monster? I don't know how you dare to show your face here.' His control began to slip; he snatched up the rusty axe-blade.

'Manuel – *no*!' exclaimed de Larra. He, like the rest of us, had been held, watching Conchita in absolute fascination – though I could see by the look in his strange, light luminous eyes that he loathed her and would be glad to see her blown by a gale off the face of the earth. But now he darted forward and knocked the rusty blade from Manuel's hand.

'Leave her alone, Manuel, you fool! She is not worth a straw. She is trash!'

But Don Manuel moved on towards his wife with such a look of awful, terrifying resolution upon his face – indeed he looked like the Cyclops itself, with wide nostrils and compressed lips and that one blazing eye – that she, with a faint scream, took to her heels.

'*Mama!*' wailed little Pilar, 'Mama!' and scampered to intercept her mother.

'Oh, get out of my way, you wretched little changeling! Haven't you done enough harm? You were supposed to give the book to your father – not your sister—'

Conchita thrust the child aside and ran for a gap in the wall, crying 'Amador! Stop him, help me, help!'

And Don Manuel went striding after her.

At that, we were suddenly all galvanised. De Larra was first through the gap, after Don Manuel, and I was close behind him, with Juana just after me, and Don Amador trailing unhappily behind us all.

Beyond the wall which encircled the keep a rough, wide slope of grass and boulders, scattered with ruined masonry, ran down to the outer bailey wall, which, on this side, was not complete. The wall, topping the cliff that surrounded the castle on three sides, had been built so as to take advantage of natural crags. And in a dozen places the masonry had crumbled, leaving the crags like teeth in a lower jaw with wide gaps between.

Down towards this wall Conchita ran at a crazy, terrified speed, stumbling and slipping among the tufty grass and brambles.

'Dona Conchita! Stop!' shouted de Larra. 'We won't let him hurt you. Manuel, stop!'

'Stop!' I yelled.

'Stop!' called Juana.

Even Don Amador, somewhere far to the rear, called reedily, 'My dearest! Stop, I beg you—!'

But nothing arrested her frantic flight. Floundering, tripping, snatching brief glances over her shoulder, seeing Don Manuel gain on her, Conchita only ran the faster.

Arrived at the wall, where it was only five or six feet high, but rough and ragged, crumbling on the inside, she flung herself upon it. In her dress she looked like a black lizard. Up the uneven slope of loose masonry she scrambled, and paused to look back only when she was out of her husband's reach.

De Larra had come up with Don Manuel by then·

and caught hold of his arm. The touch seemed to recall him to sanity; he halted, shook his head with a dazed look, and rubbed his forearm across his eyes.

'Conchita! I beg you, come down, my angel, or you will fall!' begged Don Amador. The poor fat man looked ludicrously useless, gasping and exhorting his lady as he came puffing down the slope.

Now we were all ranged in a row below her while she crouched on the broken wall above us calling out, 'Do not let him touch me!'

'No one shall harm you, my precious angel!' promised Don Amador.

And then I heard little Pilar's voice behind me upraised in a scream of utter terror. '*Mama!*'

She, farther up the hill, had seen – her sharp child's eyes had seen – what was not so clear to us, close at hand: the whole piece of masonry, loosened by Conchita's headlong assault on it, was starting to topple outwards.

With what seemed a dreamlike slowness, though it can have taken but a few seconds, she and the wall tilted away from us, describing an arc like the setting sun – then, with one harrowing, horror-stricken cry, she vanished from our view among a cataract of tumbling rock and stone.

'*Jesu!*' said de Larra.

Leaving go of Don Manuel, he went gingerly to another part of the wall, a few yards to the side, and looked over. Returning, he shook his head and spread out his hands.

'Not a hope . . . She is three hundred feet down, under a ton of rubble. And no particular loss to the world,' he added in an undertone, but little Pilar was sobbing hysterically, 'Mama – Mama – Mama—' and Juana was trying to comfort her, while Don Amador, looking utterly dazed with shock, repeated over and over, 'How could you, how could you? Oh, Conchita, my dearest, how *could* you?'

I caught de Larra's eye and muttered to him, 'The advice that Juana gave was good. If *they* came by the way of the tunnel, others may. Why don't you just go – now – take him away before anything else can happen. We will look after the children. Just go!' I repeated.

'Yes, you are right. Come, my friend.' De Larra took Don Manuel's arm. 'We can do nothing here. The esquiladores will be waiting, with wings to carry you over the mountains into France. Come, kiss your son goodbye and we must be off.'

'Suppose they are intercepted in the tunnel?' Juana asked in a low voice.

De Larra shrugged.

'In that case Manuel will blow up everybody – them and us as well! But I think it unlikely that anyone else will come that way. It is too narrow and difficult. If a whole party of troops is expected, they will be waiting across the river for some signal from Don Amador. Well – if you hear an explosion, you will know that was the end of us.' He smiled, his strange pale eyes throwing out sparks of light. 'If not – then, perhaps, one day, Senor Felix, I shall see you in Madrid. Ask for Figaro . . . And in that case no doubt we shall be hearing from our friend in Mexico or Argentina. *Adios!*'

And he led off Don Manuel, who went with him biddably, like a man in a trance.

10

We leave the castillo; crossing the rope bridge; Pedro is shot; I become unconscious

The rope brought by de Larra, which had not been needed, still lay in the upstairs chamber of the keep.

While Juana, with great care, sip by sip, silently fed the unconscious boy water from a wooden cup, I busied myself cutting the rope into lengths and forming these into a net. That was a skill I had learned from my sailor friend Sam, years ago, while crossing the Gulf of Gascony on a Basque felucca. Now I thanked God for it. He is a thrifty planner; He wastes nothing, I thought.

Little Pilar huddled sorrowfully close to me, sucking

her thumb, clutching the blue bead on her plaited necklace. When Don Manuel had kissed his son good-bye, he had passed her with averted face, ignoring her; and she had lacked the spirit even to call after him. I wondered if she realised, poor little wretch, the full implication of what had happened. She seemed to accept that she had no claim on Don Manuel. What if Amador also rejects her? I wondered. It is fortunate that Juana made that promise.

Because of the children's presence, Juana and I could not discuss their mother's frightfully sudden death and her previous acts; and perhaps this was just as well. No doubt time would bring charity. At the moment I could not help feeling, with Don Jose, that the world was well rid of Conchita de la Trava, who had brought death to one, perhaps two, of her children, ruin to her husband, and great unhappiness to her fat lover. Where, by the way, was Don Amador? Had he followed the other two men through the tunnel? Just as I was thinking that I ought to find out how he was occupying himself, he appeared, looking utterly wretched and lugubrious. Outside, a heavy mountain rain was falling, and sodden drenched clothes added to his generally dismal appearance.

'Why do you sit there making a net?' he demanded fretfully. 'What in the world is the good of *that*?' but wandered away again without waiting for an answer. He was like a great fat bluebottle fly in a confined space, buzzing and blundering. I could not help feeling sorry for him.

Letting out a great gusty sigh he went and stood by Juana and Nico.

'It were best if the poor child dies too . . . His mother gone, his father disgraced . . . And suppose you bring him back to life, only to find that his wits are flown?'

Juana flashed him a furious glance from her copper-dark eyes as she carefully trickled a little more water between the boy's open lips.

'We certainly dare not go through the tunnel now,' Don Amador muttered, ambling back to me again.

'Oh? Why not?'

Not that I had intended to. The tunnel, de Larra had said, ran north into the Sobordan valley; it was nearly half a league in length and very narrow and slippery – only sheer necessity must have impelled Dona Conchita along it. The task of carrying Nico such a distance would be almost beyond our powers; and then we would come out a long way from where we needed to be.

'Conchita told me – Don Ignacio warned her – that, after rain, the tunnel fills with water, and one must wait a day before it drains away. There was a storm last night; now it rains again; perhaps Manuel and de Larra will never reach their journey's end.'

He spoke with childish spite, and seemed almost glad of the mountain rain, lashing in through the un-glazed windows.

'When is this troop of soldiery supposed to arrive from Pamplona?'

'Oh, who knows? Who knows? Maybe they will not come at all.'

Don Amador sounded much less confident about the troop than he had yesterday. Perhaps, sure that their trick with the poison had worked, Conchita and he had sent a message by Pepe and Esteban to count-ermand the request for the troop. I wondered where the outriders were now.

'That is a pity,' I remarked. 'They might have helped us carry the children back to Berdun.'

'Please let us not wait for the chance of their coming,' said Juana. 'I think we should move this poor boy as soon as we can.'

'I agree,' said I, and, standing up, measured the net I had made against the boy's body. 'Another half-hour's work should do it.'

'Oh! Is Nico going down in a net?' exclaimed Pilar.

'Certainly. How else can we get him down?'

295

'Can I go down in the net too?'

I would have rapped out a short *No!* but Juana said thoughtfully, 'You could, of course, but it seems a pity that someone so clever at climbing should not go down in the loop, like the rest of us.'

That changed Pilar's views at once, and I began to see that the control of this wayward little creature was an art which had to be learned.

As I worked on, Pilar, just a little cheered by the prospect of descending the cliff, said, 'Uncle Dor-Dor?'

'Well?'

'*Why* did you bring Mama the paste for painting the book's pages? If it was going to make Luisa mad?'

'Indeed you are quite mistaken, child,' he said hastily. 'I did no such thing!'

'But you brought her a little pot.'

'It held ointment for her lips. Salve. Nothing at all to do with that accursed book. And perhaps it was not the book at all that killed Luisa. Maybe it was a sickness caused by hunger and cold.'

Pilar looked wholly unconvinced, but he took himself off to the far end of the room and stood there with a look of great uneasiness, alternately balancing on toes and heels, until I had finished my work on the net. Then I proposed that he come with me and observe the workings of the ratchet, to which he agreed with a show of alacrity. The storm had passed over by now, and the world outside was wet and sparkling.

'I trust you do not think that *I* had any connection with that hideous trick of the book,' he said virtuously as soon as we were out of doors. 'Indeed I had not the least knowledge of it in the world. I did not know the brat was carrying it, even. For sure, that was why Conchita sent me to hunt for the tunnel in the wrong place – just to give that little demon a chance to make her way up the cliff—'

'I have had no thoughts about the matter, senor,' I replied politely.

Don Amador was a weak, variable man, I thought. Harmless enough, perhaps, if left to himself, but, subject to another influence such as that of Conchita, I could believe him capable of crime. His manner of speech suggested this variability. Sometimes it seemed quite sincere, as when he had talked about the children last night; but at other times what he said had an airy falsity that would not deceive even a half-wit. Now he looked at me sidelong, as if wondering whether I believed him.

'She was after his money, of course,' he went on.

'But I thought that Dona Conchita's family were so rich.'

'Indeed they were, the old Escaroz. But they have

paid out thousands and thousands of reales, assisting the cause of the Carlists.'

The Carlists, I knew, were the political party most savagely opposed to Liberals such as Don Manuel and my grandfather. The Liberals wished Spain to be governed by a written constitution, for all men to be taxed equally, for all to have a vote, and equal rights. King Ferdinand had promised these reforms but, once he was supported by armies from overseas, forswore all his promises and restored the old tyrannical ways. But there was yet a third party who thought the king was not severe enough; and at their head was the king's brother, Don Carlos, a most bigoted zealot, who wished to carry oppression even further, and for no changes of any kind to be made in the laws, ever. (He also wanted the throne for himself: King Ferdinand's children were both girls, and Don Carlos claimed that, by the Salic law, they were not eligible to inherit the throne.)

A large number of the Carlists lived in the Basque territories or in Catalonia; it did not at all surprise me to hear that Conchita's parents were of this faction. In old times the Basques had been exempt from a great many taxes; they had what were known as *fueros*, statute laws freeing them from military service and from other ordinances laid down by the central government in Madrid. The Basques claimed they had the rights of an ancient, independent kingdom, and should be treated differently from folk living in other Spanish provinces.

Whether they are right or wrong, I cannot pretend to say. But old customs, I believe, should not be lightly cast off.

'Don Manuel, you see, had not come to trial at the time he escaped from jail,' Don Amador was going on. 'So his estates were not yet forfeit, as those of a condemned felon would be.'

'I see . . . so Conchita would have inherited if he had died.'

'And now Nico will – if the poor boy survives, which seems unlikely,' Don Amador said carelessly.

I felt a fierce resolve that Nico *should* survive, if I could help it, but said merely, 'Don Manuel has not died, however, so this is idle talk. Now, here is how the ratchet works—'

'We must go down *there*?' Don Amador gazed at the fearsome drop with starting eyes. His fat cheeks paled visibly.

'That was the way we came up, senor.'

'Ay, *Madre de Dios!*'

Just at that moment I heard two shots from below. My heart lightened, wonderfully. Holding on to the crane arm and peering over, I called, 'Pedro, is that you?'

'Felix!' his shout came back, 'Ay! – am I glad to hear your voice! How goes it, up there?'

'You shall hear, by and by. But now we have to come down – and one of the children is sick. Wait there, at the bottom, and we will be with you soon.'

'Come with me,' I told Don Amador, 'and help me carry Nico.'

I did not want him meddling with the crane mechanism while I was out of the way. So he accompanied me, not very willingly, back to the keep, and we placed Nico in my net, as in a hammock. He was still only half conscious, murmuring the word 'thirsty' from time to time.

We carried him back to the cliff-top – he was a light weight, poor child – little Pilar bounding alongside. She had picked up from somewhere her mother's great plumy black fan, which she importantly flourished about. It struck me that both she and Don Amador were recovering quite speedily from Dona Conchita's death. Which told a good deal about the lady.

I fastened Nico completely into the net, joining the edges together and knotting them. Then I fastened the net to the crane rope.

'Now,' I said to Juana, who had come with us, 'can

you go down with him, sitting in the loop, so as to fend him off and prevent his striking himself against the rock?'

'Yes, of course,' she said, gulping, and I pressed her hand briefly as I helped her into the loop. The descent was far worse than being pulled up, for the moment of stepping off the cliff-top and looking down into that giddy void was so dreadful; but she concealed her fears as well as she could, gave little Pilar a wry smile, and, as we wound her down, kept her attention on the boy. They vanished from view past the overhang, we felt the rope vibrate, then, after what seemed a sickeningly long stretch of time, we heard Pedro's cheerful shout.

'*Muy bien!* I have them!' – and the rope, coming free, suddenly lightened as we wound it up.

'Now you,' I said to little Pilar.

Her lip thrust out angrily.

'But I want to *climb* down!'

'That would take too long. We want to get your brother to a doctor. Also,' I whispered in her ear, 'you have to show your Uncle Dor-Dor that there is nothing to be afraid of.'

Her expression cleared.

'Of course I will show him!' And she skipped over to the crane, still clutching the plumy fan.

Despite her vehement protests, I tied her in, making a kind of harness.

'Now, don't forget to keep pushing yourself away from the rock with your hands. Otherwise you might get scraped.'

'Of course! I'm not stupid,' she said crossly; and down she went, briskly as a fisherman's bait into the water.

By the time it came to Don Amador's turn, I could see that he was in a jelly of terror.

'B-but will the rope b-bear me?' he demanded, his teeth chattering. 'For I am a man of ample frame – you may have observed—' Now, for the first time, he seemed to regret all those good dinners he had been eating all his life.

'Indeed, senor, it is a strong, brand-new rope which I just purchased myself in Pamplona,' I said soothingly, not mentioning that the crane-arm which supported it was an old, weathered piece of timber upheld by some crumbling masonry.

At last he suffered himself to be lowered, but only after countless hesitations and fidgetings, and uttering many shrill cries of fright and discomfort; and he clung on so tightly with both hands to the rope that, in spite of my warning, he was thumped against the cliff face in what must have been a most bruising manner. Well, his fat frame can stand a few bruises, I thought; at least he is well-padded.

He had not thought to inquire how I was going to get down, with no one to wind the wheel; and indeed I had purposely not discussed the matter for fear that Juana might raise difficulties. Now, taking the remnant of de Larra's rope, I made a loop at either end, one small, one large, passed the large one over my shoulders, and hooked the small one over the last of the cramping-irons which I had fastened into the rock when Pilar and I made our ascent of the cliff.

Going up had not been bad; going down was liable to be far, far harder.

So I found it, indeed. Some stretches of the climb I was able to remember; and that helped greatly, for then I knew in which direction to move. But the face of the cliff seemed very different now that I was climbing down, not up; while descending, I could not look down and see what lay below my feet, whereas on the ascent it had been easy to look upward and scan the area above me.

Once, the iron, which had not been jammed in firmly enough, dropped out of the rock, and I slid my own height down the cliff (luckily not quite sheer at that point) and landed on a narrow rock ledge; it was too narrow to support me but, by half falling, half lurching to my left, I managed to reach a wider section of it. The rope round my shoulders helped to give me confidence, but sometimes it was hard to shake it loose from the iron above – once I nearly shook myself loose in the process; then I would loop it over another iron, farther down, and so scramble on my way.

Luckily, at the moment when I fell, I was hidden from those below by the overhang, but a scatter of dust and pebbles cascaded past me and I had to shout, 'Beware, down there!' and I heard anxious cries from the foot of the cliff.

When I finally came within view of them the climb was not too difficult, and there were more hand-holds; now I had reached the point that little Pilar had climbed to when I first saw her.

She is a courageous little ant, I thought, if terribly undisciplined; perhaps Juana will be able to make something good of her: heaven send that the poor child never comes to realise the full extent of the harm that was done when she carried that book into the castillo . . .

At last, with bleeding hands and (I must confess) with weak and shaky knees, I reached the foot of the cliff, and little Pilar ran at once to upbraid me furiously.

'Why did you not let *me* climb down too? If you

were going to? Instead of making me go down like a baby on the rope?'

'Oh, come, Pilar,' said Juana – she seemed to be trembling too – 'the rest of us went down on the rope, Don Amador too, it was not babyish—'

'How does Nico seem?' I asked quickly. 'Did the descent do him any harm?'

'I do not think that he is any worse,' Juana said doubtfully. 'But the sooner we can get him into care, the better – I only wish Sister Belen were here—'

Plainly, while Don Amador and I had been descending the cliff, Juana had given Pedro a fairly full account of what had been happening. His eyes met mine expressively; and he came over and gave me a hug that was half a shake. 'If only I could have been up there to help you—' he muttered.

'There is plenty of help yet needed, Pedro.'

So he and I picked up Nico, still fastened in his net, and carried him along the narrow brambly path to the rope bridge. Pilar darted ahead, dragging Juana by the hand, Don Amador followed, limping and complaining, in the rear.

Across the gorge, two horses could be seen, tethered by the door of the foresters' hut. And as we came closer I observed, without joy, the two outriders Pepe and Esteban come out of the hut and look us over.

They seemed well-disposed enough, however. Don Amador shouted to them that we were coming over with the children, and they made gestures, indicating that they would stand by to give help, if needed.

'I can go by myself!' clamoured little Pilar.

'Very well – only take care,' said Juana.

Pilar cast her a lofty look, stuck the black fan into her waistband, then went across, hand over hand, as nimbly as a monkey.

'She belongs in a circus, that one,' muttered Pedro.

Don Amador went next, puffing, groaning, swaying, and making a great to-do. He was a comical sight, I suppose, but none of us felt like laughing. Too many sad and dreadful events had taken place. Pepe and Esteban, on the far bank, however, did seem to have some difficulty in concealing their amusement; I saw Pepe turn away with his shoulders shaking, and Esteban gave him a great cuff on the ear.

After some discussion it had been decided that Juana and I, as the lightest of the group, should cross together with Nico slung between us. I was mortally anxious about this, for the ropes from which the bridge was constructed, unlike mine from Pamplona, were old and decidedly worn. Would the weight of three together be too much? However there was really no other way in which the crossing with Nico could be achieved; he was too heavy for one person to carry on that flimsy, swaying spiderweb of cords.

'And if the bridge bears Don Amador, it should surely support you and me and this poor child,' whispered Juana. 'I do not believe that the three of us together weigh as much as he does – the fat pig!'

Pedro helped us by lifting up Nico, in his net, and supporting his weight until we were ready for him, balanced on either side of the ropes, facing one another. I had left loops of rope at each end of the hammock, which were slung round our necks, leaving our hands free to grip the bridge. The strain on our necks was punishing; it seemed amazing that Nico, a small, slight boy, could be such a dead weight. My neck began to feel as if it would never be able to hold my head up straight again – and if mine felt so, what must Juana, small-boned and slender, be enduring? She had turned very white, her lips were pressed tight together, there were deep lines on her face from mouth to nostril.

As we moved sideways, with extreme difficulty, I asked her, to keep her mind off the horrible and frightening sway of the bridge, 'Do you think that the old Escaroz will raise any objections to your taking charge of Conchita's children?'

'I suppose,' she answered after a moment, raising

her eyes from the torrent rushing among its boulders a long distance below our feet, 'I suppose they well may. If there is money involved. If Don Manuel were to die – then the grandparents would certainly lay claim to his estate on behalf of their grandchildren. But, so long as he lives, they may not—'

'Oh, I hope so *much* that he escapes,' I said fervently. 'He is such a fine man. One of the best in Spain, I am sure.'

'What do you know about it?' she said crossly. 'How many of the best men in Spain have you met?' and I grinned a little, inwardly, at my success in distracting her, if only for a moment, from the strain and terror of our position. What I feared most of all was that Nico should move, or twitch, and unbalance us, for then we would all plunge into the gorge together.

'Felix,' Juana went on, 'I want to say to you that I am sorry – very, very sorry – that you have been dragged into this bad business. If I had not told Conchita about you, she would never have known, never have had you summoned. It is all my fault—'

Impetuously I interrupted her.

'Listen, Juana. *Whatever* happens – even if there is more trouble, more danger – I could never regret it. Because, for the last five years, my deepest wish has been to see you again—'

She suddenly looked up, and I met the full glance of her coppery eyes. I went on, 'And, now that I have seen you, my only wish is to help you in any way that I can. If you would—'

She was beginning to say something in return, but voices from the edge of the bridge broke in. Pepe and Esteban were standing there with arms extended, ready to relieve us of the weight of Nico. We had not realised that we were so far across.

'Ay, *de mi*,' sighed Juana, in a moment, edging herself gingerly off the rope and on to firm ground, then vigorously rubbing her neck. 'I do not think I shall ever be able to stand up straight again—' and she knelt down at once by Nico, to see how he did. 'Have you any water?' she asked the men, and one of them went into the hut.

Having satisfied myself that Pedro, also, was now on his way across the bridge, and that it was not too hard for him, I too knelt down by Nico and began to unknot the net which had kept him safe but which must, if he was conscious of it, feel very constricting for the poor boy.

Behind me I heard Don Amador give some low voiced order to one of the men. The other was offering a flask to Juana, who opened it, sniffed it warily, and tasted a little of the contents on her finger before venturing to administer it to the boy.

Pedro by this time was past the middle of the bridge, moving slowly and with care.

'Now!' I heard Don Amador mutter, and turned round just in time to see Pepe discharge his musket at Pedro, only about fifteen cubits distant now. Pedro spun round and dropped into the gorge like a shot partridge.

At the same moment a stunning blow on the back of my head reduced me to unconsciousness.

11

In the tartana; little Pilar makes herself useful; arrival at Berdun; a use for the rubbish chute; we find a doctor; we return to Bilbao where I receive bad news from home

My wits returned to me by slow degrees. Violent physical discomfort was the first token that I was still alive.

Now I know how Nico must have felt, I thought – like a sardine in a net. Ropes were tightly crisscrossed all over my body. My hands were fastened behind me, my ankles were tied, and I seemed to be lying in a lumpy, knotted sling, with various heavy weights piled on top of me. Perhaps I am dreaming? Am I really still crossing the rope bridge? Or creeping down the cliff-face, entangled somehow in my own climbing rope? Cords, cables, rope, I was lying in a mesh, like a fly in a web, and something rough and thick was pressed against my face. For a while I wondered if I could be in a boat, for I and everything around me seemed to be swaying about in a horrible manner, it was like a nightmare . . .

The dark made it all much worse.

Then I began to receive the impression that there were other live bodies pressed against mine – shifting, struggling, the other sardines in the net – and, I suppose, I must have let out a stifled groan. A creature – some small, active body – rubbed close against me, writhing upward towards my face, and after a while I felt a warm tickling breath against my ear, and heard a tiny voice, which whispered, 'Senor Felix? Are you alive?'

'Yes, I think so.'

'Hush – don't speak aloud!'

'*Que tal?* Where am I?'

'In the tartana.'

Now, all of a sudden, my surroundings made sense. The rope, the swaying motion . . .

'Is it night?' I asked.

'Yes; but wait a moment. I will try and see if I can pull with my teeth—'

I felt a sudden sharp tug at my hair, and let out an involuntary hiss of pain. But then a fold of thick cloth which had enwrapped my head was partially twitched aside. Now the darkness was not quite so dark, and I could breathe more easily; I was able to distinguish night sky and dark trees overhead, also hear the clip-clop of mules, pulling the cart along.

At this point, remembrance came back to me with a most agonising rush. *Pedro*, I thought. Oh, Pedro. How will I ever tell Grandfather? How can I bear to face him with such news? Or Pedro's aunt Prudencia?

Alongside remembrance and grief came deep rage, boiling up inside me, so that I wrestled furiously and vainly with the cords that tied my wrists and ankles. How *dared* they kill Pedro – who was so good, so cheerful, never grumbled, never harmed a living soul – how dared they? This had not been his affair, he had come on the mission out of duty to my grandfather and friendship to me – it was the most wicked injustice that he should have been shot down, with such callous disregard, too, as if he were no more than a rabbit or a wild deer. Just let them wait till I get at them, I thought, battling with my bonds. And when my struggles had not the slightest effect, some angry tears rolled down my face, of which I was heartily ashamed.

The little voice came again.

'Senor Felix?'

'Yes? Who is that? Is it Pilar?'

'Yes.'

'Can you undo my hands?'

'No,' she whispered, sounding subdued. 'Mine are tied too.'

'Where are Nico and Dona Juana and Don Amador?'

'Uncle Dor-Dor is driving the tartana. He is a pig. I hate him,' she muttered. 'Nico and Cousin Juana are at the other end of the cart; I think they are tied up too. And there are a lot of things on top of them.'

'So there are on me too.'

'I know,' Pilar whispered. 'It is all Mama's clothes – her cloaks and furs and the bedding she brought. And stones and branches on top of that. They piled them on to hide us. I could hardly breathe at first but I managed to move my head about and make a space.'

'Where do you suppose they are taking us?'

'Back to Berdun, they said. To Don Ignacio's house, perhaps.'

This gave me plenty of matter for thought, as the tartana plodded on its way. It seemed to be moving at quite a speedy pace; I supposed they had Pedro's and my mules harnessed, besides the original pair.

On whose side, I wondered, was Don Ignacio? Was he a Royalist? A Carlist? Or simply interested in his brother's inheritance? And Don Amador? Where did he stand, now Conchita was dead?

314

'Where are Pepe and Esteban?' I whispered.

'Riding ahead,' said Pilar.

If only I could locate Juana and talk to her. Was she asleep? Unconscious? Stifled, gagged? I tried to move, but only evoked a squeak from Pilar, who said I was crushing her.

After what seemed like a couple of hours' travel we halted, to rest the beasts, I supposed. It was still dark, but we had come out of the forest; I could see the jagged edges of mountain peaks, a deeper black against the starry sky.

Footsteps echoed alongside the tartana, and a hand reached in and dragged me to a semi-sitting position. I could just make out the fat form of Don Amador.

'So: you are waking,' he said, peering at me closely. 'Are you sensible?'

I made some noise of assent.

'Listen then. God knows I do not wish to send you to prison—'

'To *prison*? Are you mad, senor, or am I? What have I done to justify my being sent to prison?'

'My friend – I could send you off to Montjuich just like *that* –' I heard him snap his fingers – 'by writing your name on a slip of paper. I have friends on the Council of Regency; the Bishop of Osma is my brother-in-law's cousin. Chaperon, the President of the

Military Commission, is the brother of my sister's husband's—'

'But what have I—'

'Assisting a felon to escape! Women, even children, are sent to jail for lesser crimes. You have not only yourself to think about, my young friend, remember. What about Dona Juana? The children? Do you want your grandfather the Conde to be impeached – his estates seized by the Crown?'

'But why should—'

'God knows,' he repeated in his thin, reedy voice, 'I do not wish you or your grandfather – or, indeed, Dona Juana or the children – any harm, not the least in the world . . .'

'Then why are you threatening me, senor?' I asked angrily. I saw his fat face shine in the moonlight, like an overripe fruit, beaded with sweat. He was, I realised, more frightened than I.

All that filled *me*, just then, was rage.

'You killed my friend Pedro!' I burst out. 'You killed him like a farmyard beast – with no more thought than that!'

'Friend? He was your servant.' Don Amador sounded genuinely surprised.

'I knew him since I was born!'

'He was only a servant,' the fat man repeated.

'How can his death be of concern to you?'

'Only a servant!' I was almost strangled with fury.

'*Listen.*' Don Amador leaned closer and spoke more urgently. 'You are in bad danger, boy. The *only* way you can avoid terrible trouble for yourself and your loved ones – *are* you listening?' He spoke lower, and shook my arm, which he still clutched. 'The only way is to pretend to know nothing, pretend that you saw nothing – that Manuel was gone when you entered the castillo, or that you never entered it – do you understand?'

He is afraid for himself, I thought; that I will betray his part in the death of Luisa, and so, also, of her mother; that I will tell about Pedro.

'I cannot pretend, senor.'

'Fool!' he hissed. And then, suddenly, in a much louder voice, 'Come, now – what we must know is the whereabouts of those casks of silver dollars. For sure, you and your grandfather still have them.'

Briefly, I thought that he must have gone mad. Silver dollars? And then, looming up behind him, I saw the figures of the two outriders. He was speaking, evidently, for their ears.

'I know nothing about any silver dollars, senor,' I said curtly.

'It is stupid to pretend. You know perfectly well what I am talking about. It happened at the village of

Cerezal in January of the year 1809, when the English general Paget would not release draught oxen to draw the carts with the British army paychests. And so all the money was left behind, hidden on the mountain-side. You know perfectly well,' he repeated.

'That old tale! If my grandfather had known where it was, he would long ago have restored it to its rightful owners. *He* is an *honourable* man!' I snapped.

'And he has not restored it,' said Don Amador smoothly. 'Therefore it still lies where it was hidden. *You* know its whereabouts. A letter was sent to you about it.'

'Not true,' I told him wearily. 'The letter that the Englishman, Smith, sent me was not about any treasure. He was warning me of a threat to my life. And that was five years ago. If he had told me about any treasure, I would have informed my grandfather.'

'You know where the money is,' repeated Don Amador stubbornly. 'And if you are wise, you will tell us.' He gave my arm a warning nip.

'Enough, enough now, senor,' Esteban said roughly. 'We must hurry on our way. We need to reach the house of Don Ignacio before daylight. The young man may be questioned again later.'

And then, to my utter consternation and surprise, he stepped behind Don Amador and swiftly garrotted him by twisting a knotted kerchief about his throat; the fat man gave one piteous, gasping cry, then crumpled to the ground, dead as a shot hare. The two postilions speedily dragged him to the side of the road and tumbled him down the bank. We had halted near a high-arched bridge; he was deposited in the water under the bridge, where he might lie for months until he was nibbled down to his bones by fish, before anybody discovered him.

Then Esteban took the driver's seat, his mule was tethered at the rear of the cart, and we resumed our journey in silence. The whole assassination had been so lightning-quick, so merciless, and so unexpected, that I could still hardly credit what I had seen. Don Amador had been a worthless, venal man, quite prepared, I was sure, to sacrifice anybody else for his own ends – except Conchita; I suppose he had truly loved her in his way – but still, his murder came as a fearful shock. And came, also, as a stark message showing what the rest of us might expect.

Indeed, after a few miles, Esteban addressed me.

'*Ingles*? Can you hear me?'

'I can hear you,' I said. 'But I am not English. I am as Spanish as you.'

'I am not Spanish, I am Catalan. Did you take notice of how we dealt with that fat fool?'

'I could hardly avoid it.'

'Well! Take warning! If you and your grandfather do not lead us to that treasure, you will go the same way as Don Amador. The Conde will be glad enough to tell us where the treasure lies, when we send him a few of your fingers and toes.'

I did not reply. What was the use? He would never believe my assertion that we did not know where the treasure lay – if, indeed, there was any treasure left by now.

The postilions' act had shown them to be ruthless, professional assassins; to hope for mercy or reason in them would be like hoping for sweet water in mid-ocean.

I heard Pilar snuffling quietly beside me, and realised, with some compunction, that she was weeping for Don Amador. His murder had come as a terrible shock for her too.

'Poor Uncle Dor-Dor! He bought me turron in Zamora . . .'

Wretched little creature, I thought. In the space of a few hours she has seen both her parents die unexpected and brutal deaths; if, indeed, Don Amador was her father. And if her father is Don Manuel he shows no intention of acknowledging her, and has gone away, God knows where.

Had he succeeded in making his way along the tunnel? How many hours had elapsed since he and de Larra left the castillo? More than twelve, I guessed; they must have met the gypsy horse-shearers long ago. Supposing that the tunnel was not flooded . . .

I tried to whisper consolations to Pilar. 'Never mind; I am sure Dona Juana will look after you lovingly—'

But where was Dona Juana? Deeper and deeper grew my worry about her. Why was there no sound from the other end of the tartana? What had they done to her?

'I am going to try to wriggle along to Juana,' I whispered to Pilar.

'I want to come too,' she answered instantly.

'Not just yet. You stay here. Otherwise Esteban will notice.'

It had never occurred to me, in my life hitherto, to ask myself what a worm must feel like, as it bores its weary way through the solid earth. Now I did not wonder; I *knew*. For my hands and feet were tied, reducing me to the shape of a worm; I could not use my arms to assist motion, but only my feet, elbows, and leg muscles. Moreover I had to fold my body like a jack-knife in order to impel myself in the direction towards which my feet were pointing; and all these movements had to take place under a weight of clothes, cloaks, blankets, stockings and petticoats (it seemed Conchita had equipped herself with enough garments to supply the whole Convento de la Encarnacion); these, furthermore, pressed down by stones and pine branches.

Writhing my way through this mass of material was a slow and laborious business; I dared not push too hard or I would make the tartana sway suspiciously.

At last, after what seemed like hours of struggle among the various shapes and textures, I encountered one that was warm, and moved; and I thought I heard a stifled cry.

'Don't be afraid; it's I, Felix,' I whispered re-assuringly. I had no answer, save another muffled sound; can she be suffocating under all those layers of petticoats, I thought in horror, and tried to increase my speed. Fortunately I was now at the rear of the cart, farther from the driver.

At last, pushing through a mass of lace and feathers, I saw, ahead of me, Juana's unmistakable profile – or part of it; now I understood why she had not been able to communicate, for the poor girl was gagged with a couple of mantillas, part of one thrust into her mouth, and the other tied round her head. I saw the despairing flash of her eyes as she rolled her head, trying vainly to convey some meaning.

'Ah, those devils,' I muttered. 'Wait a little, I'll try to pull it loose.'

Pulling a lace mantilla from somebody else's head with one's teeth is no easier than boring through mounds of petticoats with hands tied. The task took many minutes. Often my cheek had to press against Juana's, while I gnawed and bit; sometimes I could feel her shake – whether with laughter or tears I did not know. At last I had the lace chewed through, and thought I felt her signal to me by moving her head; then I could plainly feel the actions of her jaw, as she painfully expelled the gag from her mouth, blowing and pushing and thrusting it out; at last she took in a great gulp of air.

'Haaaah! No one ever did me such a service before! Thank you!' she whispered; now I did think I could detect a smile in her tone, though it was too dark to read the expression on her face.

All *I* could think of to say was, 'I love you, Juana!' and then I lay for a while with my cheek pressed against hers, and my chin resting on her shoulder.

'Oh, my *dear* Felix!'

Her answer, perhaps, was meant as a protest at my choosing such a time for such a declaration, but I caught a hint of laughter there too, and thought that she did not entirely reject my devotion. Indeed the comfort and joy of that moment, as we lay, cheek against cheek, in the crammed and crowded cart, was so inexpressibly great that, for a short while, everything else faded into insignificance.

Then Juana said prosaically, 'My hands are tied behind me. Are yours?'

'Yes. That was why I had to chew the mantilla. And my feet. I suppose they did not trouble to gag me as I was unconscious.'

'I was so terrified that Pepe had killed you. He hit you terribly hard with a log of wood. How are we to escape from these evil men?'

'If only I could get my hands undone.'

'Turn round, so that our hands are touching. I will see if I can do anything.'

We both struggled round, until we lay back to back, and our hands could meet, exploring the bonds that tied our wrists, but it was hopeless; the cords were cruelly tight, wound many times round, so that our fingers were already swelled, numb and weak.

'What, what can we do?' said Juana despairingly.

'If only that troop of soldiers could come now – we could shout—'

'It is no use,' she said. 'They are not going to come. I heard Pepe tell Don Amador. There has been a big revolt in Catalonia, of the *agraviados*, who complain that the king is not permitted to rule as he should, that his acts are controlled by Freemasons; all the soldiers in north Spain have been sent off to the mountains of Catalonia. I daresay Don Ignacio knew all about it.'

'Is Don Ignacio for the Carlists, do you think?'

'I fancy he is for nobody but Don Ignacio. Tell me, do you really know about such a great treasure at Cerezal?'

'No, no, of course not, it is all moonshine.'

My mind ranged about, like a tethered dog, hunting for ways of escape.

'Is Nico there?' I asked.

'Yes, he is beyond me – I can just feel his feet. Poor boy, I am afraid he is still terribly ill.'

So that was another complication. Even if, by some miracle, we could free ourselves from our bonds, there would still be little chance of overpowering the murderers, and none of escaping them, hampered as we were by the presence of the children.

It was hopeless . . .

'Senor Felix,' said a little voice. 'I can undo your cords.'

A small fidgety shape thrust itself up between Juana and me.

'Pilar!' Juana gasped in astonishment. 'Where did you come from?'

'The other end of the tartana. And I have already undone *my* hands. I bit through the string. Now I'll cut yours.'

'*Bit?*'

'Yes, my teeth are sharp. But yours I can cut—'

'Have you a knife, then?'

'Mama's fan. Don't you remember? It has a knife blade in the handle.'

Sure enough, I felt a midget sawing begin on the tight cords wound so bruisingly round my wrists. Sometimes the blade sank into my flesh; but I would not complain of that. Would she ever manage, though, to sever all those strands? The sawing went on and on, indefatigably, and after many minutes I felt one of the cords give, and then snap.

'I have it! I have done it!' whispered Pilar triumphantly.

'Bless you, little one! Now give me the knife and I will do Dona Juana.'

'No, I wish to do it,' she whispered crossly.

So I allowed her to complete her rescue, though impatient to take the knife and see if I could not do it faster. While she worked I chafed my own numbed and bruised wrists, and when Juana's hands were free – they took even longer than mine had – Pilar was weary enough to agree that we might be permitted to undo our own feet. This was hard to manage without making such an upheaval and swaying in the tartana that our captors would notice. For a time Pepe came and rode alongside the cart while he and Esteban talked in low voices; I heard them mention towns in Catalonia, Pedray and Llinas, and supposed they were talking about the uprising there. Was it to support this revolt that the silver dollars were wanted?

We were obliged to wait until he had drawn ahead again before going to work on our ankle-bonds.

Now we were out in the flat plain of the Aragon valley, travelling westward towards Berdun; the distant shapes of the mountains could be seen, sharp as saw-teeth, along the horizon; and, ahead of us, the little town like a sleeping black cat hunched on its hillock. Dawn was still far distant, I judged; no cocks could be heard, only owls.

As we approached Berdun more closely I heard the sound of rapid hoofs, and two riders neared and then passed us at a gallop. Obliged to keep our heads down, so as not to alert our captors, we could not see the riders until they were beside us on the road, and then it was too late to call out, as they dashed past.

But – 'That was Sister Belen!' whispered Juana in a tone of astonishment. 'Who was the man, do you know?'

'I've no idea. He looked like a gypsy, with his head-kerchief and peaked hat. Where do you think they can have been going?'

'On some errand of mercy perhaps—'

This complicated my plan – which had been to wait until we arrived at Berdun, where there might be people about, where the two delinquentes could hardly do us violence in the public street – then leap boldly out of the cart and demand to see the local Corregidor. There were flaws to this plan, one of them being that the Corregidor was probably Don Ignacio, but, at least, I thought, it would avert our instant death. We could demand to ride, under escort, to the nearest Court, probably Pamplona. But, if Sister Belen was away on an errand, was not available . . .

Well, Sister Belen must just take her chance, I thought; she can look after herself, she is no fool.

I was sorry for her absence though; she would have spoken in our favour, she was well-respected in Berdun already, and I knew that Juana had been banking on her diagnosis of Nico's poisoning and her opinions about antidotes.

Now the tartana began creeping up the steep zigzag ascent into the town. I wondered if it would go under the arched gateway that led into the centre – but it did not, we turned aside, taking the dusty cobbled track that ran leftward, outside the ramparts; along this we rolled slowly for a few hundred yards, then came to a stop.

Now good fortune dealt us a superb card.

'Wait you there,' said Pepe to Esteban. 'I will tell Don Ignacio that we are back—' tethering his mule to a hook in the wall. 'I'll return directly,' and he disappeared up a flight of steps, and through a narrow entrance in the rampart.

Esteban, still seated on the box of the tartana, turned and addressed me in a low, threatening voice. 'Do you see this knife?'

He had drawn it from his belt: a foot and a half of shining steel. 'Shout, or make any disturbance, and you'll have that in your gullet. Anyway, there's no one to shout *to*.'

This was true. The night was still black; no one stirred in the town; also, the spot where we had halted was by a row of granaries or warehouses, set in the town wall – they were occupied only by stores of grain, cats, and rats.

Esteban pulled out flint and steel, lit a cigarillo, and sat smoking. This was the moment I had been waiting for. During the last quarter of an hour I had quickly and quietly occupied myself by collecting some of the rocks and stones that weighed down Conchita's clothes and by stuffing them into one of her thick silk stockings. Now I crawled forward until I was within reach of Esteban, swung the stocking back, and brought it down with all the force I could command on his head.

He toppled straight forward off the box.

Leaping out of the cart, I dragged him from between the mules' feet.

By excellent chance, the tartana had drawn up close to that curious wooden chute, leading down the steep slope on the northerly aspect of Berdun, by means of which the inhabitants got rid of their garbage. Making a huge effort, of which at a normal time I would certainly not have been capable, I heaved Esteban up on my shoulder and thrust him on to the smooth, greasy wood of the chute, then gave him a vigorous push. He vanished from view, down into the dark.

I heard Pilar give a squeak of delight – '*Well done*, Senor Felix!'

'Hush!' I whispered, for now footsteps were returning.

Quick as thought, I snatched Esteban's hat – which had fallen off – grabbed his cigarillo, which lay on the cobbles, and sat myself up on the box, shoulders hunched forward, puffing on the cigarillo, as Esteban had sat.

Pepe came out of the alley-mouth.

'Here's a to-do!' he whispered peevishly. 'Seems that Don Ignacio's very sick – like to die – Dona Calixta, the whey-faced housekeeper, won't even let me see him. Now what do we do?'

I was quite clear what *I* meant to do. Bounding down off the box, I swung my arm back and prepared to deal him such a blow as I had dealt his companion. Alerted at the last moment, he started aside, and it hit him only sidelong; he came at me directly, and aimed a ferocious blow at my head, which would have felled me if I had not ducked out of the way.

'*Dios!* it's the Ingles – where, then, is Esteban?' he gasped, and drew his knife.

With a lucky kick, I managed to knock the blade from his hand. Again I swung my stocking. He sprang back and made a stoop for the knife, but I shoved it out of his reach. Pilar and Juana had now scrambled out of the cart and were hovering, looking for ways to help.

'The knife!' I panted, and Juana snatched it up.

Pepe came at me like a bull, with his bare hands; he was twice my size and, once he got them round my throat, I feared I was done for. But, by a kick, and a slip, and a hip-throw which Pedro had once taught me – poor Pedro – I managed to unbalance him, and he fell heavily on the cobbles.

'Now – help me, quickly!'

I grabbed his arms, Juana and Pilar each took a leg, and, struggling all together, we heaved him up on to the rubbish chute and sent him sliding after his fellow.

'*Bueno*, BUENO!' chanted Pilar, dancing round us like a little imp from the pit. 'We did for them, we did them!'

'Hush, we are not out of the wood yet!' said I. 'Let us get away from this town. Back into the cart, please, senoras!' and, springing on to the box, as soon as they were in, I whipped the mules on their way. The track, I recalled, circled around the ramparts and rejoined the entry road, so that it was not necessary to turn, merely to continue ahead. In ten minutes we had descended the zigzag, turned to our right, and were travelling west, towards Pamplona.

We went for a long time in silence, being, I suppose, all of us quite bewildered at the speed with which our fortunes had changed; also somewhat horrified (evil though they were) by the horrid and sudden end of the two men. I did not think they could survive that drop – the chute was too long, and then at the bottom they had another twenty cubits to fall.

Juana's mind was running in the same direction, for presently, from close behind me, she asked in a low voice, 'Can they possibly still be alive? Will they raise a hue and cry after us?'

332

'I think Esteban must be dead – I am not quite certain about Pepe—'

'Well, I hope they die!' said Juana vindictively. Hardly the sentiments for a postulant nun, I thought. She went on, 'When I think of poor Pedro – oh, poor, *poor* Pedro. Felix, I am so *sorry* about him. He was so kind, so cheerful. I blame myself dreadfully for everything that has happened – but that most of all—'

'That's foolishness,' I said. 'God would tell you to stop at once, if you paid any attention to Him. What use is blame? You must look ahead and make plans.'

'But, oh, Felix! Will somebody really impeach your grandfather, the Conde? Don Ignacio, perhaps? Or Conchita's parents? What do you think they will do?'

'Heaven only knows. Anyway, my grandfather wished me to come on this errand. I know that. So, if there are any ill results, he, at least, will impute no blame. I doubt if he will even be surprised; very few things surprise Grandfather.'

A small town now came into view, ahead of us on the side of the valley, a couple of leagues distant. Like Berdun, it was perched on a little hill. Behind us, the sun was rising, and the town's red-tiled roofs caught the light.

'That is Tiermas,' I said, remembering it from our former journey. 'I think we should stop there. It is a watering-place – there are hot springs. And where there are hot springs there will be sick people and there must be doctors.'

'Oh, yes!' said Juana eagerly. 'That is well thought, Felix!'

For dreadful anxiety about Nico lay beneath everything we said and did.

So, presently reaching Tiermas, we turned aside from the main carretera and found a meadow and a patch of shade behind a barn where we could halt the cart and give the poor mules a rest. There I left Juana with the children (Pilar wanted to come with me but was dissuaded by the promise of breakfast on my return).

People were abroad now, for the sun was well up, and, by asking a woman with a pail of milk, I learned the way to the house of Dr Zigarra, who had a new villa, not up in the heart of town, but down at the side, in an orchard, not far from where I had left the cart.

The doctor was a kindly, grey-haired man, very patient at being interrupted in the middle of his morning chocolate and churros.

He told me to bring him the sick child, and he would do what he could. But he was somewhat surprised by the sight of Nico when, ten minutes later, Juana and I carried him in. I suppose we were all dirty and dishevelled enough to startle anybody, our clothes torn and soiled, all of us pale with exhaustion, and poor Nico white as lard and only half conscious.

'What happened to him?' With great courtesy the doctor added, 'I don't want to intrude on your privacy, senor and senora, but I must know something, in order to treat him.'

'You are very good, sir,' Juana replied with equal courtesy. 'The affair relates to politics – so, for your own sake, the less you know the better. But the boy, who is the son of a man well-known in Madrid, was abducted and then poisoned.'

'Poisoned with what – a herb, a tincture?'

'We do not know, senor, except that it was smeared on the pages of a book, and that the same poison killed the boy's sister. First she ran mad, then she died.'

Pilar, who, of necessity, was with us, began to whimper dolefully. I picked her up to quiet her.

'And how long ago was this?'

The doctor asked other questions, then proceeded to take various measures, drenching Nico with draughts containing, I supposed, different antidotes, warming him, rubbing him, forcing him to vomit. While these remedies were being applied, since the doctor, a sensible man, seemed to know his business well, I murmured to Juana that I would withdraw and occupy myself with some business in the town.

'I'll come too,' said Pilar instantly.

Juana nodded, and we left.

On my way to the doctor's house I had noticed what I thought was an encampment of esquiladores in a meadow not far distant, and, going to the place, I found I was right; there were men in velveteen breeches and bright cotton handkerchiefs, their faces obscured by black bushy whiskers; there were Arabian-looking women with flowing black hair, huge earrings as long as my hand, and flounced, brightly-coloured dresses; there were boys in coloured shirts and loose linen trousers. Merry, half-naked children frolicked about (who looked sharply at Pilar and she at them); already the men were hard at work, shearing horses and mules which stood in patient rows, waiting for their attentions.

I asked to speak to the leader, and was introduced to a grizzle-bearded man whose jacket was buttoned with silver coins. To him I said in a low voice that I believed some friends of his had helped some friends of mine who came to them from *under the earth*.

He nodded at once, with shrewd intelligence, and asked me what I wished. I told him: to get rid of the tartana; would he and his people, in exchange for the clothes which it contained, all of good quality, undertake to return it to the place from which it came, a village called Anso? And he could have two of the mules, also at a very low price, if he could put me in the way of buying two others and some smaller, faster vehicle, to take me on to Bilbao.

The gypsy came to inspect the tartana and its contents, nodded gravely, laid his finger alongside his nose, and murmured, 'Tragala, tragala, tragala.' Some money changed hands, and the deal was concluded.

Then Pilar and I went up into the town, where we discovered stone-arched grottoes in the hillside, guarded by old dames in felt slippers, where, for a few reales, you could have a wash in natural hot water that gushed out of the rock. At one of these I obliged Pilar to have a thorough clean-up, she protesting fiercely all the while.

'I want something to eat!'

'That comes after. First, a wash.'

Attempting to tidy her a little, I found that she still had the leather necklace with the blue bead that I had made her; well, I thought, it had brought us considerable luck.

Next, with indescribable pleasure, I washed myself; then we bought some food and returned to the doctor's house.

There we found Nico sleeping: pale and damp as to

the temples, but with a more natural and peaceful aspect than he had worn hitherto.

'He will very likely sleep for many hours,' said Dr Zigarra, 'after all I have done to him. In my opinion the best thing you can do for him now is to carry him to the young lady's convent in Bilbao.' I could see that Juana must have confided in him a good deal during my absence. 'There he will receive excellent care. For it will be many days yet, I fear, before it can be certain whether he makes a full recovery.'

Whatever Juana had told the doctor must have predisposed him in our favour, for when I offered pay, he waved his hand dismissively, and said, '*Nada, nada! What I do, I do for love. And I hope the young man may grow up like his father.*' Glancing nervously about – although we were in his courtyard, where there was no one to hear – he whispered, '*Viva la Constitucion! Viva La Libertad!*' and, ignoring our thanks, hurried back indoors to his cold chocolate.

Returning to the barn, we found that the gypsy, true to his word, had removed the tartana and left us with a four-wheeled open chariot, a kind of phaeton, which would be faster than the clumsy tartana. We laid Nico on one of its seats, covered with a couple of cloaks, which I had kept, and then applied ourselves to the rolls and fruit which I had bought, for we were all ravenous.

That finished, we climbed into our new equipage, and started off at speed. The gypsy had further done excellently in procuring a pair of *machoes*, fine spirited mules who bolted along at an extra-fast trot, covering the miles at a fine pace.

We thought it best not to stop at any of the inns where we had put up on the outward journey, and so bought food at markets along the way and spent a night in the woods north of Vitoria – no hardship for me or Juana, who had spent many nights in woods on our former travels together. The doctor had supplied us with various draughts and tinctures for Nico, which he swallowed biddably enough and then returned to what, we hoped, was a restorative sleep.

During the journey we talked. What did we talk about? I hardly remember. Nothing very momentous. We both, I believe, felt the need for a space of gentleness and tranquillity, a rest, after the violent and disturbing events of the preceding day. Also, the fidgety presence of Pilar on the box between us prevented the discussion of many topics that were in the forefront of our minds. For myself, I did not object to this quiet interlude; I was very content to ride by Juana in friendship among the green fields, without impatiently demanding: what next? What is going to happen to us? And God rewarded me for this patience by Juana's sudden demand, on the second day, 'Have we any paper, Felix? Any writing materials?'

I told her, yes; in Tiermas, a well-provided little place, I had bought ink and a writing tablet. She retired with these to the floor of the carriage and curled up there chewing her quill, with that look of utter concentration which I well remembered from our previous association when she was occupied in the process of writing a poem.

It must, I thought, have been a strange and painful hardship for Juana to be debarred from writing her poems; how could a thing so natural to her be considered sinful, or insulting to God? It was like forbidding her to breathe.

'What is Cousin Juana doing?' demanded Pilar.

'Writing.'

'Why?'

'*You* like to climb. *She* likes to write.'

'Oh . . .'

The memory of climbing perhaps led Pilar's thoughts back to the castillo and the deaths that had taken place there. She began to sob quietly, and, after a while, brought out, in a small, piteous, aggrieved voice, 'I don't *want* Weeza to be dead,' looking up at me, her face all shiny with tears.

'I know,' I agreed sadly, 'It is very bad. But there is just nothing we can do about it.'

I wiped her face with a corner of my cloak and let her hold the reins, which cheered her a little.

'Will Nico die too?' she said by and by.

'We hope not. You will have to help look after him. He may be sick for some time.'

Her lip trembled again, so I stopped the mules and picked her some rushes from a stream bank and showed her how to plait them into a whip.

Presently Juana came out of her trance and told Pilar about the poem she had been writing, which was an argument between an owl and a nightingale.

'Which of them won?' demanded Pilar.

'Neither of them. Listen and I will tell you—'

So we passed the journey.

On the evening of the second day, late, we reached Bilbao, and I saw, without any pleasure at all, its roofs, smoking in rain, huddled down in their narrow valley. I could have wished that this part of the journey would never come to an end, for Juana and I, though we had talked so little, had seemed so much in harmony. Still I had no idea what she had in mind for the future; that she felt she must at present return to the convent I understood, for there she had unfinished business, and arrangements must be made for the children. But what then?

I did not dare say, '*Juana! Marry me!*' for she was, after all, a professed nun, and that would be outrageous; but I hoped, I believed, that she knew what was in my mind.

We reached the convent gate, in its high wall, and knocked for admission.

How similar this moment seemed to that one, not so very long ago, when I had first stood there knocking, with my heart frozen in fright. How many things, and some of them terrible, had happened since then. The portress opened, and gave a cry of recognition at sight of Juana.

'Sister Felicita! Come in, come in! But where is Sister Belen?'

'She – she will be coming later. But here we have a very sick boy. Can he be carried at once to the infirmarian?'

'Of course—' and the portress summoned help.

Juana was suddenly swamped by nuns, in their black robes; they took charge, clucking and exclaiming, took charge of Nico, took charge of Pilar, who threw me a frantic glance as she was swept off, helpless, in a storm of black bombazine.

'Reverend Mother wishes to see you as soon as possible,' said the portress to Juana. Would she wish to see me too? I wondered, but then the portress, glancing in my direction, said, 'Aie, the young senor! Wait, just a moment, my friend, I have an urgent message for you.' I recalled the nun – what was her name, Sister Milagros? – who had wanted to see me last time and had then been prevented. 'Is it Sister Milagros?' I asked, but the portress, shaking her head, went back into her cubicle and returned with a letter which she handed me. It was in the hand of Rodrigo, my grandfather's steward.

My heart fell, horribly.

My dear Don Felix

I think you should try to conclude your present business and return home *without delay*. (These words had been underlined a great many times.) Your grandfather His Excellency the Conde had a letter from the Land Commissioners in Madrid which distressed him so deeply that he suffered from a Spasm, and lay for a day, unable to speak. Now he is just a little better, but asking for you. Please come as soon as may be.

Rodrigo Pujal

Oh, God. Please, dear God, don't let Grandfather die.

Juana was coming to say something to me. She looked distracted. I muttered, 'I have had bad news

343

concerning Grandfather. They – he asks me to return at once. He is ill—' and Juana's eyes went wide with concern and pity.

'Felix, I am so very sorry – shall I give your respects to the Reverend Mother?'

'Yes – if you please – and tell her – tell her—'

'I will tell her all that is proper,' said Juana with a faint smile.

'*Please*, Juana – let us not lose touch – I will return as soon as I can—'

It felt as if we were being carried away, in different directions, by different currents. Half a dozen of the sisters were clustered around Juana, looking with some surprise at her sturdy, mud-splashed blue garments and sun-tanned, windswept appearance.

Doing my best to ignore them, I gently raised her hand, then kissed it.

'*Hasta luego*,' I said huskily, and she, '*Vaya con Dios*.'

Then I left the convent, and had to restrain from driving down the hill at a breakneck speed to the nearest posada where I could arrange to leave the chariot and hire myself a horse.

12

At Villaverde; the old ladies and their bird; goodbye to Grandfather

The journey back to Villaverde was speedy but sorrowful. I rode with a terribly heavy heart. Pedro's ghost seemed to travel by my side. As I drew closer to home, each turn of the road brought back memories of our outward, hopeful journey: Pedro asking me questions about Bilbao and the Basque ladies; and my own anxious, fervent, shimmering expectations of what might be waiting at our journey's end. How different reality had proved! And yet Juana herself was no different; the memory of her, herself, was like a glowing golden core, a certainty and warmth at the centre of my being.

Whatever decision she came to, about her life and the future of the children, would be the right decision, I knew.

I had pressed on, travelling both day and night, making the journey in four days which previously had taken seven, and came to Villaverde late one evening. White moonlight bathed the uplands so that, although the month was June, a spectral winter seemed to lie over the rugged countryside. Villaverde's great pale wall rose up like the barriers set to keep sinners from the Holy City.

Please, please, dear God, let Grandfather be alive, I prayed unceasingly as I rode up the long, gradual ascent; and help me, in whatever troubles may be coming to me now, to behave like a man.

I was praying in Spanish – as I generally do; the word *hombre* – *hombre* – *hombre* echoed hollowly in time with the beat of my horse's hoofs; but God said nothing.

As soon as I reached the house, though, all was light and turmoil. Rodrigo wrung my hands, Prudencia wept, the old ladies fluttered about like disturbed bats, crossing themselves, lamenting, hobbling in and out of the oratory with their veils, beads, and crucifixes.

'Grandfather—?' I said to Rodrigo.

'Still with us – praise to the Holy Mother – hoping for you every minute—'

'I will go to him directly.'

So Rodrigo led me away, cleaving a path through the choppy mass of the old ladies, who parted, like a bow wave, on either side of us.

My grandfather, for years past, had slept in a chamber on the ground floor, because of his infirmity and the wheelchair to which he was confined. But I had never been to his room, not once. When I was a child, we had not been fond of one another, I kept strictly to my own quarters in a distant wing; and, by the time I was grown, his habits of dignity and privacy were so fixed that no one, save Paco, his personal servant, would have dreamed of intruding on him. Now, it was with a sense of shock and awe that I saw for the first time the bleak sparseness of his own space: a tiny slip of a room, a low, narrow pallet, one hard chair, a prie-dieu, and a small window looking out over the sierra. It was like a monastic cell.

Pillows had been piled on the bed, though. Grandfather lay against a mound of them, propped upright. He was wholly inert – a log, washed up on the shore. Only his eyes turned as I entered the room. For a moment I was in terror that he was deprived of speech, but his lips moved, and he said, 'Hah! Felix, my dear boy! Rodrigo, you may leave us. But send Paco with some refreshment for the young senor.'

I stooped and kissed his brow. His face, I saw, was somewhat swollen and flushed; instead of resembling a mountain eagle he now, perhaps, looked more like an owl. And his eyes had lost their flash; indeed, at the moment, they were filled with unshed tears.

As were my own.

He is old, I thought. He is an old, weak man, near his end.

Kneeling by the bed, I took his hands, which felt thin and bony, and very cold.

'Dear Grandfather. I am sorry that you are ill.'

'Better for seeing you, my dear boy.'

His voice was not strong. It had sunk to a deeper, hoarser note than I remembered. But he had not lost his acuteness and acerbity.

'Well?' he demanded 'What befell you? Did you find the children? What happened to Manuel de la Trava?'

'One of the children died – poisoned by her own mother – who is also dead. The other two children are with Juana in the convent at Bilbao – one, the boy, very sick, also poisoned. Manuel de la Trava escaped – I devoutly hope – and will go overseas, to the Americas.'

What an immense and complicated tale it would be to tell. But at this moment Paco came in, beaming with

welcome for the 'young senorito' and a tray of bread
and cold meat, which I was glad to devour, since I had
hardly eaten for several days. Meanwhile my grandfather was supplied with restoratives and cordials
which, under protest, he swallowed.

Between bites, I gave him most of the story, and he
listened, nodding and frowning.

'So: as I thought. It was a trap.'

With an ache at my heart I remembered Pedro saying the same thing at Tiermas. 'We are being led into a
trap.'

'Grandfather – Pedro is dead. They killed him. For
no reason, except that he knew Don Amador was
implicated in Conchita's murderous plans.'

Death, I suppose, had no great importance to
Grandfather just now, he being so near his end. (That,
with sorrow, I could tell from everything about him.)
He said, 'Pedro was a good lad. And I am grieved for
your sake that he is gone, as I know how fond of him
you were – and he was like a right hand to Rodrigo.
But he died doing his duty – he saved Juana's life,
you say?'

'Yes, he did.'

'No man can do better. God knows that. He will
have his reward. And you killed his murderers?'

'Yes, I am almost sure.'

'So that chain is wound up. And the children are safe, and Don Manuel—'

'We hope—'

'Indeed I hope, very greatly, that Manuel's son may live to grow up,' said the Conde thoughtfully. 'Our country is in such a sorry and desperate state. Too many factions are warring, one with another, for wrong reasons. Men of such stature as Manuel de la Trava are needed, and will be needed, for a hundred years to come. I can see no easy way out of the pass we are in.'

I thought of Professor Redmond, how he had said the same thing. But then, harking back, I asked, 'About the trap, Grandfather?'

'It was all a Carlist plot – to get hold of you, to put pressure on me—'

'But why? Why? Why should *we* be of any importance?'

Grandfather's lips twitched in a faint parody of a smile. 'They still think I have some faint influence, I suppose. And that you may have, by and by. When the letter came from Madrid—'

'The letter—'

'A communication from the Superintendent General of Police, saying that I was suspected of complicity in a Liberal conspiracy and must stand trial; if I was found guilty my lands would be confiscated, unless I could pay a fine of a hundred thousand reales. Being old and stupid I let the letter frighten me – since I could not by any possibility pay such a fine – and I fell sick. But now I have thought about it I am not afraid any longer.'

'Grandfather, I believe it is because they all still think that the English army dollars are somewhere on our land.'

'It would be ironic, would it not, if they were really there? When I think of your poor English father, living here, all unknown, as a stable hand, when you were a boy? It fills my head with shame to think of him, Felix—'

'He chose it for himself, Grandfather,' I said stoutly. 'He *loved* horses—'

'But in any case, if the money were there – which I take leave to doubt – it must of course be returned to its rightful owners,' my grandfather pronounced.

I grinned, thinking of the fearsome difficulties this would involve. A British Army pay-load from eighteen years back . . . To whom, in England, would we have to send off all those chests of gold and silver dollars? To the War Office?

'Well,' I said, 'let us hope it is not there. Wherever *there* may be. In any case, dear Grandfather, do not trouble any further about the fine. I think I may now be entitled to claim moneys from my English estates—' and I told him the news that Don Amador had given me, about the death of the Duke of Wells. His face did clear at this information, and he nodded, slowly.

'God is wonderful. Only to think that you, a little impertinent yellow-haired boy, should rise to be an English duque! But Felix, never mind all that – though I fear that it will bind yet another heavy load upon your shoulders, which, doubtless you will bear as best you can.

'It is an inexpressible joy to see you home again. But, my dear boy, I had hoped that you would bring your Juana with you. I hoped that you would persuade her out of her convent, and marry her. Since I have seen, for years past, that your heart was set on her. And indeed she sounds a most redoubtable young lady.'

He said all this in pauses, with breaths taken between.

'She is without peer, Grandfather.'

'Did you *tell* her that you loved her?' he demanded crossly, sounding like Juana herself.

'Yes.' I smiled a little, thinking of the circumstances in which that declaration had been made, in the tartana, with Conchita's cloaks and feathers piled on top of us. 'And I am not entirely without hope. For one thing she is going to need help with those children. Nico, if he lives, may be frail – and Pilar is a little demon—'

And also, I think – I hope – that Juana loves me in return; her look as we parted, her laughter in the tartana, even her childish jealousy over Conchita . . . But this I did not say. It would have seemed like tempting Providence.

'And you, my poor child, will need help with your great-aunts,' said Grandfather. 'Not to mention the administration of your English estates – and this one; if those vultures do not snatch it away from you.' He thought for a moment, and said, 'The Mother Superior of that Convent – Mother Agnese – *she* is a real serpent, it seems. I had a letter from an old friend and correspondent in Madrid, Angel Saavedra, who informed me that Mother Agnese's brother is the Franciscan prior, Father Torrijos, who, with several others, has been implicated in a Carlist conspiracy and imprisoned for his part in it. Doubtless his sister was his accomplice.'

'Good heavens, Grandfather!'

I thought of Juana, back in the convent, subject, again, to this evil woman. Who was also a friend of the old Escaroz. Would they create trouble for us?

Demand the children? Whisk away Juana to some distant house of the Order in Cracow or Normandy before I was able to see her again?

'I will return to Bilbao as soon as possible, Grandfather. As soon as you can spare me. But first I will write to that Superintendent in Madrid, saying that you took part in no plot, and are ill, and must not be bothered, and that all correspondence must be addressed to me at present, but that if there is a fine, it will be paid. That will show them they will gain nothing by threats.'

'It will make them even more eager for your English gold,' said Grandfather drily. But he did not forbid me, and I thought he looked relieved.

'Then I will go to Bilbao and say – and say that I have your permission to pay my addresses to Senorita Esparza. Have I your permission?' I asked, smiling.

'With all my heart, dear boy.'

Now Dr Valdes, my grandfather's physician, came bustling in, to say I had tired the Conde for quite long enough. 'Though indeed I can see you have done him good,' he said kindly. 'His colour is much better.'

And I, stifling a great yawn, was glad enough to say good night, for every bone of me ached with fatigue.

'Good night, Felix,' said my grandfather. 'You have done well. As I expected.'

That gave me a glow in the heart.

Outside his bedroom door I found several of the old ladies, anxious to waylay me: Josefina and Visitacion, Natividad and Adoracion were all hanging about. 'Come,' whispered Visitacion, 'Josefina wishes to show you something. It will not take a moment.'

Two of them led me, their little birdclaw fingers clutching my arms, to the oratory, with its red light, where Natividad snatched up something that lay on the stone step before the altar, and displayed it to me.

'What in the world is it?'

'Josefina made it. Is she not clever?'

Josefina, who had not spoken for the past two years, nodded a great many times, her eyes bright with pride.

'But what is it?'

It looked like a wooden bird, about the size of a pigeon, very clumsily made. All over it, thin carpenters' shavings had been glued, to represent feathers.

'Now, we are going to show you!' whispered Adoracion, and they led me, giggling, whispering, and mumbling as before, to the parlour where, during the day, the old ladies mostly sat doing their stitchery. Here a low fire smouldered, and Josefina, with many flourishes and much ceremony, took the crazy wooden bird and laid it on the embers.

In a moment the shavings caught fire and the whole object was quickly consumed by flames.

'Do you see?' whispered Natividad in triumph. 'That is all your trouble burned away. And especially Agnese Cantarillos. Josefina was at school with *her*; she remembers her well and says that she is spiteful and not to be trusted. But now she can surely do you no more harm!'

They all smiled and looked at me expectantly, waiting for my praise and thanks.

Poor crazy old creatures! What could I do? I patted them, told them I was sure their specific would work wonders, and praised Josefina's industry. Then I reeled off towards my bedchamber, but turned aside for another visit to the chapel, to thank God for having permitted me to see Grandfather again, and to say a prayer for Pedro.

In the oratory I found Prudencia, kneeling humbly at the back of the room, her head buried in her arms, and her shoulders heaving with sobs.

Guilt smote me, for I had meant to take her the news of Pedro's death myself; plainly Paco had told her. News always travelled about the corridors at Villaverde with lightning speed.

Wordlessly, I hugged Prudencia and rubbed my cheek against her plump, downy one. She hugged me

356

back strongly, and I thought: how in the world could a great, complicated establishment such as this household ever be wound up and shut down? If it had to be done? All the folk that it contains and supports – Rodrigo, Paco, Gaspar, Prudencia, the old ladies – God give me help to take up such a burden!

Then, feeling that was as much of a prayer as I could achieve just then, I limped to my room. And, just before I slept, had a sparkle of message from God: remember, Felix, life is not *only* burdens. After all, your grandfather, in his day, in his youth, led his men to battle, rode wild horses, went hunting on the mountains . . .

That is true, I thought drowsily, and I imagined God and Grandfather chatting together somewhere, comfortably, leaning elbows on a wall and looking out over the snowy peaks of the Ancares.

Then I slept.

In the morning, there was a great deal of business to be done. The letter to Madrid, and various ones to England – for I found a whole pile of correspondence relating to my inheritance there – besides no small quantity of matters brought me by Rodrigo concerning Villaverde and its affairs.

As I walked with him about the courts and storehouses and stables, all so brimming with memories, of

Bob my father, of Pedro, of my old Gato, I thought, you do not have to be happy in a place to love it. For my childhood had not been a happy one. I had wished to run away from home and had done so. Yet suffering in it knits you to a place with tighter bonds.

When the most urgent affairs were dealt with, I went to say goodbye to Grandfather yet again. For I had his authority to return to Bilbao without delay, to hear Juana's decision, and to discover how Nico went on.

This second leavetaking was not an easy one. Grandfather was weaker today, I could see; our talk last night had tired him more than his body could afford. He lay, wax-white, on his pile of pillows, and could hardly spare the strength to speak, or to lay his hand in mine.

But— 'Embrace Dona Juana for me!' he said with the ghost of a smile.

'I will do so.'

He beckoned my head lower, near his, and I saw that, as yesterday, his old eyes were full of tears. Body and spirit were very nearly parted now; his body was hardly more than a carcass, limp and feeble; yet still his spirit breathed strongly in the words he whispered, which I had never heard from him before: 'My boy, I love you very dearly,' uttered so faintly that even a mosquito on the wall would hardly have heard.

My throat was tight; I could do nothing but press his hands, then turn to go. '*Hasta luego!*' I croaked from the doorway.

And he: '*Vaya con Dios.*'

13

Sister Milagros gives me her message at last; a surprise in the infirmary; a surprise from the Reverend Mother; our affairs are brought to a conclusion

When I knocked at the convent gate in Bilbao, and was greeted familiarly by the portress – as well she might, by now – she said, at once, 'Now *this* time, Sister Milagros declares that she is not going to be deprived of the pleasure of seeing you. Twice, three times, she has missed the chance. I shall send for her at once.'

And so, though I was itching to ask for news of the children, and dying to obtain permission to see Juana, politeness constrained me to wait while the portress hurried off through the cloister.

Presently she came back, panting out, 'It is all right,

it is all right. Be patient! I have sent word, also, to the Mother Superior that you are here, for I know she wishes to see you. Now, here is Sister Milagros, who has, for so long, had a thing to give you.'

The face of the sister who accompanied her – wrinkled, square, kindly, not young – was someway familiar.

'It was you who kindly took care of my parrot in Santander,' I said, bowing low. 'When I was on my way to England. But I think, when I returned to collect Assistenta, that you were not there?'

'You are right, young man.' Her berry-brown face creased in a smile. 'I had been sent here, to Bilbao, by that time, to look after the herbs, as their still-room sister had died. And then, some time after that a letter was sent for you, to Santander, enclosed in one to a Sister Annunciata.'

'Sister Annunciata,' I said slowly, remembering. 'I never met her. Was not she the niece of the Englishman, Smith?'

'Not his niece, his stepdaughter. And he wrote to her, when he was at the point of death, enclosing another letter directed to you. He hoped she would know where to find you. But by the time her letter arrived, she too, poor girl, was already dead of the cholera in Madrid.'

'So many deaths—' I said, saddened and confused by her story.

'Never mind, child. They are all with the angels now.'

I rather doubted if the Englishman, Smith, was so, as by his own confession he had killed half a dozen people at least, and had dealings with the Mala Gente, but I did not contradict.

'So – as she was dead when it arrived – Sister Annunciata's letter lay on a shelf in the convent in Madrid for several years, gathering dust, until somebody chanced to open it and found there was an enclosure addressed to you. This was then sent back to Santander. But, I fear the sisters in the Convent of the Esclavitud there are all very old by now—'

They were very old when I visited the place, I remembered, five years ago. By now they must be *really* old.

'None of them could remember where you had come from. But, on the chance that *I* might remember, the letter was, after some time, sent here to me. And, just around that time, our Reverend Mother happened to mention that your help had been requested by the Dona de la Trava, to save her children, and that you would be coming, perhaps, to Bilbao. So – to cut a long story short – here is the letter!'

And she ceremonially handed me a faded, tattered, stained, weatherbeaten packet which certainly looked as if it had been gathering dust, in one religious house or another, for the last five years. The wafer that sealed it was cracked, the thin cord that bound it had rotted through; anybody could have read it. Anybody probably *had*.

To Felix Brooke: from Oviedo

They have found me guilty; which was no more than I expected. I go to the galleys tomorrow, if I have not died in the night, which is more probable. Listen: I am going to give you directions where to find the money. *Caramba! Somebody* might as well have the use of it, and I'd sooner you, a decent-spoken English boy, than some doltish peasant who chances on it while plough-ing. Here's how to find it. I have amused myself by putting the directions in cypher, so no thieving nun who opens this letter can avail herself of the knowledge.

Then followed several lines of letters all run together into gibberish words, neither English nor Spanish, making no sense whatsoever. After that, there were a few more lines of English.

Do you recall, when we parted, you asked me if I knew the whereabouts of an English hostelry, and I said I did? And told you in which town it was? That name has two letters repeated in it at the beginning of words. Take that letter as the start of your alphabet. And enjoy the treasure in better peace or health than was ever granted to

Your friend, George Smith

Almost stunned, I read the few lines over and over. Of course I remembered the name of the hostelry. It was The Rose and Ring-Dove, in Bath, where I had at last been able to meet a messenger from my English family. Two letters repeated at the beginning of words – So: take R as the first letter of the alphabet—

Good heavens, I thought. No wonder the Mother Superior had been so willing to send for me. She could study those jumbled letters until the Last Trump, and she would be no wiser, lacking the key phrase. And no wonder she had been reluctant for me to see Sister Milagros, or to receive the letter, until the errand with Don Manuel was accomplished – he, preferably, dead, and myself, she perhaps hoped, beguiled by Conchita's blandishments. Married to Conchita, with all that money in my pocket, how useful I might have been.

Call me not an olive till you see me gathered,

Mother Agnese, I thought, looking forward with some relish to our interview.

Now, a shy, pink, white-robed novice came to ask me if I would please visit the infirmary, so I tucked the letter with great care into my innermost jacket pocket and gave Sister Milagros very hearty thanks for keeping it so carefully.

'I regret it took so long to reach you,' said she.

'It makes not the least difference in the world. The news it contains is eighteen years old already,' I told her, and followed the novice.

We went through a couple of cloisters and into a big, airy room where, at a distance, I saw a number of children playing. Among them I was happy to observe Nico and Pilar, he looking decidedly more like a human boy than when I had last seen him.

But what took all my attention from the children was much closer to the door, sitting in a basket chair with his leg stretched out in splints before him—

'PEDRO!'

'My very self! *Carracho!* Am I glad to see you!' said he, grinning away like a pumpkin lantern. 'Your servant, Senor Felix!' And he would have stood up, but I prevented him.

'I don't *understand*! How in the wide world did you get here? You were shot – I saw you drop like a stone

– into that frightful gorge. How were you saved? Who saved you? Tell me the whole story?'

'It is very simple. Do you remember the mother bear – who was about to devour Dona Juana when I popped a spoonful of lead down her gullet?'

'I suppose you are going to say that she saved you?'

'So she did. She had fallen in about the same spot, and stuck fast in a tree growing out of the cliff down below; there she lodged, poor thing, like a great furry bird's nest. So when that fellow's shot winged me—' he rubbed his shoulder, which was also bandaged – 'I hear by the way that you tipped him down the rubbish chute in Berdun; that was very well done, Senor Felix. My congratulations!—'

'Thank you.'

'So – when he winged me, that made me lose my hold, and down I fell, right on to Mama Bear, who broke my fall. I lay on her, getting my wits about me, with nothing worse than a broken leg, while up above, had I only know it, those two *gente* were clubbing you insensible and wheeling you off in the tartana.'

'What happened to you then?'

'Well, I won't deny that I was in poor case. There I lay, wondering every minute if I was going to roll into the gorge, and becoming a trifle light-headed with pain, but calling for help as lustily as I could, in-between times; when, lo and behold, who should come along but a group of those scissor-merchants.'

'The esquiladores!'

'The very same. And they, with their ropes and tackle, had me out of there in the hiss of an adder. Not only that, but one of them, knowing where I had come from, went off like an arrow to fetch Sister Belen, who had been making her name known as a healer of hurts all over the countryside. And – and so she came – and strapped my leg up in a twinkling, and that's the end of the matter!'

'Oh, Prudencia will be so happy! Poor soul – she thinks you are in purgatory this very minute.'

'Aie, aie, that's bad,' said he. 'But she'll soon know better. Thank heaven. I've plenty of ill deeds to repent before I take myself off *there*. Or so Sister Belen assures me!'

He looked so well, so happy, so radiant indeed, that I could not help giving him a hug. By this time the children were with us, Pilar hopping about like a grasshopper; Nico, I could see, still thin and pale, but, thank God, perfectly sensible and in control of his faculties. He thanked me, shyly and formally, for having saved him from the effects of the poison, and for saving his father.

'That, I fear, we don't know yet, my boy.'

367

'But we do. We do! One of the gypsies who brought Senor Pedro here said that Papa was safe in France. And he sent a message that we would hear from him by and by.'

'Oh, thank God for that,' said I from the bottom of my heart.

Now I was summoned to the presence of the Reverend Mother and led off, not to that dismal little reception room where I had been on previous occasions, but to a cheerful parlour with a statue of St Philomena, looking out on to an orchard. There, to my very great surprise was, not the sour-faced Gorgon who had interviewed me twice before, but a total stranger, a lady with a smiling but acute face and two extremely shrewd eyes, who surveyed me from head to foot, and then said in French, '*Bien!* After so long I meet you. And very happy to make your acquaintance, Monsieur Brooke y Cabezada.'

Seeing my surprise, she added kindly, 'Ah, you wonder not to see Mother Agnese. She has – ahem – been summoned to Madrid to give – to attend an inquiry. And it is not certain when she will return. So I am transferred from our house in Bayonne to take her place.'

She rang a little bell, and when a lay-sister appeared, asked that Sister Felicita be sent for.

When Juana arrived and saw me, she turned brilliant pink, then bit her lip and scowled at the floor.

'Thank you for coming so fast, Soeur Felicitee,' said the French nun blandly. 'Now: I am about to address you young people, so listen with care. It is for the old to speak first and be heeded by the young, *n'est-ce pas?* For our time is shorter, whereas *you* have all the time in the world, with your lives before you. So pay attention.'

She gave each of us a sharp look.

We were all three standing, the Deputy Reverend Mother because it was the custom of her Order not to be seated in the presence of guests; I, because I could not sit while a woman stood; and Juana because she could not sit in the presence of her superior. So we stood in a triangle, rather as if, I thought, we were about to begin dancing in a ring.

Juana kept her eyes fixed on the floor and would not look at me.

'Now, my daughter,' the nun said to her, 'Mother Agnese told me before she went that you were going through many deep troubles and soul-searchings, because you had given your promise to Don Manuel to look after his children, but you had also, and previously, given your promise to God to be a Religious. And Mother Agnese had advised you to

369

remain in the convent and allow the children to attend school here, where you could be in contact with them. Is that not so?'

'Yes, Mere Madeleine,' Juana said in a low tone.

'Mother Agnese suggested that the children should live with their grandparents.'

'Yes, Mere Madeleine,' Juana said again; her voice was even less enthusiastic.

'Well, child, I have raised the matter with Senor and Senora Escaroz. And I can tell you that they don't *wish* to have their grandchildren. In fact,' Mere Madeleine went on briskly, 'Senor Escaroz told me he didn't care a snap of his fingers what became of the son of a seditious madman or the misbegotten daughter of a profligate courtier from Madrid.' Mere Madeleine raised her brows disapprovingly as she pronounced these words. 'I understand that their daughter Conchita had been a great disappointment to them, and they were interested in the children only so long as they believed Don Manuel to be dead and Nico his heir. On learning that he was alive, they gave me to understand that I might place the children in the Bilbao orphanage for all they cared.'

'Well!' I said cheerfully, 'Juana, that frees you from any—'

'A moment!' Mere Madeleine raised her hand. 'My

dear Soeur Felicitee, you know I can speak to you as a friend, having been acquainted with you for the last five years. I have watched with the utmost sympathy your struggles to become a Religious. You brought energy, goodwill, courage, intelligence to the business; but, year after year, as you know, I have made you postpone taking your final vows. You asked me why, and I would never tell you. I tell you now. Your heart was not in it. You were not happy. I knew that from the start. Yet why did you call yourself Soeur Felicitee, I wonder? The truth is that you had no vocation. And the task that you have, here, of giving a home to those two children is, I believe, the one that God was saving up for you. And, believe me, it will be every bit as difficult as life in the convent. More so, perhaps! Nico will be delicate for some time to come; and I have it on good evidence that Pilar is a little Tartar.'

She smiled.

Juana looked up at Mere Madeleine – radiant, bewildered, *cross*, embarrassed, the tears peeling down her face.

'But – Mere Madeleine – a *home* – how can I give them a home? I have sold mine—'

'You forget, my daughter – when you leave you will have your dowry repaid – another factor which, I fear, may have been weighing with our dear Mother Agnese more than it ought—'

'But how can I be sure that I can care for the children properly?'

'Oh,' replied Mere Madeleine with her bland look, 'As to that – I daresay you will find some obliging person who will be prepared to help you in such a task.'

So then I made my bow and said, 'Reverend Mother, my grandfather the Conde Don Francisco Acarillo de Santibana y Escurial de la Sierra y Cabezada permits to ask you if, supposing her vows should be withdrawn, I may pay my addresses to the Senorita Esparza—'

And at that, even through her crossness, the cornered Juana could not forbear an unwilling grin.

So we were married, with no parade and little ceremony, in the convent chapel, with Pedro acting as groomsman, and the two children in attendance.

'This getting wed is such a famous notion, I'm going to work on Sister Belen to persuade her to come out of the cloister,' Pedro muttered to me just before the service, while we were waiting for Juana to appear, looking prickly and self-conscious, in her white lace and silver crown, on the arm of the convent chaplain.

'*Pedro!*'

'I plan to keep writing letters to her,' he said. 'It will be hard work.'

I did notice that Sister Belen gave him an especially friendly greeting when healths were being drunk afterwards.

We started on the return journey to Villaverde very soon after the ceremony, for I was eager to get back to Grandfather with the least possible delay.

'I am so longing for you and the children to be there. And for you to meet Grandfather – that will make me so happy—'

But – alas – that final happiness was not to be permitted.

Author's Note

When I first decided to write about Felix at the age of eighteen, I hardly realised what a fearsome period of Spanish history I was going to plunge him into. The years between 1823 and 1833 are called by some historians the 'Ominous Decade' because such a lot of bad things were going on in Spain.

After what we call the Peninsular War, 1808–14, and the Spanish call the War of Independence, during which English, French, and Spanish armies skirmished all over Spain, with the English and Spanish allied to drive out the French, the country was desperately poor and in a state of upheaval. The upper classes were worried that there would be a revolution, as in France.

King Ferdinand VII had been exiled with his parents Carlos IV and Maria Luisa when, in 1809, Napoleon enticed them out of Spain by a trick, and put his own brother Joseph Bonaparte on the Spanish throne. The Spanish people were longing to have their rightful king back, but when Ferdinand arrived in 1814, after Napoleon's downfall, they discovered that he had a mean and vindictive nature. He soon cancelled the liberal measures that had been passed during his exile and began a regime of repression that lasted till his death in 1833. Nor was the trouble ended then, for his children were both daughters, his brother, Don Carlos, claimed the throne, and a long series of 'Carlist Wars' began. (The Salic Law of 1713 had barred girls from reigning, but Ferdinand had declared that law invalid.)

So, during the late 1820s when this story is set, there were three main parties in Spain: that of the king, reactionary and repressive; the Carlists, even more reactionary (they had an idea that the king was being influenced by Freemasons); and the Liberals, a surprisingly large group. These three groups were all in conflict, but the Liberals had the worst of it.

I wish I had more space to tell about the awfulness of Ferdinand (he seems to have spent his exile knitting socks for statues of the saints) and his parents Carlos and Maria Luisa. You have only to look at their portraits by Goya to see how weak, obstinate, vain, and stupid they were. And Goya's paintings 'The Second of May' and 'The Third of May' show what happened when the French came into Spain in 1809, the year in which Felix was born.

One real character appears in this story. Mariano Jose de Larra was a Liberal journalist who spent his childhood in France during the War of Independence, with his family, who were Bonapartists. After the war, in the amnesty of 1818, they came back to Spain. De Larra soon began writing indignant essays, under the name 'Figaro', about the state of the country. One of them was called 'To Write in Madrid is to Weep'. He said that trying to reform Spain was like ploughing the sea. Sad to tell, he committed suicide at the age of twenty-eight. He would have been glad to know that in the middle of the twentieth century Spain at last became a democracy.